THE LOOKING GLASS

JESSICA ARNOLD

Month9Books

Edited by Mandy Schoen
Published by Month9Books
Cover designed by Gina Gibson
Cover Copyright © 2013 Month9Books

Month9Books

For my mother, my grandmothers,
and all the strong, beautiful, extraordinary women
I am blessed to know.

THE LOOKING GLASS

JESSICA ARNOLD

CHAPTER ONE

She could taste the blue, the water on her lips. Something solid loomed before her and she knew it was too late to turn around. There was a sound as she barreled into it, a sound that seemed too gentle for the impact. It should have been loud—earsplitting, skull-shattering—but in fact it was almost silent, dulled by the water. A whisper of a noise followed by a soundless darkness.

She blinked and the water slipped away from her like a dream.

Alice was lying on the couch in the hotel foyer. She lay there for a moment, opening and closing her eyes, alarmed by how her heart was pounding. Her throat was tight and she realized that she was choking back a scream. Was it a nightmare? Had she fallen asleep? She moved and every inch of her ached. As she tried to stand, her legs started shaking and she nearly fell over.

Moaning, she sank back into the soft leather, pressing a hand to her throbbing head.

She stared at the ceiling, trying to remember exactly how she had gotten there, but her memories were fuzzy. The more she sifted through them, the more tangled and sticky they became, as if she were digging through mounds of cotton candy. The hotel, of course, she recognized. How long had she been here? A week? Yes, they'd come to Maine on Saturday for a last-minute vacation before school started up again. Her twelve-year-old brother, Jeremy, had chosen the destination.

A haunted hotel.

She had to admit, the location had intrigued even her. True, she wasn't obsessed with ghost stories the way Jeremy was, but Maine was pretty and quiet and a completely different world for someone who had spent her entire life on the West Coast.

A yell broke the silence. "Somebody call an ambulance!"

Alice jumped to her feet, ignoring the piercing pain in her head. Years of practice had taught her to discern the many subtle levels of her mother's panic, but she had never heard this much raw fear in her voice.

"Mom?" she said, hurrying into the library just off the foyer. "Mom!"

"Is she all right?"

Alice recognized the hotel manager's voice. He, too, sounded worried. She ran back into the other room and stopped, looking around in confusion. There was no one in sight. The hotel was completely booked; it shouldn't be this empty.

"Alice!"

Her mom again.

"Alice, can you hear me? Come on, Alice. Come on!"

Even for her mother, whose overreactions were the stuff of family legend, this seemed to be going a bit far. Alice had just fallen asleep in the lobby. It wasn't as if she'd died or something.

She walked back into the dining room, frustrated. If she didn't find her mom soon, she'd be hearing about this for months.

"Where is she?" she heard the hotel manager ask. It sounded like he was in the foyer now.

"Outside, by the pool."

"Oh my God!"

"What happened?"

There were more voices now, but every room was still empty. The foyer, the library, the dining room. It was as if the whole place had suddenly been deserted. Had the man said her mom was by the pool? She realized she was clutching her cheeks, her nails digging into her skin.

"Does anyone know CPR?"

"Has someone called an ambulance?"

She froze; her hands went icy. Had something happened to her dad? Her brother? Her heart skipped a beat, then pounded faster than ever—a drumroll.

"They're by the pool!"

By the pool. There it was again. The voices grew louder as she sprinted toward the back door. Kids were crying now and people were gasping and yelling to friends. But Alice still could not find them. Everywhere she stood she heard noises; she felt sure that the voices must be coming from right beside her. She ran from room to room, sure the aching pain in her head—her entire body—had somehow affected her hearing.

They must be ahead of me, Alice thought to herself as she ran. *They're just a little bit ahead of me now.*

She reached the back of the game room and grabbed the door handle and pulled hard, frantic now, but it would not open. She flipped the lock with trembling fingers and tried again, but the door was jammed.

"Come on," she muttered. *"Come on. Come on ... "*

Somewhere outside, her mom screamed, her voice strained with growing desperation. Moving to the window next to the door, Alice yanked the curtains open and stumbled back.

"What the ... ?" she whispered. The window was there, but the glass—what had happened to the glass? It was opaque, blurry, almost as if it were covered with condensation. Alice couldn't even see the trees outside or the green of the lawn. Hesitantly, she reached out and touched the window, expecting to wipe away the water. Instead, the surface was dry.

She pulled her hand back, clutching it to her chest.

It's okay. This is all normal. Just some condensation and an old, jammed door, she thought, trying to breathe deeply. Her stomach was doing cartwheels. Her head pounded to the wild rhythm of her heart.

"She's non-responsive. Low BP."

Alice looked up, eyes darting around the room. She thought she heard sounds coming from the foyer—a distant squealing like the wheels of an old grocery cart—and she sprinted back. Still empty. Outside. They had to be outside. She ran to the front door, unlocked it, and pushed hard—no luck. Cursing under her breath, she looked around for something, anything, but there wasn't time … she couldn't wait. Alice took a step back, then threw herself against the door with all the force she could manage. She slammed against it and the door did not budge, but she was sent reeling back.

As she stumbled and nearly fell, a flash of color caught her eye. She caught herself—managed to stay standing—found herself staring at a mirror next to the front door.

It was an optical illusion; it had to be. Trapped in a nightmare, she walked slowly forward until her face drew level with the small, square mirror. This was not possible.

She wasn't there.

There was no trace of her in the glass, no flash of red hair or brown eyes. But there were other people—people she recognized. People she knew. The hotel manager, standing in the corner of the foyer, hand over his mouth. Alice whipped around, half expecting to see him standing behind her, next to the old floor lamp. But the lamp stood alone, shedding greenish light on the wall.

Head spinning, Alice turned back to the mirror. The annoying six-year-old girl from room fourteen clung to her mother's legs, blonde pigtails dripping pool water all over the polished wood floor. Alice's mom ran through the middle of the room beside two paramedics pushing a gurney, yelling hysterical instructions to everyone in sight, mascara running. The wheels on the gurney screeched as they turned, and it was hard to tell their screaming from her mother's. Jeremy and her dad trailed behind; her dad's crisp new shirt was dirty and Jeremy was wearing swim trunks.

They're okay. Relief washed down her neck and back like cool water. Then she saw the person on the gurney, and the water hardened to ice.

She lay on the stretcher in the purple, flower-patterned bikini that her mom had forced on her just the week before. Alice Montgomery. Fifteen. Waist-length, red hair. Pale, freckled skin. It was unmistakably, unequivocally her.

Alice lost it. She grabbed an umbrella from the stand by the door and charged at the mirror. Maybe it was a sort of window, and if she broke it, she'd be able to step through and replace that girl on the stretcher. She held the pointed end of the long umbrella and swung the thing forward, dashing the handle against the mirror as hard as she could. It cracked, sending lines through her parents' faces. She struck again and the mirror fell to the floor and shattered.

Alice sank to her knees, shaking. "This is a dream," she said aloud. This was all a bad dream and she just had to wake up. She closed her eyes, opened them, and stood back up. The mirror … the mirror was back on the wall, hanging unperturbed exactly where it had been before.

"You damn, freaking … "

Alice grabbed the umbrella from the floor and shattered the mirror for the second time. She stared at the shards as they bounced on the ground and settled into a pool of shimmering glass.

Before she could take a single deep breath, the glass disappeared and the mirror appeared again on the wall. Alice gaped at it. She could see the hotel manager, still standing in the corner so stiffly that he might have been frozen solid. The little girl's mother knelt on the floor, hugging her daughter. The old couple from room nine looked as though they were praying. There was a girl she hadn't seen before standing alone in the corner, wearing a black dress and black tights. She looked to be the same age as Alice and, unlike everyone else, she seemed entirely calm.

Alice collapsed on the floor in defeat. The pain, worsened by her attack on the door, was almost unbearable; her mind kept replaying the image of the girl in the purple bikini, lying on the stretcher with her hair still wet, as though she'd just been dragged out of the pool.

The pool.

Do you want to go to the pool with me, Alice?

Her brother had said that, not two hours ago. She remembered now. She remembered taking the tags off her new bathing suit and grabbing a towel from the bathroom. Her mom had made her come back and had tried to rub some extra sunscreen on her back, but Alice had grabbed the bottle away from her, irritated. *I already put some on, Mom.*

You know you burn easily, her mom's voice rang strangely in her ears.

But if she had been swimming, how did she end up on the couch in the foyer? Alice walked back to the couch and examined it, looking for wet spots. There were none. She looked down at herself and saw with a start that she was still wearing her bikini, though the fabric was dry. Her hair was also dry, with a little frizz. She was barefoot. Everything would have been perfectly normal if it all hadn't been so completely and entirely wrong.

"She'll be fine," the manager said, though his voice was shaky. "She just hit her head on the bottom of the pool. Honestly, people, there are 'no diving' signs for a reason. Honestly."

Alice, no diving. Her mother's voice hit her again, along with a slew of new memories. Only they weren't memories so much— more like three-second movie clips with bad sound.

Alice, it says no diving.

Everyone *dives, Mom.*

And then Alice remembered jumping into the water, executing the somersault dive she'd perfected the previous summer. Her legs were powerful and she jumped higher than she had in the past hour. It was a perfect flip, and then the water came rushing over her head and shoulders and legs. The impact threw her arms back to her sides and she was going fast, too fast toward the bottom of the pool. There was a sound—she remembered it now. That was where the memories stopped.

Alice began to wonder if she was dead.

But she wasn't. She pressed her hand to her wrist and felt her pulse; it was steady. Her head pounded. The lining of her swimsuit scratched her skin. Her hair was heavy on her back and when she ran her hand through it, it was soft. If she were dead, she would know it, right? She would have opened her eyes to see some beautiful, bright place and some nice, glowing person would have said she was dead now and ... she wasn't exactly sure what happened after that, but still. ... She had woken up in a hotel foyer, equidistant from both heaven and hell.

But if she wasn't dead, what *was* going on?

Dreaming, unfortunately, was out of the question too. Everything felt too real to be a dream. The colors were too vivid and Alice's mind was too awake, too alive. She was sure she was thinking clearly. She flexed her hands and then balled them up into fists. Everything seemed to be in working order.

"But if I'm not dreaming, I must be dead," she said to herself. Her voice echoed in the tall, empty room. She stood up and yelled at the ceiling. "I can't be dead! Do you hear me? I'm not dead!" She was too young to die, wasn't she? It just ... it wasn't fair.

"Not dead ... not dead." Her voice echoed back and forth in agreement, drowning out the sounds from the mirror. As the last echo died away, she heard a scream from upstairs and took off running.

"Hello?" she called. "Anyone?"

She reached the top of the staircase and stopped for a fraction of a second to figure out which room the sound was coming from. Now that she was closer, it sounded like a baby crying. She dashed toward a room at the end of the hall. The door was closed and Alice knocked.

"Is anyone there? Please—I need your help."

She waited, but no one answered. She tried the doorknob. For the first time since the beginning of this nightmare, a door swung open when she pulled.

"Excuse me," she said, poking her head inside. The baby's cries grew even louder and she took a tentative step into the room, which was empty. A little boy in a playpen and a blue onesie was screaming his lungs out in the next room, visible through a door-less doorframe.

The very ordinariness of a crying baby calmed her, and it was all too easy to dismiss the strange things that she had seen. Mental breakdowns were medical fact, weren't they? She'd just lost it for a minute there.

She wasn't entirely sure she'd pulled herself back together, though. If whoever was staying in this room found her in here, they'd assume she was either a burglar or a total creep—probably both. But she wanted to pick that baby up. If she could only feel its soft skin, its small head ... that newborn smell ... she would know, then, that everything was all right.

"Where are your parents?" Alice said, wondering how they could leave their kid all alone in the room like that. Alice hesitated, then started toward the doorway, already reaching out to grab the baby.

Her hands hit glass.

"Ouch!" She straightened, rubbed her fingers, and took a step back. Not a doorframe at all—just a frame. A mirror.

"No. No—not again. Not again."

As Alice pressed her hands against the glass, she saw in the mirror a woman hurrying around the side of the bed. Instinctively, Alice whipped around. Then back. The room where she stood was a perfect reflection of the room in the mirror, except empty—no playpen, no baby, no mother. The moment of normality shattered around her and Alice shattered with it. Her knees shook. She wrapped her arms around her stomach, as if she could hold herself together. Squeezing tightly, she felt her ribs—bone hard—and was glad for the reminder that she was still solid.

In the mirror, the woman picked up her baby and held him to her chest, rocking back and forth.

"Can you see me?" Alice screamed, truly frantic now. "Can you hear me? I'm right here! Right here!"

For a second, the woman glanced at the mirror and Alice thought she looked a little confused, but then she just wiped some smudged eyeliner off of her eyelid and walked away, bouncing the baby on her hip. As she opened the door to leave, the girl dressed all in black slipped through it and walked by the woman holding the baby. Was this her mother? Neither of them acknowledged the other—not a nod, not a glance—but Alice, who had spent whole days ignoring her mom, didn't think this was particularly strange. The girl came to stand right in front of the mirror. She stared at it intensely; for a moment Alice was sure she could see her.

"Hey!" She pressed her hands against the glass, leaned so close that her breath left a perfect circle of fog. The girl blinked and Alice banged her fist on the mirror so hard that her hand stung. "*HEY!*"

But though the mirror shook from the blows, the girl didn't react. She turned to the side and gave her reflection a coy smile, pushed a stray strand of hair behind her ear. Heavily, Alice stepped back, rubbing her hand. Her eyes burned, but not from the pain. Alice bit back tears of frustration as the girl grinned and adjusted her dress. She wore a strange necklace—black like her clothes and twined like rope—and on each wrist she wore two silver bracelets, not circles but perfect triangles. She was Alice's age—Alice's height. She reminded Alice of some of the goth kids at school, though her clothes were more understated than theirs and her bobbed, straight hair was too unremarkable. The girl wasn't particularly pretty (her face was somewhere between plain and forgettable), but her eyes were extraordinary—an almost golden brown that sparkled underneath long, black lashes.

Alice reached out to touch the mirror, hoping against hope that the girl would react somehow—that she would see her. But as she did, the girl suddenly turned and ran from the room without a word.

Alice stumbled toward the door on unsteady knees, surprised that she could walk at all. Somehow she managed to make her way out of the room, and closed the door carefully—the way she closed her own door when it was late at night and the house was too quiet. It hardly mattered; no matter how much noise she made, the woman in the real hotel would never notice. And, if she really was dead, then breaking into other people's rooms was the least of her worries. Once outside, she sank down to the floor and leaned her head against the wall, trying very hard not to think.

But thoughts descended on her like a legion of angry bees—the buzzing onslaught was almost more than she could stand.

It's real.

I'm not dreaming.

I'm not crazy.

It's real.

Real. Real.

Real.

Crying out in frustration, she tried to focus instead on the sounds around her. It was strange that a deserted hotel should be so loud. Alice could hear the distant noise of people talking and doors slamming. These noises—the ordinary sounds of life—were louder than Alice remembered, or maybe she had simply never thought about it before. So much noise, and all of it so fast. Did anyone ever sit still? She covered her ears to block out the sounds, but the confusion inside her head was little better than the tumult outside. She gave up, letting her hands fall to her sides.

Alice didn't cry; she wouldn't let herself. Her mom had always encouraged tears, saying that it was healthy to get it all out, that Alice was too quiet, that keeping things inside was her "coping mechanism." But stepping back and controlling came as naturally to her as breathing.

She looked around the hallway, searching for some sign of a trapdoor—an escape. Looking up, she saw an enormous painted face staring down at her. Alice stood up and reached out to touch it, wondering if this was yet another mirror. She didn't remember seeing this picture before. But her fingers brushed real canvas and real paint. Alice scratched the surface and a bit of green chipped off and landed on the edge of a rug.

Looking down at the green fleck, she realized that this rug was not familiar either. It was red and thick, with a gold, braided pattern around the edges. *Gaudy.* She was positive it was not in the real hotel.

Her eyes snapped up and she turned around in a long, slow circle. Her mouth fell open as she realized what she had been too distracted to notice before. This was *not* the hotel she remembered. The walls were covered with dark green paper. The molding where the floor met the ceiling was elaborately carved with fleur-de-lis.

Turning back to the painting, she ran her finger across the thick, gold frame. In the real hotel, the walls were dotted with colored-pencil sketches of the ocean and the coastline. They were cheap and badly done—framed prints by local artists. But down the hallway as far as she could see were paintings just like this one with matching gold frames. They were all large, at least three feet tall, and it was obvious that they had been painted by a master. The same blue eyes glared at her from each one.

They were all paintings of the same woman.

CHAPTER TWO

Alice examined the paintings one by one. There were five on each wall and every single one had almost the same inscription—"Ms. Elizabeth Blackwell as … "

The "as" was the only part that changed. In this one, the lady was dressed in a Grecian gown: "Ms. Elizabeth Blackwell as Helen of Troy." Here was "Ms. Elizabeth Blackwell as Cordelia," wearing a beautiful, silver-embroidered dress, sitting on a tree trunk with tears in her eyes. Here she was "Lady Macbeth," wiping her hands together with an exquisite but wild expression on her face. Each one was a different pose. Each clearly painted by a master, for only an exceptional painter would be able to capture such emotion, such beauty.

Conceited, thought Alice. She looked at the sickeningly beautiful face, somehow vaguely familiar, and tried to find a flaw. It was a kind of instinct—what she did with all the pretty girls at school. If she could find just one ugly thing, she wouldn't feel quite so inferior. But the longer Alice stared, the more bitter she became, because this woman clearly had every right to be conceited.

She had dark black curls that hung all the way to her narrow waist. Her face was heart-shaped, with high cheekbones and wide, blue eyes, and skin so pale that she almost seemed to glow. Examining the eyes again, Alice finally remembered where she'd seen the woman before—just yesterday, in a similar painting in the library.

Feeling this was somehow important, Alice hurried down the stairs and through the lobby. She glanced at the mirror, but didn't stop to look at the people still gathered in the reflection of the room. The sounds faded as she walked into the library. It was nearly quiet here, perhaps because there were no mirrors. But even in the real hotel, this room had usually been empty.

It only took her a moment to find it, although the painting wasn't where she remembered seeing it before. She'd only been in here once, looking for Jeremy, and she had glimpsed it hanging in a corner, halfway covered by the window curtains. In the real hotel, it looked as though someone had shoved it aside to make space for the bookshelves that lined most of the walls, but in this version of the library it hung over the fireplace. Alice wished it were back where it had been before. The portrait was, quite frankly, frightening.

It wasn't as if the other pictures had been exactly ... she didn't quite know the right word ... *normal*. Something in the dark colors, in the woman's face, had been disturbing even then. But in this painting it was all the more obvious. In this painting, the woman stood by a river, leaning against a tree. Her gown was so long that the ends hung in the water. Her hair was not in smooth curls anymore—it was windswept and wild. She looked straight ahead; her eyes were wide and her face stretched in odd ways, almost like a reflection in a fun-house mirror. She looked entirely mad … hardly beautiful anymore.

Alice took a step closer to read the plaque: "Ms. Elizabeth Blackwell as Ophelia." She remembered Ophelia from her last English class. *Hamlet* was the only reading assignment that hadn't bored her to tears. Ophelia in particular had been interesting: her madness, her despair, her suicide. She glanced up again at the painting and noticed letters along the bottom of the painting, in a darker blue that almost blended into the river. Two words.

READ ME

"Read me?" Alice repeated. *Read what?* She squinted at the letters, trying to figure out if she was missing something, but—six letters—that was all there was to see. The painting *was* of Elizabeth as Ophelia, so maybe the message was referring to *Hamlet*. In which case Alice could check that off her to-do list. *Read it.* She certainly wasn't planning on reading it again.

Trying to escape the painted blue eyes, Alice looked around the rest of the room. None of the furniture was as she remembered it.

There was a writing desk over by the opaque window and a couple of armchairs by the fireplace. The floor was wooden and scratched, covered in places by a thick, red rug. Everything had an old air about it, as though it had been sitting there for a very long time. The hotel, Alice knew, had been here since it was built to be a boardinghouse in the late 1800s. Maybe this was what it had looked like. Had she somehow been sent back a hundred years in time?

Or was this all a strange, injury-induced dream? The more she saw of this place, the more bizarre it became. And though everything still seemed much too real—too vivid—to be a dream, she still wondered if perhaps this was some strange place her mind had created …

Alice shook her head and walked over to the writing table, hoping to distract herself. There was a huge book lying on the desk—a collection of Shakespeare's plays. It was open to Hamlet and some of Ophelia's lines were underlined.

How should I your true love know
From another one? …
He is dead and gone, lady,
He is dead and gone.

"This was your book, wasn't it?" Alice wasn't sure why she was talking to the painting. It just seemed so real somehow—real enough to hear her. Those eyes looked more alive than most real eyes ever would. Alice kept talking because, after all, there was no one else to talk to. "Is this what I'm supposed to read? Well, I hate to break it to you, but every high school student in America is already sick of *Hamlet*. It's not exactly obscure."

Alice could have sworn the painting grinned at her—not a normal grin either. It looked as if the ends of the woman's painted lips curled up, just slightly, in a sneer. And Alice, for a fraction of a second, felt that the painting was keeping something from her.

She tore her eyes away from the woman and moved the Shakespeare book aside, careful not to lose the page. It all felt so recent—as if someone had been sitting here just a few minutes ago and would be coming back very soon. Under the volume of Shakespeare there was another book. This one was very small, almost small enough to fit in a pocket. It was bound in creamy, light brown leather and on the front there was a deep red mark that Alice, for a moment, thought was a rose. But when she picked it up for a closer look, she realized that it wasn't a picture at all. It was a bloodstain.

Alice dropped the little book as if it had burned her and wiped her hand on her leg. Her whole back was tingling and she practically ran out of the room. She felt silly doing it; after all, she wasn't a child, and here she was, running away as if she were still scared of a little blood. But she couldn't shake the feeling that there was something in that room—something that was watching her. And she was fairly certain that whatever it was, it had no particular liking for her.

The house was growing dark, the light coming through the opaque windows fading to a mere glow. Alice reached around for a light switch, dragging her hands across the walls, peeking around corners; but she couldn't find even one. The lights in the real house had always been lit in the evening; she'd never given them a second thought, barely noticed them at all.

She started looking for lamps then. There was one on the table, but it was an old oil lamp—just an antique. Probably just there for decoration. She made another quick circle around the room, noting several candles, but in the end she found herself back in front of the lamp. The thing looked brand new, perfect as it would have been fresh from the factory over a century ago.

And ... *oh*. She whipped back around. One, two ... three candles. An oil lamp. The problem wasn't that she couldn't *find* a light switch; there were just no light switches to be found. And no electricity. *Great*. Alice had never even been camping; a life without her laptop was no life at all. How was she supposed to light this lamp thing? How was she even supposed to find a match?

There was enough light still coming from the mirrors for her to see by. Alice stood in front of the one in the lobby and stared at the reflection for a while. Even though she hadn't been at the hotel for very long, that lobby with its warm lamps and shining wood floor looked almost like home compared to this haunting, dark place. The girl dressed in black was sitting on the couch, reading a magazine and chewing gum. The hotel manager was behind the desk talking on the phone, and Alice could just barely hear what he was saying.

"No. No, I do *not* want to do an interview. No! Absolutely not! This establishment meets all health standards set by the state, thank you very much. What happened to that girl is not our fault. The signs were clearly posted. No. No I don't know if they will be suing and believe me, if they do they'll have to fight to get any damages out of us. What do you mean by that? Of course I feel sorry for the family, but financially speaking we just can't be held responsible. No. No more questions, I'm sorry. Good night. *Good night!*"

He slammed the phone back on the receiver and leaned back against the chair, massaging his forehead. It had barely been three seconds when the phone started ringing again.

"Damn reporters!" The manager picked up the phone and slammed it down again. He looked so distraught that Alice was swept up in a rare moment of sympathy. If this wasn't just a strange dream, if it was (if it could possibly be) reality, then her accident would certainly not reflect well on his business. No one would want to visit a hotel where someone had …

"I'm not dead," she said. And she turned around and marched away from the mirror, up the dark stairs, and into the room where she had been staying with her family. She wasn't exactly sure if she had expected to find them sitting there waiting for her, but she was nevertheless disappointed when she saw the empty room. The bedspread here was different. It was white satin with fleur-de-lis embroidered in gold. The couch with the pullout bed she and her brother had shared was missing. There was a mirror on the wall next to the bed and she hurried over to it, but the room on the other side of the mirror was just as dark and empty as this one.

Alice bit her lip, trying to ignore the lump in her throat. She walked to the bed and curled up on the satin bedspread. It was soft and cool, but the bikini straps dug into her skin and, looking at her pale stomach, she felt naked. Just as naked as she had in the store when her mother had forced her to try the thing on. *Doesn't it look adorable on you! You're so tiny—you were made for swimsuits.* Alice had protested. The bikini left nothing to the imagination; it showed her exactly as she was—scrawny and pale and unspectacular. She didn't want it. Her mother bought it anyway.

Alice pulled the top off so roughly that she nearly pulled a chunk of hair out with it. She sat on the bed, bare and cold. She wanted clothes.

Who cares? I could walk around like this if I wanted to and no one would care, she realized. But that was just too … She remembered the way the girl had looked at the mirror—as if she could see through it— and of course she couldn't, but … after being forced to go to the pool in that bikini (her one-piece swimsuit had mysteriously gone missing), she was sick of the sight of herself. Besides, what if she suddenly found herself back in the real hotel? She'd rather not risk the embarrassment. She got up and walked over to the dresser. If this house really was just as it had been a hundred years ago, then maybe …

Pulling the first drawer open, she knew at once that her hunch had been right. She unfolded a red silk nightdress, sleeveless and lacy—exactly the sort of thing that her mom would have liked. Alice dug through the clothes and came across a pair of drawers and a frightening corset-like contraption. She considered the corset for about thirty seconds, grimacing, then slipped the nightdress on. Her bikini bottom she left on; no way was she wearing the drawers, and although she could get away without a bra, she was definitely not about to go commando. The dress fell around her in a cascade of shining folds. The neckline was lower than anything she had ever worn and her small chest made the dress sag in places it probably shouldn't have. Still, Alice wished that one of the mirrors would actually show her real reflection. She would have liked to see what she looked like in this thing.

She had a sudden impulse to spin around—a silly girl in a fancy new dress.

It was getting dark in the room now and the house was silent. Alice sprawled out on the covers, and, wearing that dress, she could almost imagine that she was an old-fashioned movie star. She closed her eyes, trying to hold onto the tiny hope that this was a wild, terrifying dream that she could escape from. That if she went to sleep, she would wake up in the real world where she and Jeremy could laugh about her wild subconscious and how bizarre dreams sometimes were. But sleep did not come. It hung just beyond her grasp; maybe she didn't need it here, the same way she didn't seem to need food—wasn't even hungry. Her thoughts began to spin faster and faster, whirring around so quickly that she could hardly keep up with them.

The memories came then—a flood of them. Pictures formed a kind of tunnel and she was falling through them, through her past. She saw herself, just a week ago, watching a movie with Jeremy.

"This is pretty scary," she had teased. Jeremy loved nothing more than a good horror film. "Sure you can handle it?"

"I'm not scared. You scared?"

"You wish."

She had lied. She was terrified.

Zombies clawed their way out of the darkness, stretching out their long bony fingers to find her hiding spot in the darkest corner of her mind.

The next scene followed quickly on the heels of the other. Two months ago—a Saturday night. She remembered so perfectly, so vividly, that it was almost like being there. Her dad was at his desk, headset on, fingers running across the keyboard in a blur of skin. She had crept in quietly, an English paper clutched in her hands.

"Dad?"

He ignored her at first. She came closer.

"Dad."

He sighed then and his fingers stopped. Muting his headset, he spun around on his chair and looked at her.

"I thought I asked you not to interrupt me when I'm on a call."

This was true—it was a long-standing rule. But, after her last C in English, he'd told her not to turn in any more papers without letting him look them over. He glowered at her and she frowned right back at him. So this was her reward for trying to be a good student. What did he expect her to do? Stay up till two in the morning waiting for him?

"You told me to let you see my paper. It's due tomorrow." She stopped; he blinked. "You said to interrupt you if I had to," she added, hoping he wouldn't remember that he'd said nothing of the sort.

But he had already spun back around.

"Ask your mother."

Doors slammed and echoed through her head. One minute she was in her dad's office, feeling very small; the next she was sitting on her mother's bed, morose.

"It's all right, sweetheart," said her mother, who was answering e-mails and sipping a glass of sparkling water ("Less calories than soda—try some, Alice," she had said). She put the cup down.

"He's just busy. But we'll go on vacation this summer. You'll see him then. We'll have such a good time—you'll see."

Do you want to go to the pool with me, Alice?

Too many thoughts in her head, spinning—a tunnel. And she was falling into it.

Alice opened her eyes, blood pounding in her ears. She couldn't stand it anymore. She had to get out of here before she went insane.

Alice tumbled off the bed and groped her way over to the window, feeling around for a latch—some way to open it. But, besides the smooth glass, she didn't feel a thing. A frustrated hiss exploded out of her mouth and she slammed her hand against the glass. If the window wouldn't open for her, she'd just have to get rid of it, wouldn't she? Maybe if she acted quickly enough. ... Alice pulled the blanket off of the bed, wrapped it around her arm, and charged at the window. It shattered under the blow and Alice attempted to dive through. But her head only hit glass—the house had magically healed itself again. Alice broke the window a few more times before she finally gave up. The house was too fast for her. Unwrapping her hand, she threw the blanket back onto the bed and stood helplessly next to the nightstand, breathing hard.

Alice knew there was no way she would be able to sleep—wasn't even sure she needed to sleep in this not dead, not quite alive state. She wished she had experimented with the lamps downstairs when it was still light enough to see.

There had to be one up here too. She ran her hands over the dresser first and brushed only dust, then felt around on the nightstand until her hands touched something cold. She grabbed it and traced the shape of it—a small, rounded contraption. Keeping one hand wrapped around the little lamp, she opened a drawer on the side of the dresser with the other. Her fingers slid past some dust and finally hit a box; she grabbed it and pulled out one of the matches. It was thin and felt a little too breakable for comfort, and trying to light it in the dark … she hesitated, but she didn't have a choice. Taking a deep breath, she gave the match a quick swipe, and a flame erupted out of the end. By the time she got the lamp lit, the fire had almost worked its way to her skin. Her fingernail was smoking.

For a minute she sat staring at the flickering light, feeling as though she had finally accomplished something. But somehow the room seemed even darker than before. The flame was a small, sickly thing.

"What now?" she said out loud to herself, and the dank air stifled her voice immediately. She didn't want to venture out of the room, but there wasn't anything interesting there and she couldn't lie around all night long doing nothing. Her mind wandered back to the bloodstained diary on the library desk.

READ ME

The flame jerked, then doubled in size.

Alice jumped to her feet. *Read me.* The little book. She didn't make the connection—it popped into her mind prepackaged—and yet she didn't doubt it.

Holding the lamp (now shining gold and strong) in front of her, she rushed out of the room, down the stairs, and into the library, her borrowed nightdress fluttering behind her like a red silk flag. Why she was running, she hardly knew, but the fact that something about this place was finally making sense gave her a burning hope. She passed scores of mirrors as she ran, and in every single one of them she thought she glanced the pale face of the girl in black. Shivers chased each other down her spine and she ran faster, keeping her eyes focused straight ahead. When she got to the library, she grabbed the book and sprinted back to the room, the way she used to run to her parents' room when she couldn't sleep at night. The whole time, she couldn't escape the feeling that something was chasing her, that any minute now it would stretch out its cold fingers and grab her shoulder.

Sissy. Jeremy would have laughed at her—she could see his wide smile and she almost smiled herself. Then she remembered where she was and the picture went out like a candle.

By the time she was safely back with the door closed and locked behind her, she was so out of breath that all she could do was place the lamp on the nightstand and collapse back onto the bed. She held the book against her stomach, feeling its tiny weight as she breathed in and out. Stupid Jeremy, talking her into watching those horror movies—far more graphic even than her anatomy class (in which a supposedly fearless football player had fainted not once but twice). She was letting her imagination get the better of her. *Cold fingers on her shoulder* ... she forced herself to laugh. Straight out of a movie, of course.

Ignoring her still-pounding heart, she examined the book closer. Trying to ignore the blood spot, she turned it over a few times. A gold glimmer on the binding caught her eye and she held it closer to the lamp.

"Lizzie Blackwell," she read in a whisper. *Elizabeth Blackwell*—it had to be. With growing curiosity, she peeled open the stiff cover.

Property of Elizabeth Blackwell, someone had written on the inside cover. The handwriting was elegant, tall, and slanted. Alice turned the page and did something she had not done of her own free will in a very long time—she began to read.

CHAPTER THREE

April 23, 1883

Tonight I wait for William. My case is all ready. Most of my things have been packed for days now. I gather everything at midnight, or whenever I can escape Father's all-seeing eye. I think he noticed when I took my Shakespeare collection from the library, but he has not said anything yet and tomorrow it will be too late.

William says that as soon as we are out of this city, he will take me across the ocean to Europe. He is going to help me establish an acting career in England. He says that once I become famous, we will tour the world together. Just imagine—me, a real European actress. It is all I have ever hoped for. William assures me that he has never seen such talent. I am very talented, of course. Everyone says so.

It is a shame that Father hates William so. I simply cannot understand it. But Father never trusts anyone he has not known since the beginning of time, and William is a newcomer here. I remember when I met him after the final run of Hamlet. *He waited for me outside of the dressing room. He is a good man—a man who can truly appreciate my talent. William likes to look at me and tell me how beautiful I am. I like to listen.*

I have already sent my valuables with William to take on the stagecoach. He took most of the luggage to the ship yesterday so that we will not have to be burdened with it tonight. We cannot waste time carrying bags out and risk waking my father. And so I wait here and start this new diary. Soon I will fill it with all of my great European adventures. And with William, of course. I will write all about William.

It is ten minutes past midnight now and I wish that William would come. I am anxious to escape this attic. I did not choose it, but, because all of the other suitable rooms are reserved for our guests, it was the only option. Father lets me have this one all to myself only because no one else wants to use it. Even Lillian wouldn't have it (she sleeps in the kitchen). But I am an actress and I will not sleep like a servant, no matter what they say happened here. You see, they say that many years ago, a witch lived in this room. They say that she killed herself—hung herself from this very chandelier—and one day the man who ran the boardinghouse came upstairs to check on her and found her hanging there, blue and rotting with a hole burned in the floor underneath her.

They tell terrible stories about the witch—even worse than the ones they tell about Mother.

I do not like to think about it, but I do not believe that the room will ever forget. Sometimes I think I feel someone creeping up behind me and I imagine that it is her. Father says that I am too old to have such fancies, but he has not slept here as I have. He does not understand. The witch may have left long ago, but this room still bears traces of dark magic. I feel it quivering around me—it is in the very furniture.

The furniture is odd. I wanted Father to change it, but he says that it is valuable. I think that he wants to sell it to a museum one day. I wish I didn't have to use it. Take the bed, for instance. Four-poster beds are common enough, but who has ever heard of a three-poster bed? This is the only one that I have ever seen. It is a perfect triangle. I usually sleep with my head to the wide side against the wall and my feet to the point, but I have to be very careful not to roll off in the night. It seems that everything in this room has either three points or six. The windows are hexagons and the desk is a triangle. The mirror is worst of all. It is a triangle divided into four smaller triangles by three bars of wood through the middle. I have told Father that there is something wrong with the glass, but he can see no problem. I don't know why—it is so obvious to me. The glass distorts my face in strange ways. Some days my eyes look too large, some days too small. Once I had a terrible scare when it seemed my nose had doubled in size overnight.

Oh where is William! It is almost one o'clock in the morning now. I have watched out the window constantly for the past half hour, but there is no sign of him. Where could he possibly be? I have kept the lamps lit, but I hate to risk the light. I often catch Father wandering around at night. Neither of us is a very good sleeper. What if he should see that my light is still on? I suppose I could say that I was reading, but he would see that I am still dressed. He would see the case on the bed and he would know the truth. Sometimes I am frightened of my father. He hasn't been the same since Mother died in this very room ten years ago. She had just given birth to my younger sister. They say that she went mad. They say that she killed herself.

My father has never spoken of it.

William has not come, and I am afraid. I spent almost half an hour combing and combing and combing my hair. It is so long. It is beautiful— black and silky and curled. William always tells me how much he loves my hair. I braided it when my arm began to ache from holding the comb; I twisted it into a bun at the nape of my neck.

Where is William? I am beginning to wonder if it has happened as I feared it would. I wonder if he has changed his mind.

No. No, it cannot be.

I went to the mirror to look at my face; it was distorted, but still beautiful. The candlelight flickered on my ivory brow and in my eyes. I am beautiful and William must come for me.

I left the mirror then and hurried to my desk. My newspaper clippings are arranged in a neat pile and tied with a red ribbon. I began to read through them one by one, although I already have them all memorized. Each paper is soft and faded from so much handling; my fingers know the feel of them.

"Miss Elizabeth Blackwell's portrayal of Lady Macbeth was truly marvelous," says one. "The lovely Miss Blackwell is the shining star of our local actresses," says another. Some praise the nuances of my acting, some praise my stage presence, some praise my beauty. I have well over thirty of them and I receive more every month. Father clips them out of the newspaper for me. He never gives me any negative reviews and I do not ask to see any.

Heavens it is late. I have kept the newspaper clippings out to keep me company. I am reading them for a third time.

William is not here.

William is still not here. I have thrown the clippings out the window and watched them flutter to the ground.

I am frightened for William. He has never been late before. What if something has happened to him? I couldn't bear it. But the sun is almost up and still he has not come. I don't even need the lamps anymore. Soon my father will be awake and working on the garden. He has asked Monsieur Létourneau to come sometime soon—he wishes to have a painting of me as Ophelia for the drawing room. Father believes that it was my finest role. Monsieur Létourneau is a fine painter, but he is cheap and my father is a stingy man, so it is a perfect match. I do believe that Lillian will come to wake me; she usually does. She wants me to do her hair up for the dance she's been asked to today.

William has only been delayed, I am sure. I will wait for him tomorrow. Lillian is knocking now and I must pretend that I slept tonight.

***

Alice stopped reading, overwhelmed. She wasn't a voracious reader like Jeremy and she hadn't ever understood what people saw in books, how they could lose themselves in a string of letters. But the diary … she had never felt this way about words before. They echoed through her mind and lodged themselves there—not words any longer but feelings—translated, reflected. The book was a mirror and when she read it she thought she saw shadows of her own past lurking behind Elizabeth's strange world, peeping out from behind the walls.

A sound jarred her from her thoughts and she jumped so hard that the diary slipped out of her hands and landed on the blanket.

There had been a knock at the door. She was sure of it. But—no—it couldn't be. Could it?

On a sudden instinct, she tucked the diary under the covers. Shaking from head to toe, she walked over to the door. The room was quite bright now—the windows were letting in so much light that she could almost believe there was a real sun outside shining on them, that they were more than just the illusion that the rest of the house seemed to be. She'd spent more time reading than she realized; the woman's handwriting was very difficult to decipher, though it looked beautiful on the page. She reached over and opened the door, half expecting to see Lillian waiting outside. But there was no one.

"Hello?" Alice called. It was easier to be brave now that the house was light again. Her hands had stopped quivering altogether. "Hello!" she called again. There was no answer, but no sooner had she closed the door than she heard the knock again. There was a man's voice now.

"Anyone in there? Could you please let us in?"

Alice realized now that the sound was not coming from the door at all, but rather from the mirror, which hung on a wall across from the bed. She turned around and hurried over to look through it, but the room on the other side was still empty.

"Is there a problem?" she heard the hotel manager say.

"This door is locked," the same man said again.

"Well, of course it's locked. We do believe in some security here. Didn't I give you a key?"

"A key?"

"Don't tell me you've lost it already."

"You put it in your pocket, Dad." Now it sounded as if a teenage boy had joined the conversation. His voice was steady. Alice liked it at once.

"Oh! And so I did. Thank you, Tony."

The door opened and an older, balding man came in, followed by a boy (clearly his son) carrying two enormous plastic tubs, and the hotel manager, who looked harassed.

"Is there anything else you need?" the manager asked, though it was abundantly clear that he hoped there wasn't. He stepped through the door and right behind him stood the girl with the triangle bracelets. She wandered into the room and no one even noticed. Alice watched her walk forward to the mirror and run her fingers across the glass.

"Hush," she said. It was the first time Alice had heard her speak, and she was surprised to hear how high—almost childish—the girl's voice was. The girl, her eyes closed, traced circles on the glass, and the back of Alice's neck tingled.

There was clearly something wrong with her, and Alice suspected that she wasn't "all there" mentally. Maybe she was the hotel manager's daughter, allowed to go wherever she wanted. Alice's autistic cousin had always been allowed this kind of freedom (growing up Alice had almost envied him for it). But if the girl *had* been wandering around, why hadn't Alice ever seen her before the accident?

"Actually, there is." The older man put his suitcase down by the bed and pulled a notepad out of his pocket. "Now tell me exactly what happened yesterday—just one more time."

Absentmindedly combing through her hair, the girl wandered away from the mirror.

The manager pinched his lips together so hard that they began to turn white. "I have already told you everything. The girl dove when she shouldn't have. She cracked her head and now she's in a coma in the hospital."

The man wrote this down very quickly on his notepad; his son walked around the room, staring stonily at the walls, occasionally throwing his dad frustrated glances. He was nice-looking, but not in the way that Alice had come to expect from boys her age. Everything about his face was one extreme or another. The California surfer boys were all one shade of sandy bronze, from their hair to their skin. But this boy had skin almost as pale as Alice's and black hair that fell in waves to the tops of his ears. His eyes were large and blue; his square, black-framed glasses made him look intelligent and older than Alice suspected he was.

She liked the way he looked. She liked it too much. A second later he turned away and, staring only at the back of his head, it was easy to convince herself that the boy wasn't nearly as attractive as she thought he had been. It was a trick of the light. That was all.

"Crush," laughed the girl.

Remembering that her cousin would often say crazy, random things, Alice did what came most naturally to her and ignored the girl, pressing her hand against the cool glass, watching the boy behind it. He frowned again at his dad, as the older man tried to squeeze more details out of the manager.

"But you haven't answered the question—has there been any paranormal activity of any sort? Any strange noises? Anything out of the ordinary?"

The hotel manager looked as though he had had just about enough. "Sir," he said through lips so tight that they hardly moved at all, "a girl was injured while playing in the pool. That is all there is to it. If you continue to badger me, I will kindly ask you to leave the premises." He walked into the hallway and began to close the door. "Enjoy your stay." It sounded more like a death wish than anything else. The door slammed shut behind him. The girl remained in the room and the man and his son didn't seem to care. She perched herself on a fluffy pink armchair and observed the scene with glittering eyes, like a queen, like she owned it.

The man shook his head and looked at his son. "This is what I've warned you about time and time again, Tony. Some people are so close-minded that they can't see the supernatural when it's right in front of them."

The girl laughed.

"I wish you'd leave him alone," said Tony, examining the pattern on the curtains.

"How else am I going to get the information I need? I can't base an investigation on nothing."

"It's just ... I don't know. It seems a little ... "

"A little what?"

Tony shrugged. "Insensitive."

The man, George, shook his head. "You're forgetting that what we're doing here may help the girl. If we can appease the angry spirit, maybe it will release her."

Tony still looked uncertain. "Why are you so sure that this is supernatural, anyway?"

"Why am I sure? You've seen the evidence. You've read the newspapers—always the same story. Girl injures herself, falls into a coma, dies a week later. In 1890, a guest fell out of a second-story window; 1905, off a ladder; 1926, down the stairs ... 1960, 1983 ... you know how it goes. Now this girl's hit her head on the bottom of a pool and—big surprise—comatose in the hospital. I'm no doctor, but I give her a week."

He paused and Alice gulped over the lump that had formed in her throat. She felt suddenly dizzy and grabbed the side of the mirror, forcing herself to stay standing.

George shook his head and asked, "Can you honestly say that's just a coincidence?"

As he had been speaking, whenever he said a date, the girl had put up a finger. Now she was wagging five fingers in the air. "Then the last one," she said, lifting another finger. "And you forgot the first." She put up a seventh finger. "Seven!" She had an unsettling laugh. "That's important. Seven."

Then she turned and looked straight at the mirror. Alice, whose arms were already covered in goose bumps, had a sudden desire to duck out of sight. "She's just babbling," she told herself. But then the girl's grin widened, as though she had heard Alice talking and was amused by it.

Alice reminded herself to breathe. Slowly, not daring to take her eyes off the girl, she edged her way to the side of the mirror. Leaning against the wall beside it, she pressed her hands against her stomach and closed her eyes. If the girl could see and hear her through the glass ... that was a good thing. A *really* good thing. But the girl's eyes ... the way they shone ... her pointy-toothed smile ... Alice wanted to run and hide, even though she knew she should be throwing herself against the glass and begging the girl to tell her what was going on here.

Tony was grudgingly answering his dad's question. "Well ... it is a little hard to explain."

"Exactly—you can't. And we're here to figure out why it's happening."

"I just don't see how—"

"This is our first trip together. Are you going to spend it doubting what I do for a living?"

"Are you going to write a book about this case too?" Tony said.

"Of course. It's going in my newest collection. I think I'm going to title it *Spirited Away: The Unhappy Dead*. What do you think?"

"It's nice."

Alice took a deep breath, opened her eyes, and peeked around the edge of the mirror, only to see the girl standing not five inches away from it on the other side—just standing there, grinning from ear to ear like the Cheshire Cat. Screaming, Alice jumped backwards.

"Boo," said the girl.

And in that moment, just for a second, Alice was reminded of Jeremy. He would make a game of sneaking up on her, scaring her half to death. She could almost see him there—shorter than the girl, his red hair wild, wearing that same glee on his face. Alice blinked and there was the girl again, but at least for a moment Alice was not afraid of her at all.

She rushed forward. "Tell me what's going on," she demanded. "Tell me how to get out of here."

The girl didn't answer.

"*Tell me!*" Alice pressed a hand to the glass.

Sighing, the girl wandered back to the chair, acting as if she had not heard anything. Alice lifted her hand and curled it into a fist to bang on the glass, as though she could knock down the wall. But when the girl sat down and started examining her nails, Alice froze, then put her hand down. This too was something Jeremy would have done, just to egg her on. Well, if the girl was going to play like that, Alice *wasn't* going to give her the satisfaction of a response.

Crossing her arms, Alice bit her tongue and didn't say a word. Silence was a game Alice was good at.

CHAPTER FOUR

The father, sitting on the bed by his son, rocked back on his hands. "You've wanted to come with me on an investigation since you were just a little boy. Aren't you excited that Madeline's finally let you tag along? She's always so worried about you, thinks I'm going to corrupt you or something. But you'll see. And she'll see too. We'll have a wonderful time."

Whatever the boy was feeling, it was far from excitement. He smiled anyway, and Alice could tell that it was forced. She'd used that same smile on her parents plenty of times.

"Yeah. It's really going to be something."

Alice snorted at the boy's pained expression. *Stop playing the martyr.* As if it were such a *terrible* burden to have your dad thrilled to spend time with you. Alice could hardly have a decent conversation with her distracted father, who regularly multitasked his relationships to death.

"That's my boy! You bet it is."

Tony smiled again, though this one was no more genuine than the last. "So. Where do we start?"

His father fumbled through his notes. He finally stopped on a page toward the front of the notebook. "Ah yes, here we are. We start with Elizabeth Blackwell."

"The actress."

"Yes, the actress. She was fabulous, according to the newspapers I've looked at. Quite famous, in fact; she was on the road to stardom before she died. She stayed in the attic room for many years, then suddenly went mad. The attic burned down in the fire, though—never got rebuilt. It's unfortunate too. I would have killed to look around up there."

Attic? Alice hadn't seen an attic.

Tony crossed his legs on the bed and leaned back, giving his father his undivided attention for the first time. "She went crazy?"

"Lies," said the girl, sitting up straighter now.

Alice, figuring this broke the silence war, tried to call the girl over. But the girl didn't react—not even with a glance. She was focused completely on Tony and his dad, though they seemed unaware of her.

George was nodding. "Oh yes—she lost it. No one knows how it happened, but they say that before she died she started fooling with things she shouldn't have. Her sister, Lillian, died years ago, but I got my hands on an interview someone did with her just before she passed away. Lillian inherited the boardinghouse after

Elizabeth and Mr. Blackwell died. She said some pretty interesting things."

"And you've been researching the story all this time, hoping someone would get hurt," the boy said, frowning.

"Well, I wouldn't say *hoping* necessarily. I was just waiting, on the lookout, you know?"

Yeah, like a vulture after carrion, Alice thought.

Tony didn't look entirely pleased with this answer either, but he let it go. "So she went nuts?" he prompted.

"Yes. Anyway, Lillian said that whenever she went up to see Elizabeth, she was reading strange old books, chanting things."

"Magic," said the girl, pacing the elaborate rug.

"Why?"

"That," said the man, "is the mystery. Sometimes I think that Lillian knew more than she admitted to, but who's to say? If we can isolate Elizabeth's spirit, we may be able to get the answer straight from her. "

"How did she die anyway?"

"Suicide—nasty business. She almost burned the house down. They found her drowned in the pond with a knife through her heart and the attic in flames above her. Her father ... well, they found him dead too. Burned to death tied to a bedpost in the attic."

Tony grimaced and Alice gulped. She looked at the lump in the bed where she'd hidden the bloodstained diary. Elizabeth had held that diary, written in it. Alice felt suddenly very close to her and it sent a horrified sort of thrill through her. When she looked up, the girl was looking at her. *Finally.*

"We are all of us alike," whispered the girl. She turned around before Alice could respond.

"*I know you can hear me!*" said Alice, so forcefully that specks of spit dotted the mirror. But once again the girl walked away from her. Alice threw both of her fists against the glass.

"And no one knows what happened?" Tony asked.

His father shook his head. "No one ever figured it out. The police investigated for a while, but found no one with motive. The sister was less than cooperative. And the real story was never told."

They sat in silence on the bed for a moment, Tony looking somber, his dad eager. Then George jumped to his feet and reached for the nearest plastic tub.

"You ready to start setting up?"

Tony nodded; George opened one of the tubs and started pulling out some strange-looking contraptions. Alice had never seen anything like them. Tony was screwing rods together while his father ran microphones around the room and tried to get a tiny video camera mounted on the dresser. He turned on a funny-looking flashlight and tiny pricks of light littered the wall across from him.

"This will help us check for disturbances in the air—any spirits walking by," the father explained. As he did, the girl exaggeratedly tiptoed up behind him, laughing like a maniac. She waved her arms and made as if to poke him in the back of the head. Her finger never actually touched him; it stopped an inch from his hair. No one's crazy daughter—not even the hotel manager's—would have gotten away with that unnoticed. They couldn't see her; Alice was sure that, like her, the girl was visible to no one else.

Stepping away from the mirror, Alice sat down on the bed. *All those girls in comas*, she thought to herself, *and all of them died a week later.* Had the other women been trapped in this house as well? Had they slept in this bed—read this same diary?

And what about her? Would she die too? Would she somehow float out of this phantom house and into ... somewhere else? Would it hurt? Alice had no idea and she found herself watching Tony and his father with something like hope. Maybe they'd be able to free her—if she couldn't find her own way out.

She stepped up to the mirror and caught the girl's eye. The girl stopped turning the lamp on the nightstand on and off and stared straight back.

"Tell me how to get out," begged Alice, holding onto some silly, fragile dream that the girl would open her mouth and answers would come pouring out.

But the girl did not answer. She looked at the mirror for a moment longer, then turned on the heel of her jet-black shoe and marched to the door. Yanking it open, she walked out and disappeared into the hallway.

Alice threw herself back onto the bed and sank her fist deep into one of the pillows.

She didn't turn back to the mirror for a few minutes, just sat breathing heavily, feeling the sharp bite of air hissing between her teeth. Slightly calmer then, she watched the boy and his father mount video cameras on tripods and carry them out of the room.

Both the man in the mirror and Elizabeth's diary had mentioned an attic. Tony's father said that it had been demolished after Elizabeth died, but if this was in fact how the house had looked during Elizabeth's life, then perhaps the attic room still existed. If Alice could get to it, then maybe she could find a way to communicate to Tony's father what he needed to know—the details that might tell him what was really going on here and how to get her out. There had to be a way to break through the glass. After all, ghosts could go where they wanted. If she could figure out how to communicate with the real world, then there would be no one better to talk to than someone who made a living examining the supernatural.

The room in the mirror was empty now and Alice left her room as well. The silk lingerie was cool against her skin. She glanced at the mirror in the hallway as she walked by, but neither Tony nor his father were anywhere to be seen. At the top of the staircase Alice stopped. The second story of the boardinghouse only covered the back half. Was it possible that the attic room was somewhere above one of the lower-level rooms? Or was there a third story? She closed her eyes and thought back to the night when her family had driven up to the hotel to check in. But it had been so dark and for the life of her she could not remember whether there had been another floor or not.

As she looked around, searching for something (she didn't know what), her eyes stopped on the tapestry hanging from a rod at the end of the hall—one that she knew hadn't been in the real hotel. It showed a deer in a forest, framed with a fringe of gold thread, and there was an odd lump on one side, just where she would expect a doorknob to be. She hurried over to it and lifted the fabric.

Eureka.

She tried to open the door in the paneling, but the knob refused to turn. Only then did Alice notice the keyhole, and she knelt down to take a closer look. The opening was two inches tall, and she placed her eye to it, but could see nothing on the other side. Sitting back on her heels, she stared at the copper plating, sure that she should be looking for a large, old-fashioned key. She was tempted to try to pick the lock, but she didn't dare mess with it. When she was younger, she had tried to pick the lock on her parents' door once and the bobby pin broke. The locksmith hadn't arrived to free her parents until three hours later. Alice wasn't sure if the house would heal itself from a jammed lock.

She let the tapestry fall back over the door. Where would Elizabeth have kept the key? Alice couldn't exactly ask her.

The diary. Maybe she wrote about it in the diary.

She started walking back down the hallway, but halfway to the room, she heard loud voices coming from one of the mirrors on the hallway wall and ran back to see what the fuss was about.

"I don't care if it's life or death!" the hotel manager was

shouting. Tony's father was running wires across the carpeting; he wiped his hands on his jeans, then stood up.

Tony slunk behind his dad. It couldn't have been clearer that he didn't want to be involved in this.

"I didn't say life or death," George said heavily, as though he thought the manager was being deliberately slow. "I said it's important for *life* that we know more about *death*."

"Good Lord!" The manager threw his hands up in despair. "I don't give a ... look—what is your name again?"

George bent down to adjust a cable, clearly insulted.

"Well, it doesn't matter who you are. I'm going to have to ask you to clear up this ... this mess, or I will have you removed from the building." Alice saw the girl peeking out from behind him and clasped her hands tightly behind her back, biting back the urge to shout at her.

Very slowly, George got back to his feet and turned to the red-faced hotel manager. Alice could not see the expression on George's face, but judging by the way the hotel manager's eyebrows went up, it wasn't friendly. Tony snuck a bit farther away. A few people down the hall stuck their heads out of their rooms to see what was going on.

"Do you understand the significance of what we are doing here?" said George at last.

"We?" said the manager, throwing a pointed glance at Tony, who was looking more embarrassed by the second. This was obviously not the right thing to say. George stuck his finger right into the manager's chest and started speaking very loudly.

"Now look here. I know that this may be hard for a close-minded man like yourself to understand, but my son and I have a once-in-a-lifetime opportunity to witness the supernatural as it has never been seen before. Would you stand in the way of that?"

The hotel manager looked entirely unfazed by the news that he might be disturbing a paranormal phenomenon. He pushed George's finger away and pointed furiously at the floor, waving his arm around as he spoke. "I will stand in the way of *anything* that disturbs my patrons, *sir*, and I have been receiving complaints about your little setup here. This is a health hazard and I will not stand for it! If you want to create a spiderweb of trip wires in your own room, you are welcome to do so. But this hallway is a public area, and I will *not* allow you or anyone else to booby-trap it."

"Already a trap," said the girl.

She's messing with me—just like Jeremy does. Like a bored kid poking a worm with a stick, the girl was trying to make her squirm. But Alice began to back away from the mirror all the same, eyeing the wires on the other side. They couldn't affect her, could they? If she couldn't touch that world, surely it couldn't touch her.

The hotel manager whipped around and marched down the stairs. "You have half an hour before I contact the police." The girl stepped out of the way as he passed, then pointed her toe at one of the wires on the floor, winked at the mirror, and ran down the stairs.

Letting her nerves get the best of her, Alice began to back down the hallway, craning her neck to see what was going on in the mirror. She could still see George—he had turned around, his face scrunched up and red.

"Some people have *no* appreciation for anything beyond their miserable lives. *None!*"

"We should probably take it down," said Tony. Unlike his father, he didn't seem at all disappointed by this sudden turn of events.

But his father ignored him. With a quick glance downstairs to make sure that the hotel manager wasn't watching, he turned around and grabbed a plug.

"We have thirty more minutes. You better believe we're going to use them."

With that, he stuck the plug in the nearest outlet. In the shadow house behind the glass, Alice screamed in agony.

CHAPTER FIVE

Alice had never felt pain like this before. It felt as if someone were sticking knives up her feet and spilling fire through her body. It hurt so terribly that she couldn't move; all she could do was yell at the mirror.

"Stop! *Please stop!* Turn it off!"

No one heard her. George was bent over a square device with an antenna and a flat screen.

"I'll be damned. Tony, get over here—you've got to see this!"

Tony walked over slowly … excruciatingly slowly—every moment was interminable and Alice, gasping, thought she would not, surely could not last any longer. Finally, he reached his dad's side and took the monitor George was shoving in his face.

"Do you see that heat signature right there? That's a person if I ever saw one, only a few feet away." He was speaking softly—reverently. Alice's ears were ringing; she could hear her heart. His voice sounded distant and strange.

Tony peered more closely at the screen, as though he couldn't quite believe what he was seeing. Then he looked up at the spot where Alice was standing in her version of the house.

"Make him stop!" she screamed. "Please, Tony!"

He gave a funny little jump when she said his name, and—a flicker of hope, quickly lost in the raging fire that consumed her.

"Did you hear something?"

"It must be speaking to you!" George said. His beady eyes were open wider than Alice would have guessed that they could go. "Say something! It wants to communicate with you; talk to it!"

"What—what do I say?" Tony said, looking back and forth between the monitor and his father in a panic.

"Just say something! And hurry! We don't know how long it will stay."

George pushed his son forward, toward where Alice was frozen to the floor behind the mirror.

"Help!" she gasped, unable to bear the thought of even one more second. But the seconds came and kept coming, and each one took her breath away but left her more full of fire than before.

"Um ... what's your name?" Tony said after a moment of hesitation.

"*Turn it off! Turn it off!*"

Tony shrugged. "I can't hear it anymore. It must have been my imagination."

No. I'm here. She tried to lean forward, to break free, but the effort made her vision blur and the pain grow sharper still. She would not last until the hotel manager returned to check on George; she would wither, collapse, burst into flame … the flames, the fire would eat her up. It licked her bones now. It was ravenous and Alice's eyes stung from tears and she cried out and …

Tony stepped on the wire. The one that had her trapped.

He flinched, then buckled in pain as the oddest sensation came over Alice. The pain was still tearing her apart, but there was something else, too—something more. It almost felt as if there were another soul inside of her body, and she thought she could hear someone else's thoughts. She was still herself, but she was someone else as well. And that someone was hurting too.

Alice arched her back, trying to lessen the pain shooting down her spine. Her arms and legs were on fire; her head was pounding fit to burst. She screamed at the ceiling the only word that seemed to work.

"*Tony!*"

"Dad, it's in pain!"

"What?" George looked startled. "What? It's dead. How could it be in pain?"

"*Tony!*"

"You need to turn it off!" Tony said, and Alice felt the panic in his voice; she felt it in her own body, felt his soul pulsing next to hers.

"I can't! These readings are incredible!"

"*Turn this damn thing off!*" It was Tony who shouted it, but Alice could have sworn the words came from her as well. She watched as Tony ran to the outlet, shoved his dad aside, and yanked the plug. The pain disappeared as suddenly as it had come and Alice collapsed to the floor, barely aware of the voices from the mirror. The other presence was gone and somehow Alice felt terribly lonely without it.

"What the hell do you think you're doing?" George was shouting. "I've been in this profession for fifteen years and I have never once seen readings like those. They were almost as strong as heat readings off a real person! This is enough to prove the reality of spirit existence to the most skeptical scientist in the world. So *plug the thing back in!*"

Tony's voice was shaking. "You were hurting it."

"How could you possibly know that? Give me the plug!"

"I felt it, Dad! It was in pain!"

"This is the moment I've been waiting for my *whole life*, Tony!"

"I don't care!"

"*Give it back!*"

Every bit of Alice's body felt as if it had been pummeled with a sledgehammer, but she was so frightened of what would happen if George managed to plug his device back in that she pushed herself to her knees and crawled into the bedroom. She pulled her body onto the satin-covered bed and lay motionless on the covers. When she had woken up in this place, her body had ached. The pain now was sharper and pointed—it made the soreness of earlier seem gentle, almost made her wish for it. She could still hear the shouts from the hallway, but she couldn't understand what they were saying. Alice closed her eyes and wandered the closest to sleep that she had come since she'd woken up here in the first place, only it wasn't so much sleep as a fevered exhaustion.

I'm wasting time, she thought hazily. *I can't afford to waste any time …*

It was like floating. She knew that she was lying on the bed, but with her eyes closed she thought she felt herself drifting toward the ceiling, through the ceiling, into a world that was only light. Light and voices—a chorus of them. They whispered and sighed all around her and Alice was spinning, arms outstretched, trying to find them. She thought she saw shadows flitting into the distance, running away from her, as if they were caught up in a strange game of tag and now she was it—now it was her turn to find them and no one had told her.

Waking up wasn't exactly the right word for what happened no more than an hour later. It was more of an urge that forced her to open her eyes. A need to do something. Alice couldn't remember what at first, but the discomfort of not knowing was enough to jar her back to consciousness. She slowly became aware of her body lying on the covers. The pain was gone, but the weakness remained.

Was that a whisper? She craned her neck to look behind her, but saw nothing and no one. For a moment she thought she was still in the dream—was it a dream? But what else could it have been? The light had been warm as sunshine, and without it everything seemed twice as cold. Without the voices, twice as lonely.

She felt a tiny, hard square digging into the small of her back and she began to remember what it was that had woken her. *The key—I've forgotten about the key.* Alice pulled the book from under the covers where she'd left it that morning. If the diary said where the key was hidden, she needed to know about it, because the fact that she (and only she) could get into the room was the one thing that kept her from helplessness. What would she find in there? She had no idea. But she couldn't lie here and wait for someone to save her (or not), doing nothing at all. And what if the door was the way out of here? Could that be the secret? Could it be that simple? If she couldn't find the key, she would never know.

She could hardly hold her arms up. Propping herself up against the pillows, she pressed the book open on her legs. She flipped to the end, then started flicking through pages, looking for anything about a key. But while the handwriting at the beginning of the book had been difficult, the handwriting at the end was nearly impossible to read. Skimming the mess of words was hardly a possibility and, worried that she would miss something important if she skipped, Alice hunted down the page she had left off on.

***

April 30, 1883

A week I have waited and still he has not come. I do not know what to think. I do not want to think. What if he has deserted me? What if he has found another woman? But no one—no one could be more beautiful than I am. William told me so himself. And yet I wonder and I am afraid, because I have always had this feeling that there is something dreadfully wrong with me.

For the past eight years I have spent as little time in this room as possible and now I will not leave it. Father believes that I am sick; I cannot tell him that I watch for William. Monsieur Létourneau has been convinced to paint my portrait here so that I will not tire myself with too much moving about. He made a terrible fuss at first, for he says the light in this room is dreadful and the scenery even worse, but, as I told him, he is a painter of exceptional skill and he can paint whatever background he likes. Now he paints quietly but quickly. I believe that the room wears on him. He will be happy to finish.

I stand by the window for many hours every day, with nothing to do but look at my face in the mirror. At first I tried to avoid looking at it, for I do not like what the glass does to my reflection, but now I watch very carefully indeed.

You see, I have figured out the secret of the mirror at last. The witch didn't ever truly escape this room. She died here and locked her spirit inside the glass so that she would never have to leave. It took me many hours to discover this, but after staring for an entire portrait session, I saw her at last. She was at the very bottom, in the right triangle. First I saw her forehead and then her brown eyes, but I believe that I frightened her, for I gasped and she ducked back out of sight. I think that I startled Monsieur Létourneau as well. He asked me what I was looking at, but I refused to tell him. Sometimes I see him staring at the mirror in a most curious way. What if I told him the truth, and he took the mirror away? I will not allow it. Surely the world would not be so cruel as to take away the one thing that keeps me alive.

It is my first thought in the morning, my last in the night.

The mirror's secret is not the only one that I have uncovered, either. There is one floorboard that creaks when I step on it. I have always borne it with patience, but it creaks louder now—like a scream—and sets my heart pounding. One night, nearly driven mad by the noise, I decided to take it out. There was a crack on one side, almost large enough for me to stick my hand into. I tore at it until it was big enough, then I stuck my hand in and pulled until the board came flying out. It scraped the skin off my palm when it came free, and oh I am so afraid that it will scar. Father says my hands are perfect as little white doves. I wrap it tightly each night and pray it will heal. But would you believe what I found in the floor? I hardly dare to write it for fear that Lillian will read this journal and take my new treasures for herself. But I must tell someone. You must promise never to tell. Promise.

Very well, I will tell you.

I have found the old witch's spell books.

Isn't it marvelous? The books are so old that they almost fall apart in my hands, but the ink is still readable. The larger one is full of curses and the other of spells. I read them all night while I watch for William.

They have the oddest smell.

Sometimes while I am reading I see the witch watching me from the mirror. She pops out all over the place now! One moment she will be in one triangle and then—poof!—she will appear in another, always wearing the most alarming grin on her face. I even heard her whisper something to me once.

"Elizabeth"—that is what she said.

Now isn't it odd that she knows my name? But I suppose that if she has been up here the whole time I have, she has surely heard someone say my name one time or another. She is a clever witch—I see it in her eyes. Sometimes I am frightened of her. Sometimes I see the rope she hanged herself with still lying around her neck like a necklace. I told her that she should take it off, but of course she doesn't listen to me.

I think that I am going to try one of the curses.

***

Alice's head flew up. *The rope lying around her neck like a necklace.* Her eyes went to the mirror above the dresser, where she had seen the girl last. But the room in the real hotel was empty. Sitting stick-straight, Alice stared into space, trying to remember every detail of the girl's appearance. There were those triangle bracelets she wore around her wrist. There was the necklace that looked so much like rope ...

She clutched the diary so tightly that her fingernails dug into the soft leather cover. The whole time she had been reading the diary, she had imagined the witch wizened and ugly and old, with sagging eyelids and hands like talons. Now the only face she could see was the girl's—those golden-brown eyes.

Brown eyes ... Alice flipped back through the pages, running her finger across line after line of loopy handwriting until she found where Elizabeth had written it. The witch had brown eyes.

Alice's heart was pounding out a frantic rhythm against her chest. Eyes, necklace, odd grin ... the girl. The witch. It explained at least why no one in the hotel paid the least attention to her— only Elizabeth could see the witch in her mirror and only Alice could see her now. But if the witch was still in the hotel, wandering the mirrors like some lost spirit, then why hadn't she approached Alice? Could she get free of the glass? Could she come into Alice's side of the house? As much as the thought of the witch hiding in the mirrors frightened her, the thought of the witch in this version of the house—walking the halls, sitting in dark corners—terrified her even more.

Alice leaned over the diary again. If the girl really was the witch, then Alice needed to know more about her—what she wanted and whether she could get free.

***

May 5, 1883

I think that Lillian suspects my discovery. She is always popping in, trying to catch me with the books, trying to see the witch in the mirror. Each time she so much as glances at the mirror, I ask her what she is looking for. But the little devil won't admit it. She shakes her head at me and says I am losing my mind, as if she were fooling anyone. I know what she is up to and I am too clever for her. I have a spot under my bed where I put the books when I hear her coming. The witch can take care of herself, of course. She ducks out of sight just as soon as Lillian walks into the room. The witch trusts no one but me with her secrets. I am the only one worthy—the only one clever enough to understand them. My sister is young and silly and empty-headed. I am full to brimming with life. I shine with it.

Once I locked my door so that Lillian would not disturb us, but Lillian threw an absolute fit when she could not get in. Lillian has always been one for throwing fits—by the time she was three she could yell so loudly that the whole neighborhood would hear. I heard her talking to Father outside my door and do you know what she said? She said that it is dangerous for me to be up here by myself with no one to look after me. That's when I knew. She wants access to the room so that she can take the books for herself.

When I finally let her and Father inside, she took the key right out of my hand and threw it out the window. I went down to look for it, but I couldn't find it in the bushes. I sleep with the books under my pillow now.

***

Alice stopped reading. *Outside?* If the key was outside the house, there was no chance that she would be able to find it. None of the doors would open and, quite frankly, she wasn't even certain that there *was* anything outside of these walls. She had a funny feeling that this place existed outside of reality.

The windows were almost dark now. On the other side of the mirror, George and Tony were watching television. Alice wasn't exactly sure what had happened out in the hallway, but neither of them looked happy. They were sitting as far apart from each other as possible on the bed and a coil of wire lay limply in the corner of the room. A video camera was sitting on the nightstand, forgotten.

She thought of her parents, how she had often seen them sitting like that at night, on opposite sides of the bed, television making the wall into a flickering rainbow of color. They watched comedies—the kind with laugh tracks and jokes that got stale after a while. But they were always so quiet, as if TV were a sport that required the utmost concentration. It was strange. The TV audience would laugh and laugh and her mom and dad would lie there with stiff half-grins on their faces and occasional real smiles that were gone faster than a blink. But they never laughed. Not once. Alice could see them so clearly in her head that it made her stomach clench. Though the picture wasn't a happy one, it made her miss them so terribly that she forced it away as best she could. She focused instead on the father and son in the mirror. They were real. This was real and memories were only shadows.

As Alice watched, Tony got up and grabbed a book from his suitcase. He muttered something about needing fresh air.

"Of course, of course. Whatever makes you happy," said George, in a voice so hearty that it was obviously forced. Tony frowned and walked out. His father flipped the channel.

A second later, Tony popped his head back through the door.

George looked up, then muted the television and said heavily, "Tony, is there something you want to talk about?"

Tony took a deep breath and opened his mouth, then shut it again. His eyes wandered from his dad's face to the TV screen, then back again, and finally he said, "Never mind. You wouldn't listen anyway."

"Why don't you give me a chance?" George said, but Tony had already turned around and shut the door behind him. George leaned back against the headboard and frowned at the remote for a minute. Then he whispered, "Space. He needs some space," and he turned the sound back on.

Alice got up to follow Tony into the hallway. She wanted to see if her ability to communicate with him was a freak of his father's wiring or something that could happen again. If she could tell him about the key, maybe he could look around outside for her. Maybe it was still buried somewhere in the yard. If he brought it into the house, would it appear in her version as well? There was only one way to find out. She tucked the diary safely under the covers and walked toward the door.

But she didn't even make it to the doorknob.

At that very moment, a grandfather clock in the hall began to strike midnight.

Dong.

It was as if she had stepped into an elevator going down. The room grew taller around her—was she shrinking? She looked down at her feet. Her feet ... her feet were gone. Her legs sprouted straight out of the floor.

She flailed, cried out, reached for the doorknob, but it was just beyond her fingertips. She clutched frantically at the floor, but her hands sank right through it and she, drowning in the quicksand the floor had become, thrashed and pulled at her legs. It was no use. Pulling her hands out, she tried to grab onto the bottom of the nightstand. For a moment she touched it, brushed it with her fingertips, but they slid off as her hips disappeared, then her stomach, her chest, her arms, her neck. She took a huge breath of air, strained upward one last time.

And then there was only water.

CHAPTER SIX

The water was cold and black and pressed so hard against her she thought her skull would surely burst under the pressure of it. She was suspended in motion, her arms still stretched out toward a nightstand that was no longer there, her feet on a smooth, cool surface. At first she didn't realize where she was—all she knew was that everything seemed dark and murky and her eyes stung. But then she saw the white tile she was standing on; she saw the side of the pool in the distance. As she tried to breathe, her lungs filled with water. Her head was spinning.

Air.

Alice pushed off the bottom of the pool as hard as she could, but she floated to the surface slowly, barely making it all the way up. Gasping, she threw her head free, and for a split second she saw the garden and the trees and the dark hotel in the moonlight. She was coughing so hard that she hardly registered that she was outside—she saw, but did not comprehend, though a tiny voice in the back of her mind whispered that something had happened and something was wrong. But breathing and coughing were all she could think about, and in the entire world there was not enough air to satisfy her. She had only managed to take in a few short breaths, though, when the water started to suck her back in. Her flailing arms seemed to make no difference and her legs, which she kicked with every bit of strength she had, might as well have been thrashing in midair. She pulled harder, but the water was so heavy around her; it felt solid and yet it seemed to go right through her hands. Alice realized that her mouth was open—that she was screaming. She was sinking.

"Oh my God!" a familiar voice yelled just before the water completely engulfed her head. She heard a muffled splash behind her and then an arm wrapped around her waist. Someone pulled her up and toward the surface, and Alice flailed uselessly, weakly now. Her vision was blurry and all she could think about was how it would feel to breathe. Her head broke the surface of the water again.

"Calm down!" the same voice yelled. "You're going to be okay! Just calm down, will you?"

Air filled her lungs and Alice stopped fighting. Her head felt tight, as if it had been stuck in a vice, and the blood pounded so hard in her ears that she thought her eardrums might burst. She started to cough and felt herself being dragged onto the pool deck. Coughing. Why couldn't she stop coughing? The second she gulped down air, it exploded out of her. She couldn't get enough and she started to panic again, hunching over and stretching out her arms as if reaching for something—she didn't know what.

"No, just stay calm. Breathe slow. There you go. The coughing's okay—you've got to get the water out. Here, I'm gonna go get you a towel."

Alice was too weak to respond. She coughed more water up and knelt down on the pavement, breathing heavily. Her head was spinning and she doubled over and pressed her forehead against her knees. He laid a heavy, fluffy towel over her, then took a few quick steps away and stood waiting to the side.

"You okay? Did you fall in?"

Alice managed to lift her head and turn it just enough to see the person's face.

"My name's Tony," he said.

Her jaw had gone slack and she knew she was gaping at him like a total idiot, but no matter how much she stared, she just couldn't wrap her head around it. She started hacking again, her whole back shaking. Was this even possible? How could she be back in the real world?

"What … " she moaned, wanting to bury her face in her knees again—she was so dizzy. Tony was watching her with unmistakable worry in his eyes and, whether this was the real world or a dream or something even stranger, there was a very real rush of embarrassment making her cheeks burn. *He must be thinking …* She stopped herself mid-thought. *Seriously?* No—she needed to focus.

She needed to figure out what was going on. When was her head going to straighten out? Everything was such a blur.

"Just give yourself a minute." Tony was talking as if they had just met over dinner at a nice restaurant and there she was, dripping onto the pool deck and shivering under her towel, wearing only a ... *oh no*. Alice peeked under the towel and winced as her suspicions were confirmed. She was still wearing the little red lingerie dress. Through some miracle it had stayed on through the whole drowning experience, but still . . .

"I ... I would have been fine ... on my own," she said, pulling the towel more tightly around her, moving a little farther away from him.

"I'm sure. Um ... how *did* you end up in the pool?" asked Tony.

He seemed real. She blinked a few times and squinted up at his face; there was a solidity to his chin and his mouth, how it moved when he talked. Tony exhaled heavily and then forced an awkward half-smile in her direction. Surely she couldn't be imagining this, but she had to know for sure.

"Do you believe in ghosts?" Alice blurted out. Not that she was a ghost. She wasn't. But how else could she explain that she wasn't in her body somehow and she'd been trapped in this house that wasn't the hotel and ... She was breathing heavily.

Tony laughed; it was clipped, half-hearted. He stared at her with an empty grin frozen on his face. "Did a ghost push you in?" He asked it as if it were a legitimate question—or at least as if he expected her to say yes.

"What?"

"You know … " He shrugged and glanced at the back door of the hotel. "You were walking and suddenly you fell in and … maybe it was a ghost that pushed you. Really, who knows? But I think you need help and … I'll just be a minute, let me go and—"

He was edging away from her—inch by inch.

"*Please*," Alice gasped out.

Tony stopped. "Do you need me to call an ambulance or something? I will—I mean, I can do that."

"Yes, I need help. I need *your* help." How could she make him understand? *Coma, mirrors, diary* … it sounded crazy even in her head. "Look," she said, "I didn't die, okay? At least I don't think I died—"

"Okay I think you're in shock and so I'm going to go get my dad and—"

"No!"

Her entire body seized up at the thought of George. The wires, the pain like fire … in all her life she had not felt anything like it. She remembered it perfectly—how sharply it had cut through every inch of her—and her skin prickled.

"Can I just ask you some questions? Please?"

"Um … "

She recognized the look on his face—the way he was grimacing, the pity in his eyes. It was the expression people got when they saw a crazy person and had no idea what to do. It was the look she'd had on her face when they visited her dying aunt in the hospital and she hadn't known what to say, because, really, what was there to say?

"I promise I'm not crazy," she said, and realized a second too late how desperate that sounded. *Nicely done, Alice.* She squinted at the hotel, then up at the stars. The sky was a deep blue-black and seeing it stretched out above her—no fogged windows, no old ceilings—made her heart pound faster.

Tony still had not answered; she looked back up at him and saw that same helpless, frightened grin.

"Of course you're not crazy. I didn't say you were *crazy.*" He started to laugh, but then coughed into his hand instead. "Look, I'm just going to be gone for a minute. I'll call the hotel manager— get my dad—if you don't want an ambulance, then you should at least come inside, get warm … "

He was going to tell everyone and there would be panicking and then the questions and … There wasn't time for this. She needed him to help her figure out where her family was and where she was—not *she* herself but *she* her body. (Or was this her body? Was that possible? Maybe this was a bizarre case of coma-walking. Maybe she'd been dreaming. Maybe she was still dreaming. Maybe …) She needed his help.

"No … really—"

"Please just wait here. Stay calm *please.*" Tony put a hand out, as if she were a dog he could order to sit and stay. Then he turned around and started to hurry toward the hotel.

Alice tried to clamber to her feet, but the towel slipped from her back and got tangled around her ankles. In the time it took her to reach down and free herself (the towel was unusually heavy, or maybe she was just tired), Tony got halfway across the lawn. Alice threw the towel to the pool deck and started to run after him.

"No—*Tony!*"

He stopped so suddenly that, if she'd been a faster runner, she might have crashed right into him. Turning around, he stared at her face as if he were seeing it for the first time. Her stomach tingled—tickled—and a shiver shot down her spine. Something ... she couldn't explain it ... but it was as if something had passed between them, as if the air had gone hot.

"Do I know you?" Tony said at last. His eyebrows bunched together in the middle and his lips thinned, a slight frown. "Your voice sounds ... I don't know ... "

But Alice knew. She remembered the pain most of all, but then there had been that moment when she had heard his voice—not just heard it, felt it echoing inside of her own mind. And those seconds when they had been stuck together, like two birds in one cage. It hadn't occurred to her before, but if she had been able to hear him, then it only made sense that he would have heard her, too.

"The thing is ... " She had sidetracked him, but only barely, only for a second. And though she wanted to blurt out the truth, the chance that he would turn around and walk away was just too much. He already thought she was nuts. Alice paused, then started over. "My family was staying at the hotel. Maybe we passed each other in the hall."

"*Was* staying? They left? Why are you still here? Wait—no, I need to get you help—wait a minute—"

He tried to turn around again, but she grabbed his hand and held on tight.

"I'm fine. I promise you that I'm fine. I don't need a doctor or anything. And my family ..." When she spoke, she tried to sound casual and normal—sane. "Is staying ... *are* staying. We're here. All of us. Now."

"I see." He looked down at her hand, wrapped around his. But he didn't try to pull away. "Strong grip." He frowned at her. "You do *seem* okay. But I still think ..." Tony's frown deepened. He brushed his hair off his forehead, then stared into her eyes for a long time, squinting slightly. "It's strange—I was sure I recognized ... maybe you just remind me of someone."

But he sounded uncertain.

"Right ... maybe." What could she say to keep him there? She had to figure out if he knew anything about the Alice in a coma, and if the truth was going to make him think she was crazy or in shock and go running for help, then she needed a new tactic, a different truth ...

"The truth is that I tripped," she said, nodding toward the pool. "I couldn't sleep and so I came out here. I didn't mean to go swimming." She dared to let go of his hand now; continuing to hold onto him for dear life wasn't going to make her look particularly lucid.

"Yeah, I didn't think so. You aren't dressed for it." Tony stuck his hands in his pockets; his shoulders were tight. But he gave her a genuine smile for once.

She looked down at her skimpy, soaked nightgown and realized that the waterlogged fabric was nearly see-through. Humiliated, she quickly crossed her arms over her chest. At least it was dark outside; he couldn't have seen *that* much, could he? "I didn't think anyone would be out here."

"Neither did I."

"Well I guess it was lucky I was wrong; I mean, I could have drowned … or worse. You know, a girl hit her head on the bottom of that pool the other day. I heard she's in a coma." Maybe a labored transition, but it worked.

"Believe me, I know."

Tony rolled his eyes, and the fact that he didn't seem to care stung her. It was hard to keep her voice level as she asked, "I guess it doesn't matter to you, then?"

"Of course it matters. It's just that my dad … " He brushed his hair away from his face again; water was dripping down his forehead. "My dad—he's into ghosts—and he's all excited about it—thinks it's proof that the hotel is haunted. And it just seems kind of morbid to me. I mean, a girl might die and all he cares about is a good story for his next book."

"Did your dad say anything else about that girl? Which hospital she's in? Where her family is staying?" Maybe, if this was—if it could possibly be—real, she could get to her parents and tell them what was going on and ... but how could they possibly believe her? And what would she do if she finally got to her "real" body in the hospital? Would she somehow climb inside?

"Not exactly. I mean, I know her family checked out right after the accident so they could get a hotel closer to the hospital. Me and my dad are in their room. It's kind of creepy, actually. Sometimes I wonder if I'm sleeping where she was sleeping before she ... well ... "

"You're not." Alice said. Tony looked at her, one eyebrow raised.

"How would you know?"

"I mean, well, what I meant is that it's highly unlikely ... to be sleeping in *exactly* the same spot. You may be a couple of inches off ... " Alice let her voice trail off.

Now both of his eyebrows were up. A drop of water went bumping down his wrinkled forehead and he wiped it off with his sleeve. Alice's face was hot again. She was a pro at lying to her mom—why was she fumbling this up?

"You don't think ... " she began again.

"Don't think what?"

"Maybe we could try to find out more about that girl—how she's doing. It's just so sad. I wonder if she's woken up and ... I would run up to my room and get my laptop, but I don't want to wake up my family. They kind of don't know I'm out here ... "

There was, of course, a free-for-all desktop in the hotel lobby, but there was no way she was walking back into that place. What if she couldn't get back out? What if she looked behind her and the doors were locked and the windows were fogged and … No, she couldn't go inside.

"Oh. That's too bad," he said.

She should have known that he wouldn't pick up on her not-so-subtle hint. Her mom always told her this about guys (usually while complaining about how her dad didn't do this or that or wasn't romantic or spontaneous enough). She would look Alice in the eye then and say, "Remember that: men don't think like women. You've got to tell them what you want or they'll never figure it out." And though Alice didn't exactly treasure her mother's pearls of wisdom, she had to admit—on this her mom had been spot-on.

"Do *you* have a laptop?" Alice asked pointedly.

"Yeah, but—"

"And you know the WiFi password?"

"Yeah—"

"Then why don't we use yours?"

He exhaled heavily and made a show of twisting the bottom of his shirt to wring the water out.

"Look," he said. "I'm soaked and you're soaked and it's late and maybe it would be better if you just waited until—"

"My family's leaving tomorrow—early in the morning."

Tony was biting his lip now; his eyes kept darting from her to the hotel. "Well," he said, "It's just that—"

"You know what? Never mind." Alice shook her head and laughed, but watched his face as closely as she dared. This was a dangerous move, but the chance that she might lose him was just too much. She had to risk it. Alice quickly thought back to the conversation she had seen him have with his dad right before he went outside, and she realized that this was the only advantage she had. "You should just go. It was nice to meet you, anyway. I'll probably just stay out here for a while—the longer I can stay away from my parents the better. Sometimes I just get so frustrated, you know? Like they don't even listen and they think they want me to explain things to them, but what's the point? They don't hear me. I might as well be talking to the TV."

It worked. His eyes widened and he gaped at her for a second, then shook his head in disbelief. "You have no idea—I mean, just now, with my dad, I was thinking that exact same … " He trailed off for a second, staring at her. "You know, if you're gonna be out here anyway—if you're leaving tomorrow—we might as well keep each other company for a bit. Just let me run upstairs and change and … I'll grab my computer. We can look up that girl."

"No, I couldn't ask you to—"

"Really—it's fine. I probably wouldn't be able to sleep anyway. You'll just wait here? You sure you don't want to go change your clothes?"

Alice grinned. "I'll be here," she assured him.

"But you must be freezing!"

Her arms were covered with goose bumps and she clasped her

hands behind her back to hide them. "I'm not cold—don't worry about me."

"Okay. Well, I'll be right back." He was watching her with the strangest look in his eyes and at first Alice wasn't sure what to make of it.

Curious, she decided at last. He was curious about her. And, more importantly, he was going to help her.

She was out of breath—as if she'd been running for her life, away from her prison, toward some empty place in the distance without walls and closed doors. She could smell the open air. It filled her mouth and it tasted like freedom.

"I'm Alice, by the way." Without thinking, she had given him her real name. She wasn't sure exactly what had made her shout it out like that. He smiled and turned away, walking toward the hotel with his towel draped around his shoulders like a cape; the minute his back was turned, she winced and pressed a palm to her forehead. Hers wasn't a super common name these days and what would happen if he put it all together? Then again, he seemed so bound and determined *not* to believe in ghosts that it would probably take a lot more than her happening to have the same name as coma girl to even make him suspect.

She breathed a little easier then, and, as soon as he was inside the hotel, she hurried back to the pool deck and grabbed the towel. It was damp and cold, but she wrapped it tightly around her anyway. It didn't help much; her teeth were at that trembling stage right before they started to chatter. There was a book lying on the ground (Tony must have left it) and Alice looked at the title—*Engineering Engines: What Wins the Race.* It was brightly colored, with a racecar on the front cover.

As she reached down to pick up the book, the towel slipped from her hands and tumbled into the pool. Quickly, Alice bent over the water to pull it out. Her hand closed around the edge of it, but then it slipped away from her. Water was soaking into the towel, a shadow that ate the edges first and then crept quickly toward the middle. She reached into the water and grabbed a corner, pulled it toward her, but the towel didn't budge and her hand came up empty.

"What the … ?"

Alice knew she wasn't what anyone would call muscled, but she wasn't *that* frail either. She watched the towel as it began to sink slowly into the water and remembered how, when she was drowning, it didn't matter how hard she pulled or how fast she kicked—nothing worked. It didn't add up. As a kid, she'd been in swim lessons for years. Drowning had always seemed like the remotest of possibilities.

Maybe—could it be there was something wrong with the water? She watched it rippling around the towel for a minute and it *did* seem sinister somehow, gleaming in folds of reflected moonlight. Tentatively, she cupped her hands and dipped them in. But when she pulled them out … no, that couldn't be right. She blinked hard and tried again. And again. But every single time her hands broke the surface, the same, completely impossible thing happened.

The water went right through her.

"No," she whispered. *No. No. No. No.*

Her teeth were chattering hard and fast as she held her hands up, pulled them close to her, then out as far as they would go—squinted at the skin. Gulping, trying to stay calm, she held one hand up to the sky so that it covered the moon ... or at least it should have. Through her palm, she could see a glowing circle, as if the moon itself were inside of her skin, shining silver. Pressing the hand into the pool deck, she felt it sink into the ground, just a little bit.

This world was real, then. But she wasn't.

She was so cold, almost trembling. And her hand shook as she pressed it against her chest—and, yes ... right there—there was her heart beating.

"Not dead," she told herself, her voice quaking. She was too plainly alive to be a ghost. If anything, she was more of a shadow. Pulling her knees to her chest, she wrapped her arms tightly around them and rocked back and forth, trying not to panic. But her stomach felt as if it were filled with lead and when she looked up at the sky now, she felt nothing like freedom. It seemed so heavy, as if it were trying to crush her. The more tightly she held herself, the less solid she felt. She rocked faster, trying to hold herself together. So maybe she wasn't totally free, as she had thought—maybe she still had to fight. She could do that. She could.

And she had to.

CHAPTER SEVEN

Looking up at the hotel, Alice saw at once where the attic room must have been. She hadn't noticed it before, but the roofing over that square of space was completely flat, not sloped like the rest. It looked as if someone had just scraped the attic off, as if they wanted so badly to be rid of it that they had cut it out carelessly, not bothering to make it match the rest of the house. Alice's eyes wandered down to the ground beneath where the attic would have been. If she was right, then it was highly likely that there was a key buried somewhere under that patch of grass.

Alice forced herself to get to her feet and walk closer to the oddly shaped roofing. She began to dig in the ground with her fingernails. But digging was not an easy task since half of her cells had made the most inconvenient choice to go missing. All she managed to do was rip out a lot of grass. It felt good, though—calmed her somehow. *Ghosts can't pull up grass.* She pulled faster. She pulled so hard that her hands hurt, and she actually relished the pain. *Dead people can't feel pain.*

"Pulling out grass."

Alice looked up, both hands full, to see that Tony had returned with his computer. She didn't know how long he had been standing there, watching her. He met her eyes, then nodded at her pile with a faint grin.

"Um ... still upset about the parents thing?"

Alice thought his face was kind. He might be looking at her as if she were a little crazy, but there was concern there too, as though he actually cared.

"Hey, if you want to take it out on the grass, go right ahead," he said. "Seems okay to me."

"I lost my ... room key," she said, prying another handful of grass free.

Tony watched her for a minute, then looked at her dress and scratched his head. "Wait, where were you keeping it in the first place? That thing doesn't exactly have pockets."

"I was sitting on the grass over here for a while. I must have put it down and forgotten to pick it up again when I walked over to the pool. I thought I'd be able to see it, but ... the grass is long and it's so dark out here."

"Do you want some help?"

Alice let the pieces of grass fall back to the ground. "Really? I mean ... I guess ... " She looked up at his face, then down at her own hand. It was dark enough outside that her skin looked pale, but normal enough. He wouldn't notice (would he?) that the tips of her fingers were just a tad too translucent. At least he hadn't noticed yet. "Okay," she said. It would only make him more suspicious if she turned him down.

He got on his hands and knees beside her and started running his fingers through the grass. He was wearing jeans and a dark blue sweatshirt now; he looked warm.

"You lied to me," he said.

She sat straight up. Did he know? How *could* he know? "Lied?" she asked, hand clenched so tightly around a bunch of grass that she might have been trying to strangle it. "What did I lie about?"

Pointing to her goose-bump–covered arm with one hand, he unzipped his sweatshirt with the other. "Look at you—you're freezing cold."

Alice exhaled heavily in relief. "Oh—that, yeah … I'm getting a little—wait, what are you—?"

He was putting his sweatshirt around her shoulders. "No, really. You don't have to—" she protested. Having him this close to her was not a good idea—what if (her heart skipped a beat) the sweatshirt went through her skin or something? He'd freak out, run off.

"Here," he said, holding up the sleeve, "I need your arm."

"I'd really rather—"

"I'm not gonna sit here and watch you freeze to death. Now—your arm."

Very gingerly, she stuck her arm into the sleeve, half expecting to see her elbow pop through the fabric at any moment. But it didn't, and the other arm went in without incident. She held her breath as Tony zipped the thing up. (On him, it was loose; on her, it looked like a tent.) He reached over and pulled the hood over her head; his hands brushed against her hair and when he pulled them away the strands fell onto her face like a wet curtain closing.

"Thanks," she said, keeping her voice completely emotionless, afraid that he would see how nervous she was.

"Look," he said, folding his arms, "I know you don't want to wake your family, but once we find your room key, don't you want to get some dry clothes? Maybe it would be worth risking it."

She shrugged. "Yeah, maybe." It really didn't matter what she said; they weren't going to find the key like this anyway. She ran her fingers through the grass in a circular pattern, tracing the outline first, then filling in the middle, but she knew it wouldn't be enough. A shovel would be useful—and maybe a metal detector. But how could she get Tony to help her find one? He would never believe that her key had somehow gotten buried if it had only been missing for a few minutes.

And then it hit her: she couldn't keep this up. If he was going to be of any use to her at all, she would have to tell him the truth.

"So I'm gonna come clean with you," he was saying.

She took a deep breath. "Yeah, there's something I need to tell you, too … "

"We can take turns. Here—here's mine. I lied to you, too.

Remember when I said I thought you weren't crazy? Well, actually I kind of did."

Her heart fell; she brushed her fingertips over the grass mechanically. "Oh."

"Not anymore—I don't think so *now*," he said. "But when you were saying all that stuff about ghosts and not being dead ... you must have just been confused. Maybe in shock—just a little. And I guess—" He shook his head. "I'm sorry for treating you weird at first."

"No." Her voice sounded small. "I get it."

"Do you remember what you were talking about?"

This was her moment. This was when she told him everything. She opened her mouth, mentally rehearsing her story. *Actually, Tony, I was trying to tell you that I* am *the girl that almost drowned and I think my body's in a coma somewhere and ...* But when she spoke, what she heard herself say was, "I don't remember."

She wanted to slap herself the minute she said it. But there was this knot of fear in her, choking her, keeping her from doing what had to be done. She kept imagining his eyes getting that glassy look again as he decided she really was crazy after all and told her that he had to go. And she would be alone. It would be like being stuck in the house all over again—on her own, helpless, with nobody.

Tony snapped his fingers and she jumped. "I know what it was," he said. "It must have had something to do with what happened today."

"Wait—what happened?"

He looked at her and there was a kind of hopefulness in his eyes. "You really didn't hear?"

"Hear what?"

"Well, you see … " It looked as though he wasn't so sure he wanted to tell her at all now. "My dad and I got into a little fight in the hall."

"Oh!" she said, nodding. "I remember now. The ghost-hunting fight. The manager almost kicked you out."

"My dad … " He ground some grass between his fingers while he talked. "He's big into ghost-hunting. Let's just say that sometimes he takes it a little bit … too far. Anyway, maybe you saw me and remembered the ghost stuff and … "

"Started babbling?"

He shrugged. "Stranger things have happened."

He had no idea.

Trying to put off the inevitable, Alice asked, "I take it you don't believe in ghosts?"

"Sometimes I think maybe … Like there was this moment this afternoon—never mind, it sounds crazy."

She gulped and came so very close to telling him, but then he started talking again and she lost her nerve.

"I wouldn't have come," he continued. "My dad and I aren't exactly on the best terms but he's trying. I live with my mom most of the time. My dad's been after her to let him take me on a trip like this for years. She must have finally gotten tired of him bugging her."

"Did your mom make you come, then?" Alice asked.

Tony didn't answer for a minute, he just stared at the patch of grass that he had flattened. Then he glanced at the engineering book on the ground. "No. My mom doesn't believe in forcing me to do stuff. It was my dad who talked me into it ... You know how it is. He was just so excited. I couldn't say no. And there was this car accident ... long story. We just haven't been super close since then."

Alice nodded, thinking of all the times her dad had talked her into watching his favorite comedy shows. He was almost never home and had free time even less often; though Alice didn't love the laugh tracks, the easy jokes, she could pretend to like them for a few hours at a time. She looked at the ground, her heart pounding fast. Long nights with the TV and her dad had never sounded so wonderful.

"I'm sorry you had to come," she said.

He looked at her. "Well, it hasn't been *all* bad. Saving someone's life—that's kind of a big plus."

Alice smiled stiffly, then resumed her sweep of the grass with too much enthusiasm, embracing the distraction. If only she'd been a normal, alive girl drowning in a perfectly normal way. It sounded so uncomplicated.

Tony came up right next to her, so close that their hands almost touched in the grass, and she immediately sat up, pretending to stretch her arms. If he got too close, even the darkness wouldn't hide the fact that her skin was more than just pale.

"So you're here with your family?" asked Tony.

Alice didn't answer at once. She supposed she should have seen this coming—the questions—and yet she had no idea how to answer them. *The truth* ... she couldn't do it. Just ... in a minute, maybe. But not yet.

"Yes," she said at last, deciding that simple was best.

"Vacation?"

"Yes."

"Has it been fun?"

"Uh-huh."

Tony glanced at her, his eyebrows raised. "What's your favorite part?" he asked, determined, it seemed, to get more than one word out of her this time.

"Swimming," said Alice immediately, blurting out the first thing that came to mind.

"Do you do a lot of swimming usually?"

"Um ... yeah. I guess."

"I ... uh ..." His eyes wandered to the pool. "I wouldn't have taken you for a swimmer. With the drowning and all."

Unnerved, Alice nodded. She had the feeling that he was onto her, that somehow she had given herself away.

"Do you know this hotel is supposed to be haunted?" asked Tony, doing little to smooth her frayed nerves.

"Oh yeah, I know all about it. You see, my little brother got to choose the vacation this year and he, well … let's just say he'd get along well with your dad. He chose this place *because* of the stories about it." Her heart was pounding so loud and fast that she was afraid he might hear it. "It's silly, of course," she added. "There's no such thing as … as ghosts." She said it as firmly as she could. She had to believe that, because whatever she was, she wasn't a ghost. Ghosts had already died.

"You know that every time you say that somewhere a ghost dies?" asked Tony. Alice was, however, not in a laughing mood.

"It was a joke," he clarified when she didn't react. "Like in *Peter Pan*, with the fairies, how you have to clap to keep them alive. Except with ghosts."

Looking him straight in the eye, she sat back on her knees and began to clap. Tony watched her with a mixture of bemusement and fascination.

"The ghosts are saved," she said, and she couldn't help but grin. She bent over the grass again and resumed her search. Beside her, Tony remained frozen for a moment, then followed suit.

"Guess you're not so popular with our spirit friends, are you?" he asked.

"Yeah, your dad had better watch out. I'll scare off all his customers."

Tony froze, and for a second Alice thought that she had offended him, but then he broke into a wide grin and pulled from the grass—

"I found it!"

It was a room key—small and silver. A tag on the end said "Reef Heron" and had a picture of a sleek bird with a long curved neck. Alice took it from him numbly; even with the sweatshirt, she shivered. Instead of blood, her heart seemed to be pumping ice water through her veins.

"Nice bird," he said, pointing to the tag. "My dad and I have a Spruce Grouse. Do you know what a grouse is? It's basically a chicken. Pretty lame if you ask me. But you got lucky. And I mean really lucky—I can't believe we found it in the dark and everything!"

"Yeah. That's me. Lucky."

The key glittered in her hand. She didn't know what to say, what to do. This lie was swallowing her whole, and as she sat there with the room key that wasn't hers, she felt it growing up around her like walls. She had a sudden impulse to throw the key as far away from her as she could, bird tag and all, but she couldn't make herself do it.

"Why don't you go change? I'll stay here and hunt down the news story about that girl."

She didn't answer and he added, "Unless you want to just go to bed ... I mean, I'd understand that."

"No. No, I'm not tired. Let's look up the girl now."

"But your clothes—"

"I've been wet this long, I can be wet a little longer."

"Okay," he shrugged, but looked confused. She couldn't keep

this up much longer. After she figured out what hospital she was in—then she would tell him. And then at least she would know something. She would have gotten something good out of all of this.

Tony was watching her while waiting for his computer to start up, and Alice was instantly self-conscious, her posture suddenly awkward. The way she was sitting there in his oversized sweatshirt, legs bare, tangled hair hanging out of the side of the hood—she felt underdressed and overexposed and entirely uncomfortable.

"Her name's Alice—Alice Montgomery," Alice supplied. Then held her breath, waiting to see if he would react to the name. But he didn't seem put off in the least as he typed it in.

"Seems like you know a lot about her already."

"I read it in the newspaper. And it's easy to remember—same first name, you know."

Alice crawled to his side to get a better view of the screen, still clutching the useless key. Web addresses started popping up and Alice skimmed them over Tony's shoulder. Most of them were about some B-movie actress with the same name, but then Alice spotted one with the words "pool accident."

"There!" She pointed it out to Tony and he opened it for her. The headline read, "Girl in Coma After Pool Accident in Historic Blackwell Hotel." Alice's heart started to pound faster and faster as she read.

Thursday, July 13

> *A 15-year-old girl is in a coma after a tragic accident yesterday afternoon. Witnesses report that Alice Montgomery was swimming with her brother in the Blackwell Hotel pool when she dove from the deck and hit her head on the bottom of the pool. Emergency vehicles arrived at the scene only minutes later, and the girl was rushed to the Ellsworth hospital. Physicians say that her chances of survival are low, but the family is still holding out hope.*
>
> *"Alice is a fighter," Elaine Montgomery, Alice's mother, told the press. "If anyone can make it, Alice can." The family has asked that donations be made through* www.PrayingForAlice.com. *All proceeds will help pay medical bills and expenses.*

Alice was so caught up in reading that she hardly noticed Tony staring at her. When she finally looked away from the computer screen, his expression made her jump.

"You … you're … " he spluttered, mouth hanging slightly open, blue eyes wide. Alice didn't realize what he was talking about until she glanced back at the computer screen.

Her heart stopped.

Right at the top of the article was her most recent school picture, smiling at her from the screen. Tony looked at the picture and then back at her again.

"I don't believe it. I … don't believe it."

The key slipped from her fingers. Without her even trying—without her saying a word, the lie was crashing down around her.

Intense relief swept through her, but it was also maddening to see him staring at her like that. Shock—disbelief—his eyes said everything. She was impossible and he knew it.

Her mind spun with things she could say to him—anything that would make him stay.

"Tony," she said, reaching out to grab his arm. It was instinctive, the need to grab hold of him and not let go. But Tony leapt to his feet just as her fingers were about to touch him.

"Please ... don't be afraid. Let me explain—"

Just as she was about to let the whole truth come spilling out, it happened. One moment she was sitting, solid on the grass. The next, the ground was sucking her in—knees, chest, neck. Tony watched her in horror.

"Alice!"

"No! Please—" she gasped out before she disappeared entirely. For a second everything was black, and then she found herself kneeling on hard wood, still wrapped in Tony's sweatshirt.

Somewhere in the house, a clock chimed one o'clock.

CHAPTER EIGHT

Alice closed her eyes and didn't open them for a long time. She allowed herself to slowly—so slowly—fold until her forehead hit the floor. The sweatshirt around her shoulders was warm and smelled like chlorine. She pulled it closer around her body and breathed in the scent of it. But she couldn't find any peace in it, and all she wanted was to hit something—to break something. She'd been so close. *So close.* She had even allowed herself to hope that she had escaped this place—that everything would work out.

And then there was Tony. Not that it mattered, not that she cared, but she *had* stolen his sweatshirt and he'd be totally freaking out. ... She could imagine him now, staring at the ground, eyes wide and mouth hanging open. Maybe he would tell this story on Halloween years later—the story about the ghost of the drowned girl that still appeared in the pool where she'd ... but she hadn't died. He *wouldn't* tell that story because she *wasn't* dead.

Or maybe he would tell no one. What would they think of him if he did? His dad would believe him, but everyone else ... they would think he'd lost his mind. And so he would carry the whole story with him to his grave, never whispering it to a soul. The thought of him acting as if nothing had happened made Alice unreasonably angry and she forced herself to take a deep breath.

Come on, be sensible, she told herself. *Focus. Look for a way out.* She did what she had done so many times before—since she was just a child—and pushed the disappointment into the recesses of her mind. Feeling emptier if not very much better, Alice opened her eyes.

She knew at once that something was wrong, but this change was so large that, for a moment, Alice was too overwhelmed to put her finger on it. Then she realized.

Half of the room was missing.

She wasn't sure if *missing* was exactly the right word for it. *Obscured* might have been a better choice. But either way, there was no denying the fact that where the dresser, the door to the bathroom, and half of the bed should have been, there was only mist. This wasn't ordinary mist either. Normal mist didn't stay in one place like that—it fogged up the rest of the air, obscured everything. This haze looked as though it had run up against an invisible wall; it was clean-cut, leaving the rest of the room perfectly clear. Where the mist *was*, it was thick and opaque.

Alice walked toward it in shock. She leaned over the bed and, after a moment of hesitation, stuck her hand inside. Her arm disappeared into the wall of glowing white, but she felt nothing. She expected the mist to be damp, like the inside of the cloud. Instead there was ... well, there was *nothing*. Just nothing. She pulled her hand out and was relieved to see that it was still there. The mist just hung, unperturbed. Alice felt a shiver crawl up her spine and somehow she knew that if she went into that mist, she might never come out.

The glow from the mist allowed Alice to find her way around even though the windows were dark. She ran to the door and out of the room, poking her head into the other doorways as she worked her way down the hall, growing more panicked by the minute. Everywhere it was the same. The mist had overtaken that entire side of the house.

When Alice got back to her own room, she saw her bikini top lying at the foot of the bed. If the mist crept forward (and if it had moved once before, it could easily do it again), it would swallow the bed whole. Even though she hated that bikini, the thought of it eaten up by whiteness unnerved her. Her swimsuit was real— snatched from the real world, just like her—and if it could simply cease to exist, if it could disappear. ... She grabbed her bikini top and held it close to her. The diary was sitting on the bed as well and, though she wouldn't have minded seeing that bloodstained cover swept away, the information it held was too valuable to lose, and she picked it up as well.

In the mirror, the door to the real hotel room flew open. Tony stood for a moment, silhouetted by the light from the hallway, then ran inside. Alice froze, her own danger momentarily forgotten, and scrutinized his face. In the dark, though, she couldn't see more than the round outline of his head. Even if his expression was saying something, there was no chance she would be able to see it.

He threw his laptop onto the bed and walked toward his dad. Stopping, he wavered for a moment, rocking backwards on his heels, then turned around and ran out of the room.

Alice had to remind herself to breathe. There was a growing warmth in her chest, but the heat wasn't pleasant—it was a burning need. She needed Tony to like her and the thought that he might actually be terrified of her was almost unbearable. *It makes sense*, she told herself. *I'm not crazy.* She needed him to want to help her, so of course she was afraid he wouldn't. That was all it was. Trying to keep calm, Alice looked away from the mirror, but as she did, she thought she caught a flash of short brown hair and pale skin. She whipped around for another look, alarmed, but the girl was nowhere in sight.

Alice swallowed hard. Clutching her things to her chest, she fled the room and ran downstairs to check the rest of the house. She discovered, to her horror, that the mist was not limited to just one side. It was creeping in everywhere, covering every outer wall. Half of the lobby was gone and the game room had almost disappeared completely. The living room fireplace was gone. The library was one of the few places that was completely intact, but that was to be expected. It was one of the only rooms landlocked inside the house.

Panicked, Alice curled up in the most central hallway she could find and tried to breathe. Everything around her seemed small and distant, as if her head were a faraway tower with her trapped inside. There was a mirror over the couch in the foyer and as she looked up at it, she thought for a brief second that she saw the girl again. She rubbed her eyes and looked harder; the girl was gone without a trace.

"Hey!" She got to her feet. Alice had heard that the best thing to do if you came across a bear was to wave your arms and scream and yell—make sure it knew that you were there and you weren't afraid. And even though she knew that a witch was a far cry from a bear, and even though her knees were shaking so hard it was a miracle she could stand, she shouted to the mirror at the top of her lungs, "I know who you are. I know you're in there!"

I can't hear you.

Alice reeled backwards, clapping her hands over her ears. The voice was so quiet and so piercing that she couldn't tell if it had come from the house or from her own mind. She was trembling now; she couldn't take her eyes off the mirror. The feeling that someone was watching her was so strong that tingles were running up and down her back like tiny bits of ice. The bloody diary was next to her and she grabbed it, pressing it to her stomach in the way she used to hold her teddy bears when she was frightened.

Another flash of brown (or was she just blinking?) and Alice jumped. The book tumbled out of her hand and fell open beside her and she picked it up. She looked up at the mirror one more time; the thought of not knowing someone was watching her was terrifying, but the chance that she might actually see something scared her even more.

Alice lowered her gaze to the book in her lap. It was the only escape she had left.

***

May 10, 1883

I did it! Can you believe that? It actually worked—I swear it did.

The witch is so pleased. She smiles at me from the mirror all the time now. I think that she wants to tell me something. If only I could get her out of the glass, she could talk to me face-to-face.

Maybe I will work on a new curse now—I don't know. I could try, I suppose. But birds are awfully small creatures. Just because the curse worked this time doesn't mean it will work on something larger.

Poor little bird. It was such a sweet creature. It used to sing to me all the time—it would perch right on my windowsill. The poor dear won't sing to me anymore. How I miss it! Was it too terrible of me to curse it? Now I wonder if I shouldn't have done it. I look in the mirror and I see my face and I am afraid of my own power.

No. I am not afraid. I am powerful.

The curse was truly marvelous—oh, I wish William could have seen! I waited until midnight and, right as the witching hour hit, I rubbed the salve on my forehead and spoke the incantation. The salve was very difficult. I had to boil crushed rose petals with tar and egg yolks and special salts that I found among the witch's things. I did it, though—and right under Lillian's nose, too. How jealous she would be if she found out. But she won't. She won't ever find the witch's books. I won't let her. I am too clever for her. Ha!

I am very clever, you know. Very, very clever.

The bird hasn't come since that night. I suppose it just dropped dead when the curse hit it. And I am so pleased! With these books I have the power to curse anyone I want. Even Lillian.

Poor bird.

Lillian has been doing the oddest things lately. She pops in on me unexpectedly almost every hour. She tries to catch me working magic. But I still pretend that I am sick and I am very careful to be in bed whenever she comes. She grows more desperate by the day to see me with the books. I have heard her talking to Father about me many times.

She says that I have gone mad.

The little fool. Does she really think that saying that will help her steal the books from me? She seems to have convinced Father, though. He sent Monsieur Létourneau away just the minute that he finished the painting. Or perhaps Monsieur left of his own accord? I do not remember. I was too busy watching the witch peeping out at us.

A doctor came to see me today. I told him that I am fine and I think that he believes me, he left the room so quickly. He has not been back since. He at least knows that there is nothing the matter.

And William. William is surely dead. No man would ever abandon me if he could help it. Sometimes when Lillian's not home, I creep downstairs into her room and use her mirror. I smile at myself and curl my hair around my fingers. I strike poses. And, truly, I am just as beautiful as ever. William would never leave me.

Do you know, Lillian dared to mention William's name the other day! She asked if he would be coming to see me soon. How could she ask such a thing? How could she be so insensitive? I sent her away at once.

What should my next curse be? I have asked the witch, but the only word she seems to say is "Elizabeth"; I do not know why. Perhaps it is the glass that makes it hard for me to hear her. Sometimes I am sure that she is whispering secrets to me—great secrets—but I am too deaf to understand.

The three pieces of wood that divide the mirror into four cover the glass like bars in a jail cell window. Perhaps if I pry them off, then the witch will be free to leave as she pleases.

Oh dear. I still do not know which curse to try next. There are so very many to choose from.

Maybe I will try to free the witch first.

Here comes Lillian again. I must go lie down in bed before she sees me writing.

***

One more thing: I have figured out the secret of magic. It is three and four— just like the mirror.

***

Alice put the diary down and realized to her surprise that her hands were shaking. She didn't like being so close to Elizabeth's mind. It left her with a sick feeling, as though she had just thrown up. The witch's brown eyes and crooked smile kept popping up in her head; she couldn't escape them. She felt like a cornered animal, huddled on the floor, mirrors watching her like empty faces.

She was too frightened to go back into any of the rooms. The mist working its way across the house disturbed her almost as much as the looming threat of the witch. What if she got trapped somewhere with it creeping toward her like that, alone in the middle of a white box closing in on her from every side? She wouldn't be able to stand it.

She knew it was dumb, that she was too old now, but she had an impulse to run to her parents' room—to talk to her mom. Her mom had a way of making her feel better about things, or at least she had before Alice stopped talking to her about anything important. … When had that happened anyway? Alice didn't remember. Maybe a couple years earlier, when her parents' usual arguing had subsided into stony silence, when she had started to realize that something was broken that might never be fixed— when she had clamped up inside. It wasn't important now. She couldn't talk to her mom anyway. Her parents' room was on the other side of a country she wasn't even sure she was still a part of. She was in her own shadow world now. She looked up at the wall, at the empty house, and felt so desperately lonely that her eyes started to burn and she curled up, back against the wall, wishing for something, for someone, for home.

"This *is* home."

Alice jumped—hit the back of her head on the wall. It was the girl. This time Alice was sure that she could see her there in the mirror, kneeling on the couch in the real foyer, arms crossed over the top of it. The book, which Alice had been holding against her stomach, slipped from her hands and tumbled to the floor.

"You can't leave. Not now."

Alice stood up with some difficulty; her knees shook. She wasn't sure if she was breathing.

"You can see me," she said. It wasn't a question anymore. The girl—the witch—was staring straight at her and there was simply no chance, no way that Alice was imagining things now.

The girl blinked and yawned. "I'm glad you're here. It's been lonely for years now. The house has been so very hungry with nothing to eat."

Alice's stomach turned. She thought of the mist, creeping forward, eating up all in its path. The witch's lips were slightly parted and her teeth gleamed like two rows of knives. Alice took an uncertain step toward the mirror and said breathlessly (her lungs were like popped balloons), "I know who you are."

"Yes. I'm a friend."

She smiled and Alice didn't believe her. Though Alice was tempted to simply tell the witch what she knew and try to get her to leave, there was this other nagging thought that she couldn't dismiss. If Elizabeth had been right, then the witch was powerful. Alice, trapped here, needed nothing more than power. Was it possible that even a witch could be an ally? Could this be her way out?

"I already have friends," said Alice. Then, thinking it would be best to hear it from the girl's own lips, "Tell me who you are."

"No."

"No?"

The girl tapped her fingernails on the mirror, or at least seemed to. They made no sound when they hit the glass. "No, you don't have friends."

"What's your name?" tried Alice.

"Don't need a name."

"Everyone needs a name. What do people call you?" Her fear was quickly turning to frustration. Did the girl ever stop smirking? Or was she born with that lopsided grin?

"If you have to call me something, call me Alice," said the girl after a moment's thought.

"I'm Alice."

"And I am you."

"You are not."

She rested her chin on her hand, rolling her eyes. "Bored now," she said.

"What do you want from me?" Alice asked. Maybe if she knew what the witch wanted, they could work out some kind of exchange. She would give almost anything to get out of there.

"You're the first one in a long time. I was excited," the girl said.

"Can you help me?" Alice blurted out, unable to contain it any longer. "Do you know the trick? Is there a way out of here?"

The girl broke into a wide smile. "Of course."

"What is it? Whatever you want—I can give you whatever you want."

"Want? I just want you to be happy," she said in a voice so sweet it bordered on simpering. Alice's stomach turned; this didn't feel right. *Don't talk to strangers*—the mantra of kids walking home from school—was playing on repeat in her head.

"Then tell me the way out."

"You already know it." The girl pointed through the mirror at the mist that covered the door. Alice looked at it, then back at the mirror.

"No. It can't be."

"It's easy. And it doesn't hurt."

"No."

Alice didn't know how she knew, but the instinct to stay away from the mist was stronger than anything she had ever felt. There was something strangely beautiful about the glow it shed, but it was a menacing allure, like the rippling green of a venomous snake.

"It doesn't matter. Eventually you won't have a choice." The girl shook her head at the mirror and Alice, angry that this conversation was turning up nothing useful at all, turned her back and walked to the other side of the room, taking deep breaths to calm herself. What if the girl was right? What if the mist ate up more and more space until there was nowhere left to hide? Alice clasped her trembling hands together.

At least one thing seemed clear—the witch was in no great hurry to harm her. Alice still had no idea (and wasn't about to ask) if the girl could get free of the mirror, but for now she seemed content to stay there. And Alice, oddly enough, felt much better now that she knew exactly where the witch was. It was easier when she could keep an eye on her, when she didn't have to worry about her popping up unexpectedly.

It was morning now—of that she was fairly certain. Steady sounds came from the hallway mirror and a couple of families kept coming in and out. Some little boy was screaming from inside one of the rooms. He wanted to go swimming and his mother wouldn't let him.

The girl was examining her fingernails one by one. Each one was long and perfectly shaped, like the fake nails some of the girls at Alice's school wore. She pulled one to her and rubbed it against her dress, then held her hand up to the light and stared at Alice from between her fingers. Alice was just about to attempt conversation, take two, when she heard a voice she recognized.

CHAPTER NINE

"Dad?"

It was Tony. Relieved to have found a distraction, Alice leaned closer to the mirror. The girl put her hand down and grinned, but didn't say a word.

"I need you to tell me everything again." Tony was trailing behind his dad, who still looked very grumpy. At this question, he actually stopped and turned around to face his son.

"For goodness' sake, Tony! What else is there to say? I've told you everything I know three times now. Why are you suddenly so interested in haunted houses, anyway? Is there something you're not telling me?"

So he hadn't told his dad about her. Alice was relieved; she hated to think what kind of awful contraptions George would set up if he knew she was wandering about—hotel manager or no.

Tony shrugged. "Do you remember when I told you to unplug

the sensors yesterday?" he asked. "It's like I said before—I could have sworn that I actually felt ... someone. Is that even possible?"

George shook his head. "I told you ... it's complicated. Have you even read my book?"

"I was going to ... I had homework. Could you please just tell me?" Tony said, with a hint of irritation in his voice. "Do you think it's possible ... well, no, that's not exactly what I mean ... Have you ever felt like you had one foot in your own body and one foot in somebody else's? Like you were feeling their emotions, their pain? Like, if you tried hard enough ... you could read their thoughts?"

Alice took a quick, deep breath. She remembered how Tony had cried out with words that seemed to come from her. And she wondered ... she wondered if they might be able to manage it again. Because, secretly, she would have liked very much to see into Tony's mind ... to find out how it worked, how it felt about certain people.

"I could show you how he feels," whispered the girl, and in the hotel beyond the glass she ran one of those long, perfect fingernails down the back of Tony's neck. Alice felt her heart skip a beat. "Let me help," said the girl. Now it looked as though she was digging her fingers into his hair. Tony jumped and touched his head, looked puzzled. "Don't you want to know him better?" asked the girl.

"Get away from him!" said Alice. The girl, instead of moving away, leaned forward, stuck her tongue out, and ran it down Tony's jawline. Alice felt sick. She slammed her hands against the glass so hard that the frame around the mirror shook. The witch grinned, walked back to the couch, and sat down cross-legged on the cushions.

"Well ... Tony ... " George stumbled over his words and Tony glared at him.

"Don't try to lie to me, Dad. You don't have to try to impress me; I just want the truth."

George's face went pale. "Your mother said that to me once. Has she been telling you I'm a liar?" All the blood seemed to pour into his cheeks at once. He was glowing red now, like an overripe cherry on a flaming tree.

Two middle-aged women, walking across the lobby with hiking poles and backpacks, stared pointedly at George (who'd been speaking louder the longer this conversation went on). Tony grabbed his dad by the elbow and steered him toward a small parlor that opened off of the lobby. Alice turned away from the mirror and was about to follow them when she saw through the open doorway to the parlor a wall of mist shedding a pale glow over the wood shelving. It had eaten up half of the room; a third of an armchair poked through—front legs resting heavily on the rug, back legs nowhere to be seen.

Alice glanced back at the mirror just in time to see Tony closing the door to the parlor. The girl (perched on the edge of the couch) smirked at her, then covered her face with her hands in mock consternation. Alice, cheeks flushing, stood up straighter, turned deliberately on her heel, and marched into the mist-eaten room. She kept close to the door—as far from the mist as possible—and parked herself in front of a tiny round mirror on the bookshelf. She didn't like turning her back on the mist, so she angled herself with one shoulder to the mirror and the other to the half-gone armchair.

"Please—don't bring Mom into this," Tony was saying. He cringed, and Alice could tell that, more than anything, he did not want the conversation to go in this direction.

George picked up right where he left off; if anything, he was speaking more loudly now. "And why shouldn't I? If Madeline's been calling me a liar to my own son, I have a right to know about it!" His eyes were burning blue and he looked almost menacing.

"I know you're not a liar, okay? Just don't … don't lose it on me."

"And Madeline—"

"Hasn't ever said a word against you," Tony said in a very unconvincing way. George huffed and looked away.

"Not true."

The girl was leaning against the fireplace, running her fingers through her short hair. Alice didn't remember seeing her come in; it was as though she had simply materialized. Maybe she had. "He's lying," she said, her voice somewhere between a whisper and a hum.

Alice tried to ignore her, keeping her eyes fixed on Tony. But she watched the girl out of the corner of her eye.

"You're a bad liar, Tony. Just like your mother. But, " he shook his head, "you shouldn't lie. You don't ever have to lie to me, okay?" He sounded like a parenting audiobook—practiced and sincere—but Alice wasn't sure he meant it. "As for your ... experience," George went on. He hesitated, then said, "Honestly, Tony, I haven't ever heard of anything like it. But really, anything's possible. Spirits aren't bound by our limitations. They can share thoughts, even bodies I suppose. Don't discount what you felt, Tony. Don't forget."

Tony looked disappointed with this answer, and George sighed.

"I know ... " he started to pace, "*someone* who had an experience once where she—"

His voice cut off abruptly and Alice, who could see him leaning against the back of the armchair, his lips still flapping, clapped her hands to her ears. She could hear her fingers hitting the side of her head.

"Hello," she said, and her voice was clear.

The girl yawned loudly.

George's jaw was going up and down, but Alice could hear nothing at all. She turned to the girl.

"What's going on? Why can't I hear him?"

"Oh, I see. *Now* you want my help," said the girl, her lips in a pout.

"Yes, I do."

The girl shrugged as George blabbered on. "Guess he must have left the room."

"What do you—?" Alice cut off, her eyes coming to rest on the two feet of the armchair that stuck out of the mist. She looked back up to the mirror and realized—George was leaning against the back of the chair. The mist had swallowed up that whole section of the room in her version of the house.

"You've *got* to be kidding me," she said, wringing her hands in frustration. The mirrors were her only source of information from the real world; if she didn't have them, she would be completely on her own. It was as though her senses were being ripped away from her one by one.

"And then she thought she saw a man in corduroys sitting on the end of her bed ... " Tony interrupted his dad in a very bored voice. "Dad. You've told me this story before. I know who *she* is."

George put his hands in the air and walked forward to stand just in front of the chair. Alice heard him this time when he said, "You're the one who didn't want to bring your mother into this."

Tony looked away.

"My point is," George continued, "instead of trying to call him back the next night, she convinced herself that it had been her imagination. And that was the last experience she had with the supernatural."

"So what you're telling me is I just have to believe?" Tony asked. His gaze flicked upwards, a hint of an eye-roll.

"More than that. Spirits don't appear to just anyone. If one has taken an interest in you, you've got to jump on the opportunity. You've got to do everything you possibly can to communicate with it. You might never have another chance."

Tony sighed and thrust his hands into his pockets. He looked at the door and said. "We should get breakfast before the kitchen closes."

"Did you hear me, Tony? This is your chance to prove you can be in touch with the supernatural."

"I know, Dad. I know."

He glanced at the bookshelf and for a second his gaze stopped on the mirror. Though he could not see her, Alice felt a chill run through her as his eyes swept over hers. Then he left the room, muttering something about being hungry. His dad, eyebrows furrowed, followed him out.

Alice hurried back into the lobby, but Tony and his dad were already walking into the dining room. When Alice tried to follow, she entered just in time to see the last inch of the only mirror in the room give a final twinkle as the mist swallowed it up.

CHAPTER TEN

"Nice boy," said the girl, who was lounging on the lobby couch in the mirror when Alice returned. "Too bad about his problems."

Alice was still caught up in his look, in his tone. And—he had been talking about *her*. "You don't know the first thing about him."

"Another thing we have in common, I guess," said the girl, tucking a strand of hair behind her ear.

"I don't have to listen to this." Alice turned away from the mirror and walked into a small piano room that branched off from the foyer. The mist had eaten one wall of the room, but the rest was intact. Alice sat down in a chair and fidgeted with the worn floral fabric, her eyes on the mist, her mind on Tony.

"You should listen."

Alice started. At first she thought the girl was standing right behind her, but then she turned around and saw that there was yet another mirror hanging on the wall. The girl was observing her from the glass, arms folded, expression inscrutable.

Without a word, Alice got up, grabbed the mirror, and threw it to the ground. To her surprise, the mirror's face went completely black. Then, a moment later, it reappeared on the wall.

The girl wagged her finger, unperturbed. "Naughty."

"What is with you?" asked Alice, holding the sides of the mirror so tightly that her knuckles began to turn white.

"I'm here to help you. That's all."

There was silence for a moment; the girl stared and Alice glared back at her, thinking hard.

"What do you know about Tony—*how* do you know about him?" she asked at last. Alice remembered how the girl had touched Tony's head and, for a second, Tony had looked as though he felt her do it. And Alice wondered if it was possible that the girl could read Tony's mind the way that Alice had read it for one brief second, thanks to his dad's equipment. If the girl could connect to Tony—without equipment, without anything—then maybe she would send a message to him for Alice. Maybe *this* was the way to communicate through the glass. It could be the only way.

The girl ran her tongue across the edge of a fingernail. "I have ways."

"What ways? Tell me." So the witch wanted to help? Let her prove it.

"Didn't anyone ever teach you how to just *believe*?" asked the girl.

"Believing is useless unless you have a good reason."

"Then it's not believing."

Alice grabbed the frame around the mirror. "If you can read Tony's mind, just tell me how you do it."

"Don't you want to know all the dirty secrets?"

"I don't care about that," she said, which wasn't entirely true. If she'd been alive and at home, she'd surely have Internet stalked him by now. But, being trapped in a not-real house, she had other, more important things to worry about. So she asked again, "Can you *talk* to him?"

The girl smiled; her teeth glinted. "Someone wants to send a message in a bottle."

"Can you make him hear you?"

The mist was pulsing gently, sending ripples across the surface. Alice stared at it and could have sworn she saw it inch forward, eat up another quarter of a brick on the fireplace. She shivered and came even closer to the wall, so that her toes were pressed against the molding.

"Oh you *do* want to know about him. You want to know everything—it's killing you, isn't it?"

Alice pulled back from the mirror. The girl's brown eyes looked almost black, like enormous dark holes ready to suck her right in. Her mouth was twisted into a funny little smirk. Alice glared, furious, because she realized now that she wasn't going to get anything useful from this girl. The witch was baiting her, toying with her—dangling things over her head, then pulling them away.

Alice wished she could reach through the mirror and grab

the girl by the neck and …

Tony's voice sounded in the other room. She hurried back into the foyer just in time to see him and his dad walk into the lobby and nod to the hotel manager, who was looking exceptionally tired this morning. He had purplish bags under his eyes and his cheeks were sagging. He glowered at George as he passed and George straightened, making himself seem a few inches taller. (He was still shorter than Tony.)

"So … " George said. If he was trying to start a friendly conversation, the manager was not responding well. His eyes had narrowed and one of his eyebrows was higher than the other. George cleared his throat. "I heard the girl's still not awake," he said casually, as if he were merely noting that it was a cloudy day.

But the manager's reaction was anything but calm. His eyes opened wide and he ran clawlike hands through his hair.

"How do you know that?" he said hoarsely.

"I just … just saw it on the news," George said, looking a bit taken aback.

"It's on TV now, too. Of course it is." The manager sank down into his chair, nodding to himself, his lips the thinnest of lines. "Right. Right. And they probably mentioned the hotel. Right. Dangerous hotel."

George opened his mouth to answer, but Tony elbowed him and shook his head. "No," Tony said. "They didn't mention the hotel at all."

The manager just kept nodding.

"Look," said George. "I want to apologize for what happened yesterday. I know we didn't get off on the right foot. But I was hoping to put a few of my sensors up today—very, very small pieces of equipment, I assure you. They wouldn't be in the way at all and nobody would even notice—"

"Right. Fine. Go ahead." The manager spoke in a monotone. He was rocking back and forth in his office chair now, his hands gripping the desk.

Tony and George looked at each other, stunned.

"Um ... okay, well, thank you—" George said haltingly.

"Four rooms," interrupted the manager.

"Excuse me?"

The manager held up four fingers. "I've had four rooms check out early. No reservations have come in since it happened. You go ahead—set up your equipment. At this rate, there won't be anyone to disturb."

"Can I get you a coffee? Or something?" Tony said. "You don't look ... well."

The manager ignored him. He started ranting in a voice so loud that it drew a few people out of the breakfast room to stare. "I got a call not half an hour ago from a lawyer in the city. Apparently the doctors are saying that the girl is brain-dead, that she went without air for too long. They want to pull the plug at the end of the week. The parents are upset—not that I blame them—but they're suing! Do you know what I sacrifice to keep this hotel running? And after all, how much clearer can I get? 'No diving' means no diving.

None! But they're saying that I should have had a lifeguard on duty. Imagine! I can barely afford the upkeep on this place. How am I supposed to hire a full-time lifeguard? It's incredible!"

Alice stumbled backward and leaned against the nearest wall, fingers grasping at the paint.

"Pulling the plug?" she whispered.

Her heart rate tripled in two seconds. They couldn't! They—they wouldn't! Would they? Her parents wouldn't just let her die like that.

It was just the doctors, surely. The doctors thought there wasn't any hope for her—they'd probably tried to convince her parents of it. But her parents, of course, wouldn't believe that. They would give her as long as she needed to wake up from this awful existence that was too cruel even to be a nightmare.

Still, the urgency inside of her, the urgency that nagged at her every minute to find a way to escape, started pulling even harder. Now it tingled all over her body—pinched her mind and tickled her stomach. She had to get out—wake up—go home. She had to do it soon.

"You'll never make it," said the girl, and Alice didn't answer because that thought had crossed her mind too.

Tony. Tony would help her, wouldn't he? She wondered if her strange midnight reappearance would repeat itself. And what if it didn't? What if she never touched the real world again? Or what if she appeared and Tony wasn't there? She felt temporary relief at the thought—if Tony wasn't there then George wouldn't be there either to torture her with his inventions—then more fear when she realized that if he wasn't there then no one would pull her out of the pool. What would happen then? Would she die—for real?

"I'm sorry to hear that," George said. "But we really should—"

The hotel manager was, at this point, beyond self-control. "I can't bring her back from the dead! Getting revenge on me for something that wasn't my fault doesn't even serve a purpose. It's the world we live in, I tell you! People are ... are killing justice in the name of gain."

The manager pulled out a tissue and blew his nose; it made a sound like a trumpet, shattering the silence. He glanced at the people from the breakfast room who had gathered in the doorway. At the sight of them watching, the manager threw the tissue down onto the desk.

"I'm sorry," George said, "about the lawsuit."

The manager looked up. "Oh, I imagine it's all roses and daisies for you. *You* benefit from the whole situation. Another ghost running around for you to catch—that's how you see it." He laughed.

"Look," George said, with an amount of patience that Alice thought was nothing less than heroic. "I know we've had our disagreements, but—"

"Just go," the manager said. "Go! Get out of here. Do what you want. I'm already ruined!" He laughed. "Completely ruined!"

He was laughing quite loudly now and George and Tony were staring at him with their mouths hanging open. A second later,

Tony cleared his throat, muttered a quick goodbye, and dragged his father out of the room.

The manager threw back his head, covered his eyes, and was silent.

CHAPTER ELEVEN

Alice only hesitated for a moment before running up the stairs after George and Tony. Part of her wanted to run and hide in the remotest corner of the house she could find. But she could avoid George's traps better if she knew where he put them. She had to follow.

As she reached the top of the staircase, she remembered why she had run down to the main floor in the first place. Through the open bedroom door in front of her, she could see a wall of mist that had devoured most of the room. It was worse up here than it was below; the mist was moving faster. She thought of the attic room and a twinge of panic twisted her stomach. Glancing to her left, she saw the back of George's head as he passed the hallway mirror; to her right was the deer tapestry that hid the door to the attic.

Alice wavered for a moment, then dashed down the hall to the right. In a desperate panic, she tore away the deer tapestry, and started kicking the door—toes pulled back, low roundhouse kicks that made the wood creak and moan. But the door held steady and each impact sent an even more painful shock up Alice's leg. Finally, she hobbled back and fell to the floor, clutching her red, scratched foot. Some of her frantic energy had worn off and she stared at the tiny keyhole, panting.

So much for brute force. She was going to have to do this the hard way after all. Limping, she hurried back toward George and Tony's room. She couldn't afford to waste any more time on the attic right now—not when George could be lacing the halls with death traps. Between his devices and the mist, Alice's freedom was shrinking with every moment. Hurrying down the hall, gritting her teeth against the pain in her leg, she imagined that the walls were closing in on her—the hallway getting narrower, disappearing entirely—and claustrophobia made her breathing go shallow. When she pushed the door to George and Tony's room open and saw that there was only a five-foot-square corner of the room remaining, she almost turned around. But there, in the remaining six-inch sliver of mirror, was George unpacking one of his plastic tubs (Tony stood by, arms crossed). Holding her breath, Alice forced herself inside, pressing her back against the wall. She watched George closely, but if he was saying anything, she couldn't hear a word. The mist, cottony and yet somehow severe, hung motionless before her, like a curtain.

The girl had followed her.

"You think he can help you," she said, walking into the room in the mirror, her hands lost in the black folds of her dress. "You think that he can save your life."

Alice's stomach clenched. She looked away from Tony's face and down at the floor. Her feet, bare against the carpet, seemed awkward and large. Her right foot looked red.

"He'll help," she muttered.

"Oh yes—he'll help all right." The girl grinned.

"What do you mean by that?"

The girl just shook her head and said, "Watch." She stepped right in front of the mirror, blocking Alice's view completely. Alice tried to stand on her tiptoes to see Tony more clearly, but the girl leaned forward and blew on the glass, making a wide stripe of fog right down the middle.

"What are you doing?" demanded Alice.

"Helping. You'll see."

The girl's blurred figure disappeared, leaving Alice fuming. *Helping?* The girl was helping her about as much as the mist was. Alice leaned against the wall, waiting for the fog on the mirror to fade. It didn't budge. For several moments she stood—surely it would dissolve—but it didn't. It stuck to the glass like paint, like something solid. Alice ran forward and wiped the glass with her sleeve, but that did no good at all. Hurrying back to the safety of the wall a second later, she gave up and made out the shapes behind as best she could. Everything blurred together in a soupy mess. A darkish lump that she knew was George bent over and then straightened up. He took a few steps to his left and paused for a moment (maybe he was putting something on the bookshelf? She couldn't tell), then crossed to the other side of the room. The minute he stepped across the invisible border that was the edge of the mist, his voice came clearly through the mirror.

"—that the other one goes over here." He leaned over the small coffee table in front of the armchair and worked on positioning boxes that were about the size and shape of speakers.

George turned around and held still for a minute; Alice guessed he must be listening to something. Then he said, "Not a radio frequency at all. It's more of a wireless connection. Don't you see? Radio waves can interfere with … "

You'll see.

The girl's voice did not come from anywhere in particular; it came from everywhere—from the air, from the mirror, from the wall itself. Alice looked for any sign of the girl in the mirror, but she was nowhere to be found. She looked behind her, around her, and everything seemed normal, and yet her skin prickled with goose bumps and her hands were freezing cold.

She looked back at the mirror and her heart started racing. Something *was* different.

What had been nothing more than fog had now transformed into a shimmering silver pool. As Alice leaned forward to look into it, breathless and a little afraid, the ripples flattened and the silver grew brighter and brighter. Shapes appeared, becoming faces, and Alice leaned forward farther still. It was like a television within a mirror. She saw the faces more clearly now. They were two boys—a younger but still recognizable Tony and someone else standing next to him—outside, next to an old brick wall. When the other boy spoke, Alice found that she could hear him just as if he were standing beside her.

"We're going tonight. You bringing it?"

Tony hesitated, pushing his hair out of his eyes, scratching his forehead.

"Dude, you've been bragging about it forever. You promised you'd let us try it out," said his friend, who was dressed in a polo shirt and very nice jeans. They both wore backpacks; it looked as though they had just gotten out of school.

"You know my dad's always asking me about it."

The other boy rolled his eyes. "So what? We've gone before. Nothing's ever happened. Totally safe—we're good drivers."

"We don't even have licenses."

"Don't need them. We know what we're doing. Now are you gonna let us try it out or aren't you? 'Cause if you aren't … " He shrugged and said casually, "I'm not sure you should come at all. You've got to follow through—you can't just brag about your fancy car and not give it a go. Maybe you don't even have one. How would I know?"

Tony frowned. "My mom will find out."

"Just tell her what you always do. Study group at my place."

Tony's frown deepened; he looked away. "She called your mom last time."

"Seriously?" his friend asked, and Tony shrugged. "No way—was she pissed?"

"She said I needed to be more responsible—you know. Said she was disappointed."

"Did she punish you?"

"She thinks disappointment *is* a punishment."

He laughed. "Your mom's so my favorite, man."

"She's worried now, though."

The other boy shook his head and readjusted his backpack. "So she's worried. Whatever. It's not like we're doing drugs or anything."

"We kinda ... well."

"Well, we're not. We just wanna *feel* something, you know?"

"Yeah."

They stood in silence for a moment. Tony fingered his backpack straps. "It *is* my car."

"Just what I've been telling you."

"I promised."

The boy was tapping his foot; his arms were crossed. "Yeah, you did."

Tony sighed, looked blankly at the kids walking past him, and said, "Don't leave without me."

As suddenly as it had appeared, the picture was gone. The glass rippled and the circle of silver churned. Holding her breath, Alice reached out to touch it, then changed her mind. This was just some trick that the girl—the house—was playing.

But her heart would not stop pounding. She clenched and unclenched her hands, feeling how sweaty her palms were, though her fingers were cold as ice.

"That's not what I meant."

Alice shook herself. Tony had walked over to where his dad was standing now; it seemed that almost no time had passed during her unexpected detour into what had looked like (but, she reminded herself, couldn't possibly have been) Tony's memories.

The blurry shape of Tony leaned over the two boxes. "I'm saying I don't see why these have to be set up so close if the connection is wireless. Don't you want to cover the most area possible? If it's like a net, you want to spread it wide, right? You see?"

Do you see yet?

The girl again. Alice was more prepared this time, but still her heart raced as she watched the ripples flatten and Tony's face appear in the mirror within the mirror.

A yellow sports car tore down the freeway, dodging cars left and right. Alice saw it, then found herself inside of it, looking at the two front seats like a fly on the windshield. A freckled kid with spiky hair was tapping his foot on the dashboard to loud music; he looked as though he was having the time of his life.

"Sweet! This is *awesome!* Man, I can't believe your dad got you a *car!*" He twisted around to look in the rearview mirror. "They're never gonna catch up. Not in a million years."

"Awesome," Tony said. His fingers were tight around the steering wheel, but he was smiling. He jerked the wheel to the side and screeched around another car. "Whoa." He was breathing heavily; his smile widened. "*Whoa!*"

"Nice one," said the other boy. He rubbed the leather armrests and nodded to himself. "Sweet," he said again. "I'm so jealous, man. You have no idea."

"My dad's cool," said Tony. The freeway was clear ahead of him and he accelerated. The speedometer crept up to 105 mph. He looked almost relaxed now. His fingers loosened on the wheel.

"Uh, duh. Yeah. So he just left it for you after the divorce?"

"Pretty much. Bought it when I was three—we've been fixing it up ever since. Just the two of us, you know? We did the paint job the month before he left."

His smile faded and the car decelerated.

"Hey man, don't slow down," said the other boy, craning his neck to see behind them. "They're catching up. Oh crap—they're totally on our tail!"

Tony glanced in the mirror. "I don't see them."

"Speed up—come on! They're right behind us!"

"I don't see anyone!"

"Are you freaking blind?"

For one brief moment, Tony turned around, squinting into the darkness behind them.

"Oh yeah—okay, I see their headlights. What're you talking

about? They're way behind—"

But the other boy's scream drowned out the end of his sentence. It was loud and high and piercing and sent chills down Alice's spine.

Tony whipped around. "What the—"

Alice saw his eyes widen as the car headed across the carpool lane and straight into oncoming traffic. The other boy's scream was pure panic. Tony grabbed the steering wheel with both hands and turned it sharply to the right; the car veered, turned, turned again, spun … they were spinning … they had crossed back over to the other side of the freeway. They were going so fast now that the world was a constant blur and the boys' faces were two blotches of panic and the car was a yellow bullet heading into a ditch on the side of the road.

The picture rippled and then it was gone.

George picked up one of the boxes; Alice could see only a beige blur that had to be the top of his balding head.

"You have a point," he said. "Maybe putting one out in the hall would be a good idea."

Once again, she hadn't missed a second. Could the girl really stop time? And what could the girl possibly hope to gain by showing her this?

The scream rang in her ears. … She shivered.

The mist was completely still and Alice, fairly sure it wouldn't move anytime soon, came closer to the half-gone mirror. She sidled up next to it the way people approach the edge of a cliff—inch by inch, eyes wide and unblinking. Heart pounding. She thought she might throw up. Reaching out, she ran her finger down the smooth glass. It was perfectly solid. And yet when it rippled, it seemed fluid as water, as though she might be able to stick a hand right through it. *Straight through.* Could she get to the other side? She stood poised beside the glass, hoping the girl would give her just one more little video trip.

The back of her neck was sweaty and she wiped it with her hand. She could smell herself; a wave of nausea made her clutch her stomach. She almost retreated back to the safety of the corner, but pride kept her standing there. What if the girl was still watching her? Alice refused to appear afraid, to show weakness.

Tony reached for the other box. "What if we put one up by the pool? What do you think?"

What do you think of him now, Alice?

The minute the girl's voice echoed in the room, Alice plunged her hand into the surface of the mirror. Her hand disappeared inside it and for a second her fingers felt cold, but the cold was strange—too intense—and only a second later the freezing turned to burning. It was unbearable; her skin felt as if it had gone up in flames. Cursing, she pulled her hand out and stumbled away, holding it to her. For a moment she didn't dare to look at it. She expected to see the charred, blackened remains of fingers hanging limply from her palm. But when she did finally dare a quick glance, she saw that her hand looked perfectly normal. The pain was all in her head, not that that made her feel it any less. Blinking back tears, she watched the mirror.

When the ripples flattened this time, Tony was sitting in a hospital bed, his arm in a sling, his face dotted with cuts and bruises. A woman with dark, curly hair (his mother, Alice assumed) sat on a chair next to him, listening to a white-jacketed doctor talk about fractures. When the doctor got up to leave, the woman stood and began to pace the room, her arms folded, lips pursed.

Tony was stone-faced and thoroughly unapologetic.

"They're not going to arrest you," she said at last. "They could have."

Tony nodded in response, his eyes on the floor.

His mother, a tall woman with very short brown hair, stopped pacing. She pressed her palms into the hospital bed, exhaled heavily.

"I've always tried to be honest with you, Tony. I think you know that."

Another nod. His mom bit her lip and surveyed him.

"One of the things that attracted me to your dad was his love for adventure. He would do … " She smiled. " … anything. Just for the thrill of it, you know. We went rock climbing. Scuba diving. We did so many things—and it wasn't enough."

She sat down then and Tony looked away. His expression, however, had lost some of its hardness. He looked guilty now—guilty and a bit uncertain.

"Adventure—that adrenaline rush you get—that can become an addiction," said his mom. Alice was surprised to hear that she sounded not angry, but concerned. Her parents would have screamed at her for half an hour and banished her to her room for months if she'd pulled a stunt like that.

"Part of the reason your dad is ... the way he is—always looking for the next big lead, running around the world searching for something—he's trying to *feel* something, Tony. It isn't enough for him to be content. If his heart isn't pounding, if he doesn't have that thrill, he forgets that he's alive. And so he goes from fix to fix, but he isn't happy." She paused, put her hand on Tony's knee. "This *will* eat you up. Don't let it get to that point, Tony. It's a long road back."

Tony didn't answer. He swallowed hard and blinked several times.

"Now," his mother said, businesslike, "you're going to have to appear in court. There'll be a hearing and you'll be lucky if you just end up with some community service. As for the car ... " She looked angry for the first time. Tony still couldn't meet her eyes.

"It was your car," she said. "And you decided how you were going to use it. Now you'll just have to deal with the consequences."

"Is it—"

"Totaled."

"If you'd just let me keep it—I could fix it. I could try. Dad ... Dad would let me."

His mother stood, shaking her head.

"Sometimes you can't fix things, Tony. I think your dad would agree."

He wouldn't meet her eyes, but he didn't argue. She grabbed her purse.

"You told him?" he asked softly.

Tony paled as she nodded.

"He wants to talk to you. He's angry." Her fingers tightened around her purse. "I'm angry too. But for God's sake let's get out of this hospital. We can talk at home."

The picture rippled and dissolved, and as it did the entire silver pool began to pulse. It got very bright, then faded quickly, getting smaller and smaller until—with a final burst of bright white light— it disappeared entirely. The mirror was back to normal.

Alice blinked, unclenched her hands, and crossed her arms. Her stomach was churning. She massaged her fingers, which tingled sharply—as though her circulation had been cut off and the blood was only just now coming back.

In the room, George was silent for a moment, then said, in such a soft voice that Alice almost didn't catch the words, "The pool. Sure. Absolutely."

Tony turned to face him. "Okay. What's wrong?"

"Nothing—nothing. It's just that I'm surprised. You're taking an interest. You've never seemed to care much about this sort of thing."

Shrugging, Tony answered, "Guess I've changed."

George fiddled with what looked like a knob on the box. "If Madeline could only see you now. ... She wouldn't be saying that you just came because you didn't want me to feel bad, would she? She gave me such a bad time about it, too. And she was wrong. *Wrong.*" There was a pause during which George's eyes gleamed and Tony looked a bit ashamed of himself. "Well," George continued, "we may just make a ghost hunter out of you yet."

"So ... we can put it by the pool, then?" Tony asked.

George shook his head. "You kidding? You couldn't keep me away."

They walked out of the room and Alice hurried into the hallway. She didn't get very far; she had that freezing exhaustion she associated with throwing up. Lying down on the rug, she wrapped her arms around herself, trying to remember what it felt like to be warm.

CHAPTER TWELVE

For several minutes Alice lay on the floor, clutching her goose-bump–covered arms and trying over and over again to think of a way to escape George's ghost-hunting tools should she appear again in the pool. But nothing seemed plausible. If she couldn't even get herself out of the water, then how could she run away?

She was coming up with nothing useful, and her mind started to wander. The car shooting by like a yellow bullet flashed before her eyes. She heard the scream again.

Why had the girl shown this to her? She didn't know what to believe, whether it was even possible that she had seen something real. And, even worse, if it *had* been true, where did that leave her? If the witch was powerful enough to read a person's past, could she read someone's present? Could she read minds?

I want to talk to you. Alice mentally recited the words. She thought them slowly, lingering on every consonant. She shut her eyes and thought them again, picturing the girl, calling out to her.

Can you hear me?

There was no answer. Louder, then—*Can you HEAR me?*

Still no response. "Hey!" she yelled, looking up at the mirror. She lifted herself up on her elbows, listening to her voice echoing down the hallway, but the girl did not appear. And Alice didn't even know a name to call.

"You!" she tried again. "You know I'm talking to you."

The paintings of Elizabeth glared down at her. There was utter silence. Alice shook her head. The only thing to do—the only thing that she could think of doing—was to forget it, write the whole mirror thing off as a trick. The girl was trouble. The girl was part of the house and the house only wished her harm. The girl was a witch. Alice knew it was true, but what she had seen haunted her nevertheless, like a bad taste in her mouth.

And Tony … she'd been spying on him for days now, but for the first time she felt as though she'd really intruded. Like the time she'd read her mom's journal. She'd been sick for days about it—all the complaining about being trapped, about how draining it was to be a mother. It had been like sinking into someone else's cold, used bathwater.

I didn't have a choice. I don't even know if it was true.

And she didn't—she had no idea. So why did she cringe away from thinking about what she'd seen?

I hardly know him, she answered herself.

This was what it came down to; it was an uncomfortable weight in her stomach. It didn't even matter if what the girl had shown her had actually happened. Either way, it proved the same point—she knew almost nothing about Tony. He'd lived just as long as she had and she'd spoken to him for less than an hour—how could she know that he wanted to help her or that he even would? She couldn't. The girl was right.

She sat up, shivering. Her stomach was steadier, but more than anything she wanted comfort, and comfort was hard to come by in this place. She wished she had something to eat, craved the familiarity of chewing and tasting, though she felt no hunger. Her bare legs were covered in goose bumps, and she couldn't stop thinking about her old, comfortable jeans—the ones that her mom wouldn't let her leave the house in. Tony's sweatshirt was thin, hardly enough fabric to keep her from shivering, and her bare legs were icy. It hit her that there was a closet in the library and, pulling herself to her feet, she rushed down the stairs, trying to step lightly on her right foot, hoping there would be coats inside.

Alice pulled the door open and it creaked so loudly that she jumped. There was more than she had bargained for. It looked as though every single dress Elizabeth had ever worn in a play was stuffed in here. The small space was full to bursting with silk and velvet and feathers. Alice pulled out a deep red shawl and draped it around her shoulders, but couldn't resist looking through the rest of the clothes. There was an exquisite blue velvet dress and a peach-colored toga. So many gowns she lost count.

And then, in the corner, the most beautiful sage green she had ever seen.

It was what Elizabeth was wearing the last time she was painted, Alice realized, holding the dress up and comparing it to the painting on the wall.

Her legs were freezing; she looked at the long skirt. She bit her lip, then pulled off the shawl and sweatshirt and stepped into the dress, doing her best to zip up the old-fashioned zipper on the back. Then, pulling the sweatshirt back on, she threw the shawl back into the closet and closed the door.

The weight of the dress was comforting somehow and finally, she started to feel warm. But when she looked up at the painting, she felt as if she were looking in a mirror and she quickly turned away.

The diary was on the floor where she had put it down. She walked over and stared down at it; it looked even smaller from this far up, positively miniature next to her foot. Its smallness was almost cute, nearly appealing … like candy-coated poison. Though she was tempted to leave it there—wished she could never have to open it again—there was nothing better to do now. And, after all, it was the only clue she had to go on.

***

May 13, 1883

Lillian betrayed me yesterday.

Now I shall loathe her until the day I die.

She said that William had come for me. I still don't know why I believed her, little demon that she is. William is dead. I should have remembered that if he weren't, he already would have come. Perhaps I was simply too hopeful to be cautious. Either way, I trusted her. I hurried to the front door at once. I didn't even put my books back under the floorboard for safekeeping. Lillian followed behind me. If I had been paying attention, I might have noticed that she was acting strangely. But my love was at the door and I could think of nothing else.

Only he wasn't. The person at the door wasn't my William at all.

Heavens, I can hardly write, it makes me so angry. I wish I could strangle her. I would like nothing better than to wrap my hands around her little throat and shake it, feel her head bobbing helplessly about. The witch would have done it—I know she would. She nods me on, trying to get me to do it. I, however, am above such paltry revenge. I shall find a better way to see justice served.

The witch does not always know best.

When the man at the door grabbed hold of my arm, I knew that something was wrong. And then I saw it—the carriage with words printed on the side. The door, open and waiting to receive me.

I do not know exactly what I did to the man, but I remember that he fell at my feet, groaning in pain. My sister ran toward me and tried to push me into the arms of another man waiting nearby, but I slapped her so hard that she fell to the ground. She is lucky that I did not do worse. The other man I fled from, all the way to my attic room. I have barricaded the door with my chest of drawers now. Lillian may bang on it all she likes. I shall never let her inside again. Never.

It is a miracle that she didn't steal the books while I was distracted.

I hear my father yelling outside. Creaking—there, the carriage is leaving. They are gone—Father has taken care of it. I think he is coming inside now. Is that the door? Yes, it was the door. He is outside my room, with Lillian—he is yelling again, now at her. I can hear quite clearly through the wall. He is very angry. He tells Lillian that she had no right to contact the asylum without his permission. Now she is yelling. She says that he has gone mad too. She says that it's dangerous to have me around the house, in my condition.

I don't understand what she means by "my condition." I am perfectly well. The doctor knew that I was.

Now it is Father's turn. He says that this is his property and he will do with it as he likes. He will keep me here if he wishes to. Lillian is furious. Goodness how she yells! She says that his business has always benefited from having an actress in the house to amuse the boarders. She is calling him selfish. And now she is calling me spoiled.

"You love her more!" she screams.

That is the heart of it. She is jealous of me! I always knew that she was.

Oh look! The argument is over and now it is just Father knocking on my door. I will not let him in right now. What if Lillian is watching? What if she forces her way inside?

I tell him that I will open the door later.

"Why?" he asks.

I tell him that I must wait until it is safe and he is silent for a moment. Then I hear him walking away. How heavy his footsteps sound! I have never noticed how loudly they ring before.

I am back at my desk now; I have the book of curses in my lap. I am planning. Lillian has crossed a line today. It is time for her to reap her reward.

And she shall reap it.

***

The clock began to strike midnight and Alice jumped. She braced herself ... but nothing happened. Ten ... eleven ... twelve strokes and still she stood, just as solid as before. She wasn't going anywhere tonight.

Alice slumped down onto the floor, next to the lamp that she had lit a few hours before. It was starting to smoke and she adjusted the wick. There was a lump in her throat the size of an egg; she hadn't come this close to crying in a long time.

There was no reason to believe it would happen again, she reminded herself. Nothing in this place made sense anyway; nothing was reliable. So why was she so disappointed? What was there for her out there anyway?

There was the key.

And Tony.

"You changed your colors."

The girl. For once, Alice was almost glad to see her. She ran into the entryway and straight to the mirror. The girl stared back at her—same clothes, same triangle bracelets, same rope necklace.

"What was that about? Why did you show me that?" Alice said.

The girl tilted her head. "What's to explain? I wanted to help you see what it is you can't. Because I'm your friend."

"And what is it that I can't see?"

The girl's eyes left Alice's face and swept down to her dress. She looked pleased. Meeting Alice's gaze again, she said, "That you don't know him. That he has a whole life behind him and you know nothing about it. How can you trust him?"

"I don't know you," she said, self-consciously smoothing the folds of the gown. "How do I even know you're not lying to me?"

"I guess you don't. But I think we both know that that's not really the problem here."

"What?"

"You don't want to believe me, Alice. You don't *want* me to be telling you the truth. Because you're just so desperate for anyone to swoop in and save you that you'll give your heart and soul to the first person who stops long enough for you to latch onto."

"That's ridiculous!" She could feel her cheeks coloring. At least she knew now that the girl really couldn't read minds. If she could, she would never think—not even for a second—"I don't—Tony is just ... I'm just hoping he can help me. Because I want to not *die*. There's nothing more to it than that. And he's been a whole lot more helpful than you!"

The girl cut her off. "I wasn't talking about Tony, but it's funny you should mention him ... " she said, giving Alice a look that was both significant and accusatory—her eyebrows slightly raised, her lips curled into a little smile.

Alice had always wondered what it would be like to have a sister. She thought now that it might feel something like this. It was as though the girl knew exactly which buttons to push—she knew just how to twist things to make Alice as irritated as possible.

"I was talking about your life," said the girl, which was funny coming from someone who looked as though she had known no more of life than Alice had.

"I've always been self-reliant. I don't ask people to save me. Not usually," Alice assured her.

"And you spend every day wishing you could, wishing you had friends to share the burden."

"I have friends," she said automatically.

"Yes. You have me."

Alice laughed. "I don't know who you are or what you want or what you're trying to do, but I can tell you for certain that you're not my friend."

"Of course," said the girl, taking Alice by surprise. "Of course. I'd forgotten what wonderful friends you already have. You know what? Why don't I let you spend some quality time with them?"

Before Alice had time to ask what the girl meant by this, she had blown on the glass and disappeared.

"Not again," said Alice as the now-familiar silver pool appeared. She tried to walk away, sure that she didn't want to see anything that the girl wanted to show her, but when she heard her own voice she turned around.

"What is it?"

She was sitting at her desk doing math homework. Her mom walked in and watched her for a moment before asking, "Shouldn't you be getting ready?"

Alice put her pencil down. "Ready for what?" She was wearing her pajamas and her hair was wet from the shower.

Trapped Alice swallowed hard. She remembered this. This had happened not two months ago. How could the girl possibly have known ...

"The sleepover? At Shay's?" her mom said, walking over to her dresser and pulling out a shirt. "Here, I'll pack some stuff for you."

"Sleepover? What are you talking about?"

Her mom was looking through her underwear drawer now. "Don't you ever fold anything?"

"Mom!" Alice hurried over and shut the drawer. "Mom, there isn't a sleepover."

"Yes, there is. Mollie's mom told me about it. She's going. And I know that you're friends with them so I just figured that—"

"I can't," said Alice quickly. She pulled the shirt out of her mom's hand and stuck it back in the drawer, taking her time so that her mom wouldn't see her face. Taking a deep breath, she turned back around. "Homework. Studying. Finals. I'm swamped! So don't worry about it. Shay and Mollie understand. I'll just ... get back to work now."

Alice walked back to her desk but her mom didn't leave. She sat down on the bed, frowning.

"They didn't invite you, did they?"

"Of course they did. I just ... forgot, you know?"

But the lie was no good. Her mom had a hand to her forehead and she was shaking her head violently. "I don't believe this. They can't keep excluding you. You were best friends in elementary school."

"It's high school, Mom. It's been years."

"You know what?" Her mom stood up. "I'm calling Shay's mom. You're going to that sleepover, Alice. Her mom will understand ... it's unfair to exclude ... "

"Mom! Don't!"

But her mom was already out the door. The picture fizzed and was gone.

Alice sat down weakly on the couch. She wasn't sure what disturbed her more—that what the girl had shown her wasn't a lie, or that the other things she had said might not be lies either.

***

May 14, 1883

I have opened my door again. Father has assured me that there will not be a repeat of yesterday. Lillian is being punished. She is not allowed to leave the house anymore. Instead, she must care for me and show me the sisterly kindness that she finds so hard to grasp. I find it fitting. I have always had to lead the way as far as love is concerned. I sometimes tire of being the better person.

I rather like the thought of her as my maid. She, on the other hand, is furious. She goes stomping around the house, disturbing the boarders and making Father angry. Lillian has never had much sense; she doesn't know the difference between punishing others and punishing herself.

She despises me—I am even more certain of it today than I was before. The little brat gave me the newspaper with my breakfast today. She's never done that before and I knew at once that she had some hidden, vengeful purpose in it. I was right.

I didn't find the article until I had read all the way through the first three pages. When I saw the headline, I almost didn't go on. Lillian was just trying to punish me for keeping the witch's things from her.

But I read it anyway.

A girl in New Hampshire has been swindled by a man who said he wanted to elope with her. He took all of her valuable items to the boat, promising to come back for her the next evening. He never did.

After I read that, I threw my glass against the wall, just to hear it shatter. Lillian came into the room, wearing a smile that reminded me very much of the witch's.

"Did William take all of your jewelry too, Lizzie?" she asked me.

And that is the moment when my patience with her ran out.

I think that I would have killed her had Father not interceded. I had her pinned to the wall, my hands wrapped around her scrawny throat, but he pulled me away. Father has always been a strong man. Although I fought hard, he soon had me back in my bed. Lillian screamed terrible things then. She called me mad. She called me a murderer. She said that I should be hung. Then she grabbed Mother's favorite vase from my drawers and flung it at my head.

I don't remember it hitting me. I just remember waking up to my father's face staring down at me many hours later. Poor man; he was quite beside himself. The doctor apparently would not come to tend to me—I do not know why. Father didn't even believe that I would wake.

Lillian would have liked that.

I looked at my face in the mirror tonight. My left eye is bruised and so swollen that I can hardly open it. It is red now, almost purple. Tomorrow it will be darker. There are cut marks all over my cheek and forehead.

I can no longer tell whether it is my face that is distorted or the mirror.

When I saw what Lillian had done to me, I knew what to do. In a court of law, crime is punished. Theft is met with retribution. Injustice with justice. Murder with death. I am the judge and the jury, the victim and the executor. I will repay.

***

There was a crash from the real lobby and Alice jumped so hard that the book tumbled from her hands and fell to the floor. She sat up, glancing in the mirror. It was still dark—probably about five in the morning. Tony and his dad were bending over a box of equipment that one of them had just dropped.

"Damn," said Tony's dad, "I'm going to have to replace this lens."

Alice's breath was fogging the glass. She wiped it clean with her shirt.

"I'm sorry. It just slipped right out of my hands."

They both looked very tired, staring at one another with

matching dark circles under their eyes.

"It's okay," George said with some difficulty. He was clearly trying very hard to be patient with his son. "I needed a new one anyway."

Tony looked relieved. "Okay. I'll gather everything up. You go ahead without me."

George gave a tired nod. "How about we try setting up in the garden next time? I know you wanted to set up near the pool, but it seems like a pretty dead area. I could have guessed. Spirits generally avoid the water."

"Are you sure about that?"

"Absolutely. I've never caught one by a pool. Not once."

"Oh," said Tony. He looked as though he wanted to say more, but he just bent down to pick up a piece of glass.

George started to head up the stairs, then turned around to look at his son. "Tony?"

"Yeah?"

"Look, I'm sorry we didn't come up with anything tonight. We'll pick up something tomorrow for sure."

Tony just smiled. "Don't worry, Dad. It was … fun anyway."

George looked about ready to fall down the stairs in surprised pleasure. Somehow he managed to regain his balance and fumble his way up to the second floor. As soon as he disappeared into the hallway, the smile slid right off Tony's face and he sat down on the floor with his head in his hands.

Alice watched him.

"Tony?" she whispered.

"Alice?"

She was so surprised to hear him answer that she jumped and her forehead bumped against the glass. Cringing, she called again.

"Tony! Can you hear—?"

But before she could finish, he started speaking over her, and she realized with a pang of disappointment that she had misunderstood. Tony was talking to himself, not to her.

"Alice, if you can hear me, if you're here somewhere ... I have something to say to you," he said. He was looking at the ceiling now, as if he expected to see her floating around up there, ghostly and white.

"Look, I don't know what's going on."

She pressed her palms against the glass; she could feel it bend under the pressure.

"I don't understand what's happening with you. I don't know if you're dead or alive, or just ... something else, but if I can help, just come talk to me again, okay? I want to help you if I can."

A wash of relief, so strong it nearly made her cry, swept through her. She might not be able to touch the real world, trapped behind these mirrors, but here—reality was stretching out a hand for her to grab hold of. Tony's hand. And just knowing that someone out there knew she was in here, someone hadn't given up ... Until now, with hope flooding back over her, she hadn't realized how little she'd been holding onto.

"I'll be by the pool all day tomorrow," he said. "I'll be there, so you can come whenever you want, and we'll talk about things. I can be alone if you want me to be."

Some of her relief went up in flames; if he was by the pool, she wouldn't be able to see him. How would she know what he was doing? And what good did it do her to have him out there when there was no reason to believe she'd ever escape this mirror house again?

And, a small voice in her head admitted, the thought of facing a whole day without seeing him was brutal. It felt like losing her only friend.

"I've got to go now," he said, gathering up the rest of the glass on the floor. He picked up the box, looked around the room, and sighed. "You probably can't hear any of this anyway."

Alice pushed harder on the glass, wishing more than anything that she could somehow force her way through to the other side. Tony stopped halfway up the staircase, just stood there perfectly still. He hung his head and muttered something under his breath; she leaned in to hear, banging the side of her head against the glass.

"I've never met anyone like you before, Alice."

Then he disappeared around the corner and Alice slumped onto the lobby couch. She pulled her knees to her chest. She should still be feeling relieved—she knew that. Tony was going to help her. She had an ally. She had a chance. But fear—cold, bone-chilling fear—was sweeping through her like winter, and her fingers were so cold. Alice touched her face, felt her icy skin, and all she could think of was her aunt's funeral, standing by the coffin, reaching inside and touching her hand ... it was cold.

No. No.

Alice tried to shake the thought away, but it had settled on her now and it was so heavy. She buried her face in her arms. Her body was in a hospital somewhere. She was lying there. She wasn't moving. Were her hands cold as a corpse? She wondered and she didn't know.

I've never met anyone like you before. But he hadn't met *her*. *Her* was lying on a hospital bed like a dead person. Would she ever meet him—really meet him? She imagined what it would be like, escaping this place. She'd wake up and get better and find him and thank him ... then what? Would they hug? They would shake hands. Her hand would be real and warm and solid.

It stung to think about it—she had never wanted something so badly in her life. Alice told herself that she just wanted to live, that this was perfectly normal, but underneath the mere desire for survival—she couldn't deny it—was a different kind of heartache. And it had to do with Tony. Not that he felt anything more than normal curiosity about her. That was what he had meant, she was sure. *Never met anyone like you.* Well, he hadn't met a ghost before.

So why was it that when she thought of him, she wanted so badly to be alive, wanted it more than she knew she could want anything? Maybe he reminded her of herself somehow—what she was before the accident. That was probably it. He was, after all, a lot like her in some small ways. She saw herself, sometimes, in the expression on his face, heard herself in the way he spoke. ... He had a nice voice, a very nice voice—

"'The course of true love never did run smooth.'"

The girl's voice was heavy with sarcasm. Alice looked up. This was the one thing she wanted least of all right now.

"Leave me alone," she whispered.

"Oh, but you are very much alone," said the girl, and when Alice—only moments later—dared to look in the mirror, she was nowhere to be seen.

CHAPTER THIRTEEN

May 15, 1883

I am preparing. Goodness, it's so marvelous I want to write it all down. I want to tell you all about it.

But I won't. Not yet. "Patience," says the witch. She speaks to me now—sometimes for hours. But today she says but one word. Patience.

Sometimes the witch knows best.

Today I glanced in the mirror and saw nothing beautiful at all. I saw black and blue and a swollen eye and a gaunt, misshapen face.

It is as I feared. I am not beautiful. No man can ever love me. No one can love me! I felt lost for a while then, because beauty is all I have lived for. My beauty, my talents—they are all I have.

And I have lost everything.

I picked up the scissors and went to the window. Snip! Snip! My hair is short now—it brushes my shoulders. A foot of long black curls went tumbling into the pond. They float on the surface, gleaming and making the water ripple in awful, strange ways.

My eyelashes were long and black and thick. I snipped them off too and sent them into the water with the hair. I tried to cut my eyebrows, but I only managed to cut myself and I gave up.

I look in the mirror. Now I am truly hideous.

The witch is grinning at me. You know, I've never noticed how ugly she is before. Now I see it, though. She has a cut on her eyebrow. Her hair is shaggy and tangled.

But she is still smiling that crooked smile.

Lillian came to check in on me. She screamed and ran away when she saw my face, my hair, my eyes. I laughed at her and moved my wardrobe to block the door. Now she and Father are banging on the door, yelling at me, begging me to open it.

Oh the noise! There is so much noise! I curled up against a wall and covered my ears, but it did no good—no good at all.

Please go away! Go away!

They are gone. They have given up. It's quiet now and I can think—I can prepare my curse. I sit in front of the mirror and the witch and I work together. I do most of the work myself, though. I don't need her as much as she thinks I do.

Don't tell her that.

Stop screaming, Lillian! I'm not going to open the door!

Go away!

I must think about my curse.

***

Elizabeth's handwriting was becoming more and more difficult to decipher. The first pages in the diary had been hard to read, but they had also been beautiful, with an artfulness all their own. Now Alice was nearly halfway through the tiny book and the pages looked as if a child had scribbled all over them with her hands tied together and her eyes closed.

She had trouble focusing. For a long time she sat downstairs, waiting to see if Tony would come back down dragging a pillow and blanket, off to spend the night by the pool. She knew, of course, that that would be a bad thing (she couldn't watch him if he were out there), but part of her wished he would. She wanted to know how committed he really was.

At one point in the dead of the night when everything was dark and quiet, she found herself staring blankly at the wall. Her thoughts kept returning to him. Finally, dying of curiosity, she jumped to her feet and ran up the stairs. The mist shone through the open doors on the second floor, shedding enough pale light for her to walk down the hallway without hitting any walls. Holding her breath, she opened the door to Tony and George's room. But the mist had eaten up the mirror entirely; there was nothing left to see. Heavily, she walked back down the stairs.

Alice's mood went in cycles, shooting from hopeful to angry, then plummeting to despondence. The same thoughts went circling through her mind, like ugly horses on a never-ending merry-go-round.

It might be okay, now that Tony's helping.

Tony.

But what can he possibly do? He doesn't know any more about this curse than I do. He doesn't even know there is a curse.

It isn't fair. What did I do wrong? What did I do to deserve this?

I'm a good person.

I'm a terrible person.

It's no good. I'm not going to get out. I don't get to win this game. It's just no use. The diary—all of it.

Burn it all.

By morning, Alice thought she might be losing her mind. Her thoughts were spinning in such disarray and she couldn't control them. ... She tried. She was huddled against a wall with the book clutched in her hands, her eyes exhausted from squinting at the tiny rows of text. Her body, however, wouldn't do her the favor of actually being tired. She craved sleep the way she craved food—she didn't seem to need it, but the taste of it hung on her tongue.

Her brain was like a wild animal in a cage, throwing itself against the walls.

Focus.

She tried, but she couldn't.

Finally, the sounds of morning started to come from the mirrors—the crashing of doors, the clomping of feet. The hotel manager arrived at his desk at 7:30 sharp. At 8:13 he got a phone call, lost his head, and started yelling into the receiver about lawsuits and his three children.

After a few minutes, his yelling became a meaningless drone. Her mind wandered to her parents. Just the thought of them was enough to send her spiraling down so deep into memories that she wondered if it were possible to lose her way in her own mind. It was funny the things she remembered—not the happy things, not the big things, not the good things either. Just the things that cut her deep somehow, that made an impression. Like the time she, thirteen years old and self-conscious, asked her mother if she was pretty.

"You're not unattractive, honey," her mother had said casually, unaware that her answer would haunt Alice for years.

There were the presents her dad would bring back from his business trips for her and Jeremy—so many gifts. The way his eyes would light up when he gave her a hat or jewelry or a doll ... she remembered that. He would get the strangest look on his face as he watched, a hungry kind of look, as though he needed to know that they loved him. Gifts, she realized now, had been the only way he could show them that he cared.

And Jeremy. When he was younger—only four years old—he would come running into her room during thunderstorms and climb into her bed and wrap his skinny arms around her.

"Why are you afraid?" she would ask. "Don't be afraid."

"I'm not afraid. I'm never afraid."

And he would fall asleep huddled against her. She never told him to leave—not once. Because though thunderstorms didn't scare her, the warmth of his body against hers was so comforting and so real that she wondered how she ever slept without him.

Alice didn't understand how these thoughts could affect her so deeply, but somehow they did. They worked their way inside of her, twisting like knives—good memories, bad memories. Memories were all that was left of her life and it terrified her.

Tony and George tromped downstairs at noon, carrying their equipment in big plastic tubs. The manager glanced up from his computer and exchanged a tense grimace with George.

"Hunting?" he asked.

George merely nodded. The manager's lips thinned, but he too remained silent.

Alice watched Tony until he disappeared from sight. The waves in his dark hair caught the light in a way that made her heart beat fast. She imagined the sunlight in his hair—the sunlight in the water. She hadn't seen real, blue, daytime blue sky in what felt like years. When she closed her eyes, she could imagine it. And she could imagine him in it, waiting for her by the pool as the wind blew the trees and the birds sang and …

She wanted to claw the walls. Was this what claustrophobia felt like?

There was nothing left to do but sit and try not to lose hope entirely until midnight rolled around again. As much as she wanted to appear again tonight, she felt that she had very little reason to hope. Or perhaps she simply didn't dare to wish too hard anymore. The house felt like a jinx. If she wanted something, it would make sure that it didn't happen.

But still she wore the dress.

***

May 16, 1883

I found the knife in the kitchen—stole it right out from under the cook's nose when she wasn't watching. For now, it is hidden under my pillow. Lillian mustn't know that I have it.

She hasn't come to see me today. Perhaps she is frightened. She should be frightened.

While I wait for nighttime, I write my curse. It has never been done before. The witch herself did not discover the secret of binding soul to object, but I have. Many hours have I pondered this, and I believe that I have the answer.

No human being lives forever, and, just like a human, a bound soul fades with time. The curse that an object carries becomes weaker every minute, just from the burden of existing. A curse's power, the soul, must be replenished.

The witch wrote that the bound soul must help to execute the curse. I believe that she was wrong. Must wood consent to be burned in a fire? No. A soul is nothing more than living fuel. The curse is the rider, the soul is the horse—more physically powerful, but tied up and forced to do the rider's bidding.

The only question is how to replace the old souls with the new.

The answer is in the curse.

If I am correct, and I believe that I am, I can cast a self-renewing curse—a curse that kills to satisfy its own need for survival. This house will carry a curse forever—a curse on all women who hope for love. Not all will pay the price, but some will be sacrificed to keep the curse alive. A few deaths alone can remind the world of the fragile balance on which it turns.

Lillian will be the first to serve the curse; she will become part of this place, just as the witch became part of her mirror.

Of course, every curse must be carefully crafted. Curses are like artwork, you see—they must be balanced. If the curse is to survive, there must be a way to destroy it; invincibility is against nature. I have not yet decided what the escape will be. Perhaps the witch will help.

The four elements, of course, I must include. Lillian must burn and hang, drown and be buried. Burial, of course, is simple. Hanging will be simply a matter of finding the rope. Fire will be more difficult, but this attic will do for wood. I shall burn the floorboards, I think. Water is challenging as well, but there is a pond outside my window. I shall lay the body there after it has been touched with fire.

I mentioned before that I discovered the secret of magic—three and four. The witch included four in her curse, but not three. I believe that this is the reason it was unstable. I shall remedy that in my own experiment. Three chances—that is what I will provide. The victims will each escape three times from their doom. Three times in seven—thrice in a week. This will balance the power of the curse with the victim's ability to destroy it. But, once that week is over, the victim's fate will be sealed.

And that will be the end of it.

***

So that was it.

Alice let the diary close in her hands. Her eyes drifted and she found herself watching the glow from the lamplight shimmering on the dark ceiling. Elizabeth's painting as Ophelia stared down at her, a cruel sneer in the curve of her lips. Alice had reluctantly moved into the library only a few hours before, when fear of the dark and uncontrollable nerves forced her to seek out a more enclosed space—one where she could keep a close eye on the one and only door. And yet she was still not sure if she felt any safer in here. The room itself was overbearing, and the painting gave her chills every time she caught a glimpse of it.

"Three chances, then," Alice said to the painting. "Is that the secret? But what am I supposed to do? Three chances to do *what?*"

The painting offered no answers.

Alice turned away, clenching her teeth in frustration. If she could only get into the attic—she would find some answers there, she was sure of it. Elizabeth was always talking about the witch's books that were hidden there, and Alice knew she needed to get her hands on them. If Elizabeth had adapted one of the witch's curses to her own purposes—to bind a soul to a place—then maybe the witch's books would show Alice how to break the curse as well. The fact that the attic was locked only made her more desperate to get inside; if the house was trying so hard to keep her out, then she had to try just as hard to get in. Alice hated losing at games.

Behind the armchair she was sitting in, a grandfather clock counted out the seconds. Alice had been so busy decoding the cryptic handwriting in the diary that she hadn't looked at the time for hours. Only now did she turn around to see how late it was.

One hour until midnight.

"Are you ready for the ball, Cinderella?"

Alice was so beyond sick of the girl that, as she walked out into the foyer, she had every intention of destroying that mirror, just for the momentary pleasure of it.

"You don't know me," Alice said, taking an umbrella out of the stand by the door, "and I'm just about finished with this."

The girl smiled—wide. Her teeth glinted; her voice was sharp.

"I don't know you. I *am* you," she said. She reached out and stroked the mirror with two thin fingers, and her skin didn't turn white when pressed against the glass. It was as if the mirror wasn't there at all and, if she wanted, she could reach her hand all the way through and grab Alice by the throat.

"You're not me," said Alice, preparing to swing the umbrella. "You're lying to me."

"You're lying to yourself. You do it all the time."

"Why would I—"

"In the night, in the dark, when you tell yourself that everything's okay. When you pretend that people care. That boy ... "

Alice leapt forward; the umbrella fell forgotten to the floor.

"Don't you dare bring him into this."

But the girl continued on, completely unperturbed.

"Do you want to know what he really thinks about you? I can show you."

"I don't want—"

She held up a finger, shook her head. "Lying."

"I don't care—"

"Do you ever *stop*?" The girl shook her head and sighed the careworn sigh of a much older person. She reached out toward the mirror, as if to stroke Alice's hair, but her fingers stopped again at that invisible barrier.

Alice tried to say something, tried to get the words out, think of an adequate reply. But she realized with horror that the girl was *right*. She was a walking lie; she couldn't stop. She lied to her mother all the time. She'd lied to Tony. To herself.

"I care," the girl said gently. "*I* care."

"I don't believe you," Alice whispered, stepping away from the mirror again.

"Let me prove it to you. Let me in."

"In?" A chill coursed down her spine. Surely the girl didn't mean … couldn't mean …

"In," the girl said again.

"No." Alice shook her head, crossing her arms in front of her. "Absolutely not. Even if I could—"

"But you can," crooned the girl. "You just have to wish it."

"Why would I ever … ? You … you're all wrong."

"We're both wrong. Surely you see that? Let me help you. I want to help you."

Alice was silent. Her skin tingled and she ached to turn around and run somewhere—into the library, maybe, where there were no mirrors for the girl to torture her with. But she couldn't do it, couldn't work up the will to simply turn and leave. It was as if some heavy, painful lump inside of her were weighing her down, gluing her feet to the floor. Her heart felt heavy in her chest and throbbed when the girl spoke.

Wrong. Both wrong.

The long-gone words still echoed in her ears, and she began to wonder if they were true. It seemed far too coincidental—too random—for the house to have simply singled her out. What if the curse picked her because she was different in some way? What if it picked her to destroy because somehow she was already broken?

"You see," said the girl, softly now, "I can help you understand."

Alice looked up. The throbbing inside of her was stronger now, like a drum, like an extra heart beating. Her hands shook; her mind reeled. But she wanted it so very badly—to understand, after all this confusion. She looked into the witch's eyes; they were so brilliant they seemed to glow amber through the glass. She had a slight upturn to the corners of her lips, a grin that made Alice sure she knew more than she was saying. Alice did want answers, and if the witch was really offering to tell her ...

"But I can't," she whispered. The cost was too high; the

consequences would surely be dire.

The girl looked down and clasped her hands together. Her triangle bracelets clanked like old bells when she moved her arms.

"I know what he thought when he saw you the very first time. I know how his heart was pounding."

"You don't know anything about Tony," Alice said quickly, fighting back her nearly unbearable curiosity. She told herself that it didn't matter. What was it to her if Tony felt one way or another? Knowing his heart rate—no matter how fast—wasn't going to get her out of this mess.

The girl let out a tiny laugh—barely more than a hiccup. "I know everything about him. If you would just let me show you—"

"You don't know him. It's not possible." Alice said the words, but wasn't sure she believed them. After all, the girl had shown her things from her own life that she couldn't possibly have known, or at least shouldn't have.

The girl laughed again.

"Look at yourself. *You* aren't possible. None of this is possible. Reality doesn't apply here—not the reality you've always known."

Alice tried to think of something wrong with the girl's reasoning—if she could only catch her in a lie, then she would know once and for all that the girl was not to be trusted. But she couldn't find anything to disagree with, and for a moment she found herself almost believing. She protested anyway. "I just don't—"

"Don't believe me? Why should you? You and I—we aren't

fools." Her lips were parted; she was breathing hard. "But you don't have to believe me. You just have to give me a chance to *prove* it you. Let me in—just for a minute—and if you want you can send me right back out."

Alice's heart was pounding now. Her head throbbed. Proof was what she wanted. Proof was what she needed. Her mind was whirling; the girl's proposal sounded possible ... teetered on the verge of being acceptable. "I can do that?"

The girl's lips curled into a not entirely pleasant smile. "This *is* your party."

But again Alice drew back. "If you want to help me so much, you can tell me what you know from out there. With the mirror. Just—you know—blow on it."

The girl's eyes glinted gold. "But it isn't enough to just watch. I can let you feel what he felt. And I can't describe it to you, either—not with words. It doesn't work in words, doesn't mean anything. I could tell you right now that he thought you were beautiful when he saw your face for the first time, but I can't describe to you how much he wanted to reach out and just hold your hand ... there are things that you have to feel for yourself."

"He thought ... " She swallowed hard over the sudden lump in her throat. "He thought that I ... "

"Beautiful."

Her resolve swayed dangerously, threatened to break. He had thought that? She couldn't suppress a smile. Could it be possible that the witch knew—that she was telling the truth? Maybe it was worth letting her in, just to find out. After all, if she didn't let her help, she would always wonder …

What other things had he thought about her? If the girl was right—if she could know … the idea sent a thrill through her, which was quickly followed by a rush of guilt. It was like holding her mother's diary in her hands again, turning it over and over, feeling the fabric of the cover, knowing that she shouldn't look inside … not quite able to turn away …

"I won't hurt you. I can't hurt you. I'm just a figment. I don't have any power over you."

If the girl wanted to hurt her, surely she would have already.

"Why haven't you asked to come in before?" Alice asked.

The girl shook her head. "Would you have let me?"

Alice didn't need to answer.

The girl blinked—once, twice, three times—watching Alice silently from the other side of the mirror. Witch or not, she didn't *look* dangerous. She looked very helpless and very alone and Alice was so alone and what was the harm in it? Two lonely girls helping each other to understand. No harm. No fear. What did she have to lose? Her life? But her life was already as good as lost.

Her palms were sweating. This felt wrong.

She had no right to look into Tony's mind. But she *did* need to know more about the witch—needed to learn whether she was friend or foe—and what better way to figure it out than by taking her up on all these promises she had made? *I don't* want *to do it*, she told herself, *but I have to.* And then, *He would understand.*

He would do the same thing.

"Come in," she said. The words had a dire sound to them. The girl smiled, twirled around, and then, without warning, she was next to Alice and very, very real. Her eyes sparkled and she reached out a pale hand.

"You can trust me," she said.

Alice hesitated for only a moment. She took the girl's hand and it was cold, but solid.

"Do it," Alice demanded, before she could regret this.

The girl nodded, and then …

CHAPTER FOURTEEN

The flood of feelings and sounds and images rushed into Alice's mind with a force that knocked away everything else. Fears and doubts were crushed into nothing under the weight of it. Everything was gone; even Alice herself disappeared into the smallest corner of her mind, watching the events unfolding before her as if she were watching a movie. But no movie was ever this absorbing. She didn't just see—she felt, she smelled, she touched. She was there, in Tony's body, seeing everything unfold from his perspective, feeling just what he had felt.

At first it was beautiful.

He pulled her out of the pool and her wet hair smelled like chlorine and sunshine. Her skin was soft. She felt very light in his arms—too light, as if she weren't even there. But she was there— he knew she was, because when she looked up at him with those amber eyes he felt the strangest tugging inside of him. He had seen pretty girls before, felt things before, but this girl was … she was different. She was scared and her cheeks were red from the cold and her face was so beautiful in the moonlight. Her eyes had that look about them, as though she had seen things, felt things, and he knew that look because sometimes he saw it in his own eyes when he looked in the mirror. Smart, she was smart, too—something intelligent about the arch of her eyebrow, the way she looked at him.

And he wanted—what was wrong with him?—he just wanted to make her smile at him. So he said something (What had he said? It was so stupid. Why had he said that?) and she moved farther away from him ("I would have been fine," she said) and he felt like such an idiot and he just wanted to reach out and hold her and tell her that she was all right, that she was safe now.

She moved and her thin dress clung to her body like a swimsuit. He was talking to her and every word he said seemed wrong the minute it left his lips. Was she okay? He started to wonder … she seemed upset. He wanted to get his dad but she stopped him and he couldn't break away now. She wanted his help. *His* help.

Help her. He could help her. He went to get his laptop, saw his dad asleep. He wanted to laugh, wanted to tell someone he'd just met *her*.

I just don't like anyone, Mom, okay? So stop bugging me. He'd said that not two weeks before.

Never been in love yet? You're really in for it. You just wait.

He was in for it. This was incredible.

This was terrible. He was terrified. She was sitting in the grass; her hair had fallen in messy curls around her face. Courage. He just needed a little bit of courage. She was just a girl.

When she came to sit next to him, his heart nearly stopped. She was leaning over his shoulder to see the computer screen; he could feel her breathing. He imagined he could hear her heart beating, but no—that was his own heart pounding. Surely she would hear it; she would know how scared he was.

He pulled up the article she was pointing at. *Alice*. It was a nice name. The girl in the picture smiled at him from the screen—not a full smile, but a tight-lipped one. That was the way he always smiled for school pictures. He stared at the picture, transfixed. He had never felt like this before and it frightened him to no end. Was this normal? How did people live like this? Would it ever go away?

Alice. The picture of her said everything he needed to know: she was like him, she would understand him, he could understand her ...

Alice.

No.

He blinked. The picture came into sharper focus. He looked at the girl beside him. Back at the picture.

And then—no, surely he was imagining things. *People* didn't just sink into the ground and disappear. He didn't understand. He crawled to the spot where she had vanished, whispering her name as if it was some incantation that might bring her back. He ran his fingers across the grass, felt it bend under his palms, slammed his hands into the hard dirt, pounded it, but it didn't give.

He stumbled backward and pulled his knees into his chest; his computer was still open and he numbly read the article on the screen. The girl stared at him with unblinking eyes. He slammed the computer shut and stood; he needed to move, needed to breathe.

A ghost. She was a ghost.

His breathing became panting and he paced faster—back and forth—panicking more with every step.

Then there was fear. Alice could feel it as he remembered—she remembered too now—the time he had seen a ghost before. Walking by a funeral on his way home from school—a shortcut through the graveyard. The people were talking and he was walking by, silent, and then, suddenly, she was in front of him—an old woman with wild gray hair laughing like a maniac. He screamed and people turned around to stare at him. *Can't you see her? Can't you hear her?* They stared blankly, and still she laughed and laughed and leapt forward and reached for his throat. He fell to the ground as the people watched, murmuring to each other. *She's going to kill me!* She was going to kill him. Someone was calling the police. And then the woman was gone and he ran, ran, ran all the way home and didn't leave his room for the rest of the day.

Alice. He was back now. His arms were tingling. He was still afraid. He grabbed his laptop and hurried up to his room, was tempted to wake his father. But he couldn't tell his dad about this—his dad would never let it go, and he just wanted to forget the whole thing. He hadn't even told him about the other time. He would never tell anyone. And who would believe him anyway?

He turned around and fled the room, running as fast as he could down the hallway, his feet making the floor creak as they pounded on the rug. He ran down the stairs and out the front door, stuck his key in his pocket and just kept running.

And that was when everything changed from beautiful to terrifying, when Alice felt her own body cringe and pull away from the girl's small hand. She could not break away; the pull was just too strong. The images kept coming—a horrible movie that would not stop.

He was breathing hard from running, but still was cold. The girl—she had taken his sweatshirt with her, back to wherever it was she came from. And that didn't seem right somehow. Ghosts couldn't do that, could they? He closed his eyes and tried to remember exactly what had happened—exactly how it had happened, because something about the whole thing unsettled him in a way that had nothing to do with the fact that the girl was a ghost and he had been a big enough idiot to fall for her. There was something else going on here, something strange. When he'd lifted her out of the water, she'd been light—it was true—but real weight in his arms, like a real person.

He looked at his watch—the one he had been wearing when he jumped in to save the girl from drowning. The watch was not waterproof and when he looked at it he saw that it had stopped at precisely midnight. It was broken. His mother would be ... his mother was not important right now. The girl had appeared at midnight and then—yes, he remembered now—she had disappeared just as the grandfather clock in the hotel had been chiming one. Exactly an hour. It was too precise for comfort. And the girl clearly hadn't been expecting to disappear. Since when were ghosts bound by time? It was almost as though she was stuck somewhere, as though she wasn't much of a ghost at all.

He closed his eyes. There was something very strange going on here, something that he wasn't seeing. Alice Montgomery was in a coma. So she wasn't dead—not really. Not alive either, because how was a coma—stronger and stranger than sleep—really life? And if she wasn't dead and she wasn't alive, then she had to be stuck. In limbo. Between life and death.

Or … and this thought made him stop outright … maybe the girl was in a coma *because* she was stuck. In which case what she really needed was something to help her move on. It made sense. She just needed to be nudged in the right direction and then she'd be free. A plan came to him then. He, Tony, could help her. He could use his dad's equipment. He could help the girl to die.

Because if she was dead, then he could let her go.

He turned around in the middle of the road. This was the solution. He would help her cross over no matter what the cost, get her out of his world and out of his life. Out of his mind forever.

***

Alice didn't know that she was crying until the girl pulled her hand away and she fell onto the floor, choking on words she didn't want to say, tears tumbling down her cheeks.

"He wants … " she couldn't finish.

Tony didn't want to help her live. He wanted to help her *die*.

"I just … thought … " She hadn't thought, had she? Alice pulled herself backward and hugged her knees to her chest, bracing herself against a wall as though it could swallow her up and end all of this. More than anything, she wanted to forget what she had just seen and move on as though nothing had happened. But her mind was a blackboard with no eraser, covered with miserable scrawls that she couldn't remove, and the mess confused her and she rocked back and forth and back again because she didn't know what else to do. There were no more tears now—nothing but numbness and the chill in the air around her.

The girl crept forward and put her hand on Alice's knee. Alice stared at the hand blankly; she looked up at the girl's face and saw what looked like sympathy in her eyes. At that moment—and for the very first time—she trusted her a very little bit. Maybe the girl did understand. Maybe she was the only one who could.

"Do you want to see more?"

Alice shook her head. More? She could barely handle what she *had* seen. More would surely break her.

The girl stroked her shoulder.

"It's hard to know what they really think, isn't it? Your parents … the boy … "

Her parents were planning to let her die. It was true. Nobody cared—nobody at all. They were all willing to stand by and let her disappear. Or maybe they even wanted her to die; then they could sue the manager and get their money ... a small trade, money for her life. Did she really mean so little to them?

"You mean something to me," said the girl, and Alice wondered if she could read her thoughts. The possibility didn't seem as outlandish as it once would have. "You know that, right?" the girl continued. "I *know* you, Alice. I know how much you hurt. That's why I've been trying to help you."

"Help me?" asked Alice, pulling away from the girl, sliding to a lonelier section of wall. "How—how could you say that showing me that was *helping* me? I thought that it would make me ... "

"Happy? Did you think that I would show you only what you wanted to see?"

The girl stared at her and Alice did not answer.

"How could I lie to you? You lie to yourself all the time. The last thing you need is a friend who goes along with it. I showed you what you *needed* to see."

"You knew it would hurt me," said Alice. She was angry and it felt better to hate the girl than to hate herself for going along with the whole thing. "You knew it would hurt and you did it anyway."

"But that's what love is," sighed the girl, and though she sounded exhausted there was no anger in her voice. "Love is doing what you know is best for someone even if it's going to tear them apart for a little while. You know that. You're just too upset to see it right now."

"How could *that* possibly help me? How could it help me to know that they … "—her eyes stung—"that everyone wants me *dead*?" She surprised herself by yelling the word at the top of her lungs. It echoed. The girl did not budge.

"Because once you realize that there's nothing holding you here, it will be easier for you to let go." She said it so calmly, so simply, and Alice gaped at her, wordless. Death was still echoing around the room.

"You can leave all this behind," the girl continued. "You can be with *me*. They don't want you, Alice, but I do. And if you come with me, you can have what you want—you can be happy and there won't be anyone there to stop you."

Alice felt tears in her eyes. She was swollen with anger and when the girl spoke of happiness, Alice felt the deepest, purest pang of longing. This pain could be gone—wiped away into nothing. She could start over. The thought of a blank slate was so enticing that it pushed aside all hesitations and cautious questions. It was the only thing that Alice could see anymore, the only thought in her mind.

The girl's eyes were wide and honest. Alice believed her at last. She wanted so badly to believe her.

"If my life doesn't mean anything to them then why should it mean anything to me?" she whispered.

"It's so easy to let go," said the girl. "Just come with me and—"

But her words were cut off by the chiming of the grandfather clock. For a moment, Alice met her eyes. She didn't want to be torn away from the girl, didn't want to go back to a world that did not want or need her.

"You'll be back," the girl whispered.

Alice breathed in deeply, until there was no more air to breathe.

CHAPTER FIFTEEN

She was expecting the water this time, but that didn't stop her from panicking when she emerged at the bottom of the pool. She immediately realized how foolish she had been to wear this dress. The long train weighed her down; her almost transparent hands couldn't fight the pull of the heavy fabric, and she began to feel the familiar panic of not being able to breathe.

Just as the world started to grow fuzzy, she felt a familiar arm around her waist dragging her upwards. This time, she did not fight. "You came!" Tony said as soon as her head broke the surface. He was wearing swim trunks and a tight black shirt tonight.

Alice was too busy gasping for breath to answer. Tony put his other hand under her knees and carried her over to the pool deck, where he had not one, but three fluffy towels already folded and ready to receive her. As she tried to get air back into her lungs, he wrapped one around her shoulders and another over her legs.

"I didn't think ghosts needed to breathe," he said, helping to wring out her sopping hair.

"I'm … not … a ghost," she gasped out. *Not yet.*

He reached under her towel, pulled out her hand, and held it up to the light. Alice could see every bone.

"Not a ghost," he repeated.

"No," she said firmly, though her voice was weak and strained. She saw his eyes wander to the waterlogged green silk. "Elizabeth's," she explained. "It was Elizabeth's."

"Oh," said Tony, and for some reason he looked quite grim as he examined her. Before, he had seemed happy to see her; now his eyes searched her face with unmistakable concern. This was what she had expected—him looking at her as if she had caution tape wrapped around her head, as if she were going to fall apart any second, go crazy, explode.

His eyebrows furrowed and she tried to read his expression. She knew what she was looking for—fear, discomfort—and she thought she found it there in the tightness of his lips. It was true after all. Deep inside, he'd been hoping she wouldn't reappear. Because really, who would want their summer vacation bogged down with a ghost? She wasn't his responsibility. Helping some random ghost-girl wasn't something he should have to do.

"Did you find it?" she asked, clutching the towel tightly around her. "Did you find the key?" She tried to say it with real interest, but her voice sounded hollow—even to her. Her fingernails dug into the towel and she hated how solid it felt, how heavy it was around her.

Tony sat down beside her, his wet hair dripping onto his shoulders, neck, and back.

"What key?"

"You didn't find it," Alice interrupted. The sight of him made her sick to her stomach and she looked away. She missed the girl's voice, the way the girl spoke to her.

"If you could just explain to me what's going on—"

Alice cut him off again. "You don't have the key. What else is there to say? She was right all along." The key—what did the key matter to him? He wanted her to disappear. He probably hadn't even looked for it. She'd been an idiot to think he would; fresh hot anger poured over her and she couldn't tell whether she was mad at herself or at him. Or at her parents. Or at everything.

Tony muttered a few words, as though determined to make another stab at the sentence he had been unable to finish, but then stopped quite suddenly. Alice turned around to look at him again. She would be gone soon enough; there was little point in hiding from him.

"Alice? I don't understand. Are you talking about the room key we found? … If you could just tell me … "

She pulled the towel so taut that she felt it stretch against her shoulders, pushing into her skin, past her skin. "I need to call my family," she said. Her hands were trembling and she held the towel even more tightly. Her dad would answer the phone … maybe her mom. She could hear their voices in her ears—*Hello? Who is it?*—and she wanted to scream at them, *Why? Why don't you care?* Begging to live did not cross her mind; all she wanted to do was punish them for letting her go so easily. She would make them hurt as they had hurt her.

"I need to call them."

Her voice faded. She heard a sound and whipped around, eyes wide, but it was only a bird in the bushes.

"Give me your phone," she demanded, turning back to Tony.

But he didn't move.

The buzzing of the crickets and the buzzing of her own mind blended into a feverish drone, crescendoing up and up until she could hardly stand it. She wished she could cut off her ears, her head, let it drain out. "You promised to help me!" she snapped. "Well, what are you waiting for?"

Somewhere, safe in a more serene, less panicked part of her brain, Alice knew that this behavior was quite unlike her. She wasn't one to make demands, wasn't one to be sharp. Why was she acting this way? He would never—could never—want to help her when she was bossing him around, cutting him off—not listening.

Did it even matter? Where had being kind ever gotten her? She wasn't a bad person—was never mean—and still her friends were few. Still here she was, trapped and dying. Forget karma. She hadn't done anything to deserve this; the wheel of justice was up in flames. Still ...

"I need your phone," Alice repeated, her harsh tone slightly softened.

Tony cleared his throat. "I don't know if that's the best idea," he said, his voice quiet.

All of Alice's snappishness returned immediately. "Why not?"

"Think how it would sound," he said, more loudly now. "They wouldn't believe me—or even you. They would think it was a prank."

"You don't want to help." He was making excuses. He was lying to her face and all he wanted was to keep her trapped and to let her die. The girl was right. Everyone just wanted her to fade away. To leave them alone.

"I do!" He curled his hands into fists and dug his knuckles into the ground. "But think about it. I can't call them, Alice. You can't call them. And the hospital—it's two hours away. And last time ... last time you disappeared after an hour."

He was right, of course. Right about all of it. She had been foolish to think it might work. As if her parents would believe that a boy they had never met was communing with their comatose daughter's spirit. And even if they heard her voice ... her parents were sensible people. They would think they were losing their minds or just delusional with grief. Her parents thought that the supernatural was a joke and they laughed at ghosts and God alike. Her father told her Santa Claus was a lie when she was two.

Tony was right, and Alice felt nothing but anger, frustration.

She could have forgiven him for being wrong, but somehow the fact that he had corrected her—had seen what she could not— irked her to no end. Her frustration drained into hopelessness and hopelessness faded to despair; she loosened her hold on the towel and it went limp around her. Limp, lifeless, and cold.

"It's really important, isn't it?" he asked. "This key?"

She didn't look at him; when she spoke, it was a mutter. "Clearly not to you."

He was patient—didn't even respond to the jab. "Care to explain?"

She rolled her eyes, irritated that he didn't understand even though she knew there was no way he could.

"Your dad told you about Elizabeth Blackwell, right?"

"Yeah, but … " He stopped. "How did you know that?"

She realized that she was going to have to start from the beginning. And really, what was the harm in explaining at this point? It didn't matter, but he might as well know. She spoke through clenched teeth (her head felt hot), explained how, after hitting her head, she had woken up in a different version of the hotel with no working exits. "I can see your hotel through the mirrors in mine," she told him.

"So you've been watching me?"

A wave of embarrassment welled up inside of her, but was quickly forced back by a rising tide of contained fury. Normal Alice would have apologized, cheeks blushing, but this Alice—with her ringing ears and her head on fire—didn't even answer. She simply continued with her explanation. "Elizabeth's diary is in my version of the house and I've been reading it. I think that she did something to the house—something that made me get stuck there, and if I can figure out how to break it then I can get out. There's an attic room in the house, but it's locked. If I can just get up there, I could find the witch's books. She might have written how to break the curse."

"Why do you think the key would be out here? Wouldn't it be in your hotel?"

"Elizabeth's sister threw it out the window about a century ago. If it's anywhere, then it's still buried in this lawn. There's no way we'll find it, though, not so deep underground."

"Well, there's a thought," said Tony softly, but she barely heard him. "Maybe," he began, then trailed off. "I have an idea—if you want to hear it."

But she wasn't listening and he, waiting for an answer, was silent.

The key isn't important anymore, she tried to tell herself. *Neither is Tony. There isn't a reason to be upset. I just need to think clearly.*

But she couldn't! It was like wandering through a fog, unable to concentrate, constantly distracted by dark shadows, by sounds, by passing ideas. She couldn't control her mind. She couldn't stop it. The real Alice—calm Alice—hid in a corner, held prisoner in a brain that wasn't quite her own. She thought she felt a small hand on hers and looked down, but there was nothing there. Still, she couldn't quite shake the feeling that the witch's hand was still wrapped around her fingers, that something was pouring thoughts and feelings into her and she couldn't get away, couldn't make them stop …

Alice jumped to her feet and walked away from Tony; the towel fell to the pool deck. Her legs needed to move; she needed to use some of this terrible, pent-up energy that was flooding her. Tony followed her onto the nearby lawn and, when she sat down, he followed suit.

"Alice?"

She didn't answer for a moment; there was a bird landing in a pine tree nearby and she could see its silhouette as it glided down and disappeared into the darkness of the pine needles. It was nothing to her—only a bird—and she wondered if that was the way Tony saw her. Something distant from himself, for observation only. And if she died, would he even blink? Would she feel anything at all, besides relief?

"Tony?" she said, and she was surprised by how calm her voice was. "I know that you want me to die."

"*What?*"

"You know, forget it. I … I don't want your help!" she cried, even as most of her mind screamed back that she wanted his help more than anything. "I just … want … I want to be left *alone*."

This was the right choice. To be alone, where she couldn't get hurt. She was dead either way, so why make it more difficult?

"You can't be serious."

No. Her lips formed the word, but her breath caught in her throat, as though it had run up against an invisible barrier. *No,* she didn't want his help. Did she?

Did she?

And then everything inside of her went hard. Her breath—her heart—everything seemed to stop, as if she had become a statue of steel with no moving parts. She felt cold, too—so cold—as though if she were breathing, her breath would be ice in the warm air. But when she spoke her words were fire, not ice, though they came from the freezing hole inside of her.

"Why would I need *your* help?" she spat.

Tony recoiled. And Alice laughed—she laughed at the stupid, helpless look on his face. Her unexpected power to wound rushed through her, molten lava through the steel that had become her heart. It was so overwhelming and incredible that she laughed even harder.

"Why would I need *you?*"

His eyes were shining. She could break him with her pinky finger and her own power thrilled her.

But as he bit his lip and turned away, Alice felt the tiniest twinge of sympathy, and that was enough. Her steel body shuddered and shattered. Her heart resumed its pounding. Guilt swept over her— fresh and strong—and her hands were pale and shaking.

She was panting. Her chest heaved—up, down, up, down. Her eyes were on the grass. She could hear Tony breathing, or was that her? Were those really her breaths, labored and uneven?

"What do you want, Alice?" he asked.

What do I want? Alice thought numbly. *Oh God, what do I want?*

And then the anger that had been holding her together broke—snapped like a twig. She collapsed onto the ground, sank down onto her hands and knees, not crying but taking heaving breaths, the kind that came after there were no tears left. A second ago she had been powerful, frightening even; now she knelt on the grass helpless, hardly able to breathe. She couldn't see—her eyes were blurry—but she felt Tony come closer. She felt him stop right in front of her, she felt him hesitate, and then there was an arm around her and she had her head on his chest and she was breathing in the smell of his soaking shirt.

She blinked. The world came back into focus and she was exhausted; the anger that had exploded out of her had left her empty as a smoking gun. She began to realize that, though Tony still had his arm around her, his hand, cupping her shoulder, was tense. There was something stony about the way he held her that made her feel as if she'd curled up in the cold embrace of a statue.

Alice pulled away.

"Tony?"

He wouldn't meet her eyes. When he spoke, his voice was labored and low. She watched him closely, still bitter, but also confused. She hadn't expected him to be angry. She had expected him to be ashamed.

"Do you mean it, then?" he asked.

She realized that she had never answered his question. What did she want? She still hardly knew.

He shifted his weight to his other arm. "You don't want my help."

Why couldn't she answer? Only a second ago she had been so full of words that she couldn't stop them—they came bursting out of her. Now she had nothing. She couldn't muster up even a yes or no.

He shook his head. "You know, you say that you've been watching me, but I don't believe you."

Why? She thought it so clearly that for a moment she thought she had said it. Then she realized her mouth was still shut tight and he was still frowning and looking away.

"If you'd been watching me," he continued, "you would have seen that the *only* thing I've been trying to do—ever since I saw you the first time—all I've been trying to do is help you."

She felt as if she were choking. She pressed her hand to her throat and her skin was cold. She swallowed hard, breathed in deeply; the smell of grass filled her nose.

"And I have to wonder, what *have* you been seeing? Because you haven't been seeing me. I don't think you know me at all."

"No," she gasped out.

He stared at her and she stared back. Though his eyes were open, there was something oddly closed about his face, as if she were staring at a photograph of him and he wasn't really there. Silence had rarely seemed so interminable. It stretched on and on, and the sound of the crickets didn't fill the empty space, but rather emphasized the quiet.

"The first night you saw me," she said at last, "you were afraid when you found out what … what I was."

He did not answer. He did not blink.

"You went running. You were terrified."

Finally a reaction. He sat up straighter. "How in the world did you know that?"

"She showed me."

"Who showed you? I wasn't in the hotel. How could you have seen that?" He sounded angry now.

"There's this … " He was glaring at her and, as much as she wanted to, she didn't dare look away. "There's a girl—the witch, actually. She showed me things."

Alice didn't mention that she had asked to be shown.

"A witch showed you," Tony repeated. She couldn't be sure if that was sarcasm in his voice or surprise. Maybe he didn't know either. "A witch," he said again.

"*The* witch. The one Elizabeth wrote about."

"How can you tell?"

"I just know," Alice said. She had no desire to explain; she'd sound ridiculous babbling about the feeling she got when the girl spoke—the too-bright glow of her eyes. "Who else could it be?"

He frowned, but he didn't disagree. Then, seriously—she could tell this was what he really wanted to know—he asked, "How did she show you this stuff then? How did she know?"

The fogged-up glass, the silver pool, it all seemed too ridiculous to say out loud. Alice considered lying, but couldn't come up with a better story. So she decided to be vague, because it was the details that made her sound crazy. "I just saw it. I don't know how."

"But how did she know about *me*?"

Alice threw her hands in the air. "I don't know," she said. "She knew everything about me, too. It's not just you." She paused, then repeated, "She knew me, too." This was true, and it assuaged some of the guilt Alice was fighting to keep contained. Sure, she'd looked into Tony's head, but she'd been forced to watch some of her own less-than-happy memories too. Not to mention that she'd been trapped in a creepy house for days on end with only a witch for company. If that wasn't an excuse, she didn't know what was.

Anyone would have done the same thing. She didn't have to feel bad.

She wanted to cut her nagging conscience out of her head with a carving knife and drown it in the pool.

"What else did she show you?" Tony demanded.

Alice considered mentioning the car fiasco, but Tony might totally freak out if he knew just how much of his past she had seen. Best to stick to the evening he already knew she had watched. That was what she wanted to know about anyway. She hesitated, choosing her words carefully. It was hard to keep her voice steady with the unpleasant mixture of anger and guilt churning in her stomach, leaving a taste bitter as bile on her tongue.

"She showed me that you wanted me dead."

Tony's mouth fell open. He gaped at her and then—without warning, so suddenly that she actually jumped—he *laughed*. He pulled his glasses off and wiped the corners of his eyes.

"You want me to die," Alice said, furious. "What's funny about that? *This isn't a joke!*"

"Is that what this whole thing has been about?" he asked, shaking his head. "You said it earlier, too—that I want you to die. Is that why you're so messed up tonight? Because this witch told you that I wanted you dead and you believed her?"

"No!" Alice protested. She couldn't believe he was making light of this. "I'm 'messed up' because I'm under some crazy curse and I'm probably going to die and nobody cares! My parents—you heard—they want to let my heart stop beating. Well, you know what? Let them! If nobody cares, then neither do I!" She stopped; she was breathing hard again. Then she added, almost spat, "You certainly don't care. I don't know why I ever thought you did."

This wiped the smile off his face—at least a little. He ran a hand across his forehead, sighed, and said, "Alice, I'm going to ask you that question again and I want you to listen closely to me, okay?"

She turned away.

"Fine, you don't have to look at me. But listen. A *witch*—the same witch that helped Elizabeth cast this curse or whatever it is—this same witch told you that nobody cared about you and that you should give up. This witch told you that you might as well die and you believed her?"

As he spoke, something cooler than anger and warmer than fear tugged at the corners of her mind—a calm but insistent doubt. She tried to push it away—it confused her—and she said huffily, "Do I have any reason *not* to believe her?"

"Let me tell you why I was laughing," he said. She considered turning around to look at him, but she didn't want to give him the satisfaction.

"For a minute there, I thought this girl had maybe shown you something real. But saying that I want you to die—there hasn't ever been a bigger lie than that. I was scared after I saw you—that's true. But ever since then, I've been killing myself trying to figure out how to help you *live*, not die."

"Why should I believe you?"

He laughed again, but this time it was grating. "Why do you think I'd be here if I wanted you to die? If I wanted you to die, I'd be in the hospital with your parents, begging them to let you go a little sooner. I'd go yank the plug myself—it wouldn't be hard, right? Easiest murder ever. But I'm not a killer. God, what kind of psychopath do you think I am?"

She whipped around, thinking perhaps that she would see the lie in his eyes, see a telltale smirk. But what she saw was the same face she had seen before—a face that was insistent, but no longer angry. Eyes that were bright, as blue eyes sometimes were, but that did not glow as the witch's eyes did. His mouth was set. And Alice, who had lied enough to know what it felt like, couldn't find any dishonesty about him—not in his voice, not in his body.

No. Her mind protested. It kicked against her and yelled in the witch's voice and punched at nothing with the witch's small, childlike hands.

But he was right. He was *here*. He was waiting for her and why else would he be waiting? It *would* be easy to pull the plug, to go to the hospital and break a machine or two.

And yet he was here.

She looked around her. The world suddenly seemed brighter, more sharply cut, more real. It was like in *The Wizard of Oz*, when everything changed from black and white to color.

The girl's voice still rang in her ears, but she shook her head and it faded away. She blinked. It felt as if a bubble around her had popped; she breathed in deeply and the air was fresh and cool—such a beautiful thing, breathing. Living.

The witch had lied.

CHAPTER SIXTEEN

She must have been smiling, because Tony broke into a grin. "There's Alice again," he said.

Alice opened her mouth, but then shut it. Ashamed—she was embarrassed. Should she apologize? She had called him a murderer. How could she apologize for that?

"Guess I win this round?" he asked. "Tony, one; evil witch ... well, let's give her half a point for effort. Seems only fair."

"Three-quarters of a point," Alice said, her voice soft. Her heart still pounded.

"Really?"

"She's pretty convincing." Alice shivered. She could remember so clearly—still—how Tony's thoughts had felt in her head, how strongly he had wanted her to disappear. She shook herself. Even now, it would be too easy to slip back into believing. It had been so easy.

"Fine," said Tony. "Fine, but if she gets three quarters, then I get one and a third—I think I deserve a bigger lead than a quarter point."

"That seems arbitrary."

"It is. But you know what they say—history is written by the victors."

For the first time in what felt like days, Alice smiled. Her lips had a strange, plastic feel as they curled back, as if they had hardened and shrunk.

"Fair enough," she said. It suddenly occurred to her that she was cold. The damp towel was a lump on the ground and she picked it up, wrapped it around her shoulders. It didn't help much—the heavy, cold fabric only made her shiver—but the sharpness of the chill brought her to her senses somehow. Her brain kicked into gear again and started gaining speed.

"The key," she said, remembering why this trip had been so important to her in the first place. "There's still time. We have to find it—now."

"My dad has something," Tony said. "It's kind of like … okay, not like, it *was* a metal detector."

He looked her in the eye, very serious now. He didn't question the sudden change of subject and she didn't bother to explain.

"What I'm trying to say," he said, "is that my dad modified this metal detector to read some kind of ghost residue—don't ask, I don't understand it—and I could try to, you know, put it back together the way it was before. I think we can use it to find your key."

So this was the idea he had mentioned before. Alice felt her cheeks flush; the answer had been right in front of her the whole time. "Oh, okay. That—that's great."

She paused, then added, "Thanks."

"Just give me a second," he said, and stood up and ran back into the hotel. He returned five minutes later with a haggard-looking metal detector. As he held it out, Alice saw that it looked old and unreliable, not to mention that there was a whole handful of wires looped around the outside and secured to the handle with electrical tape. He began to tug at the wires, pulling out a few, rearranging others, the tip of his tongue stuck between his teeth.

"How do you know how to do that?"

He didn't look up; his fingers were a blur. "I read a lot. And I like stuff like this. It's kind of a hobby."

"Fixing metal detectors?"

"Fixing anything." He patted the metal detector handle. It looked as if it might come apart if the wind blew too hard.

"Great," she said, as enthusiastically as she could, but she felt her newfound hope give a weak, nervous flutter. "It's … great. If the attic window was over there," she said, "then I expect that the key would have landed somewhere in this general area." She got up and Tony followed. He gave her a nervous smile, then said, "Okay, let's give this a go."

He began to pace slowly, methodically, back and forth, as he worked his way across the lawn. Alice watched him closely, her fingers crossed behind her back. In her mind she seemed to hear a quiet ticking as the seconds of her time in the real world flitted briefly into the present and were immediately absorbed into the past. She was jumpy with nerves, and when she thought she heard a footstep nearby, she started and whipped around, only to see empty green grass and a tree branch waving in the wind.

The witch ... her hands curled into fists. If the girl had threatened her, ordered her, tried to force her to give up, Alice would have been angry. But this—the manipulation, the lies, the careful scheming—it made her blood boil. It made her violently mad. Alice could imagine the witch sitting in the shadow house, waiting for Alice to come back—the grin on her face.

The metal detector beeped and Alice jumped again, hurrying forward as Tony reached down, felt around in the grass, and picked up a quarter.

"At least it works," he said, shooting her a faint grin.

Alice was so tense that she couldn't squeeze out a response. She thought she might explode, or simply crumble into a million pieces. An image of Tony using the metal detector to find pieces of her scattered across the lawn flashed through her mind and was at once sobering and bizarrely funny.

"I'm a sophomore, you know—junior next year, I guess. You are too, right? How do you like school?" said Tony. His transparent attempt at conversation calmed Alice more than it should have; the sound of something other than the wind and the metal detector muffled her worries.

"School is fine. People … not so much," she admitted. She felt oddly comfortable talking to him now. It was hard not to feel closer to him after she'd lost her head right in front of him and he'd helped her screw it back on straight. When she looked at him, she felt solid—safe. "I was popular in middle school," she admitted. "But when I started high school—I'm not sure what happened. My aunt died that summer, and … people said I was different. Boring. I just felt tired all the time. I guess I didn't care."

Tony froze for a moment, then asked, "What happened to your aunt?"

"Cancer."

Even now, two years later, everything inside of her went cold when she thought about it. Her grandmother had died of breast cancer in her late twenties; Alice had never met her. Her aunt had barely made it to thirty—she died two weeks after her birthday.

Alice's mom was thirty-two. The doctors said there was a test and that if she was positive for some gene, she'd get the cancer too. But her mom said she was fine, refused to be tested.

Would *she* want to know? Alice wasn't sure.

"Terrible," said Tony.

Alice looked at him with new respect. Everyone else at school had just said "sorry"—as if they could be sorry. Half of them didn't even know she *had* an aunt.

"It is," said Alice.

Their eyes met. His were serious and honest. Her stomach unclenched and warmth flooded through her, despite the cold towel. It spread from just above her belly button all the way up her chest and neck and into her cheeks.

Then the moment was gone and Tony resumed his search.

"I used to be pretty cool, too," he said, "when I was stupid and stuck-up and had a car. Had lots of friends then. But ... well, there was an accident and I started being responsible. They call me Mr. Wordsworth now. And I know that should be a compliment, but it isn't. They think I'm boring and I read too much."

"You crashed the car," Alice said, before she could stop herself.

"It was actually—"

He stopped.

"How did you know that?"

"Your dad ... I heard him say something about it to ... someone." She knew it was a frail lie, but she couldn't let him know how much she had seen. Shame made her cheeks burn and she was glad it was so dark.

"My dad hasn't talked about it for years." Tony hands were tight around the handle of the metal detector. He was staring and now she wished it were less dark just so she could see that look on his face more clearly. She was sure, if she were just a foot closer, if it were just a bit lighter, she would be able to read his expression and it would say something important.

But then he swung the metal detector again and she knew she'd lost her chance.

"Maybe he's finally forgiven me," he said. "And by the way, I can't imagine anyone finding you boring."

She opened her mouth to thank him, but the words got lost somewhere between her mind and mouth, tangled in a ballooning bulge of emotions. Heart beating quickly, she waited, listening to the night wind, to the crickets, to the stars and their overwhelming silence. Tony swung the metal detector and there was something hypnotic about the motion—how it went back and forth, big and gleaming and dark. Every moment seemed swollen with possibility, then lank with disappointment as it passed without discovery or progress. She didn't think she could bear being sucked back into the shadow house with nothing gained, no further discovery to aid her in her escape. And the girl to look forward to.

Just as the horrible possibility was beginning to sink in, the metal detector beeped again.

She didn't hurry forward as she had the time before; she didn't think she could bear the disappointment if this was only another coin. But when Tony began to dig in the grass, she could no longer suppress her curiosity. She darted forward and helped him expand his hole in the lawn, although her translucent fingers did little more than rearrange some pieces of dirt. They dug down three inches before Alice caught sight of something shiny sticking out of the dull brown.

"There!" she said, grabbing hold of Tony's arm. He pulled the object out and handed it to her.

"Unbelievable," he whispered.

Encased in a layer of dirt was a large, heavy, old-fashioned key—the perfect size to fit in the hidden keyhole. Alice closed her fist around it so tightly that the metal dug painfully into her skin.

"This is it," she said unnecessarily. "I don't know how to thank you."

She meant it, too, though she wasn't sure she liked it, being in someone's debt. But it was Tony and he'd pulled her out of the pool twice now. She'd lost faith in him but he hadn't ever given up on her. She owed him her life and her sanity.

Tony shrugged off her thanks and asked, "Are you sure you'll be able to bring it back with you?"

"I think so. It works with clothes. It worked with your sweatshirt."

"Yeah," he frowned. "Guess I'm never getting that back, am I?"

Alice gasped. "I completely forgot. You know, I should have tried to—"

"Alice."

"—take it with me. I could have. Tell you what—"

"*Alice.*"

"—next time I'll bring it—I will."

"Alice, it's fine. I was just teasing you."

"Oh." Of course he was. And there she was, embarrassed again. She never *had* been good at knowing when people were joking and when they were being serious.

"Well, I think the key should—I think I'll be able to get it back," she said in an attempt to cover the awkward moment.

"I hope so. Hey, if you can bring things back, what about people? I mean, if you just took my hand—"

"No," said Alice firmly. She knew what he was thinking, but she wouldn't do it. Not ever. "I'm not bringing you to that place. I'm not putting anyone else in danger."

"But I could help. I can take the risk."

"*No.*"

There must have been something in her face that warned him against repeating the request, because he dropped the subject, although he didn't look happy about it. His gaze wandered from her eyes to her dress, and that strange frown crept over his face again.

"You don't like it, do you?" Alice asked, suddenly self-conscious.

"What? Oh—no, it's not that. It looks," he paused, "very nice on you."

Alice disregarded the compliment immediately, sure that he was just being polite. "Then what is it?" she asked.

"I did some reading," said Tony, his eyes on the grass. "My dad's notes."

"I know."

He glanced up in surprise.

"I was watching," Alice explained.

"Oh, right. Of course." If anything, this made him look even more uncomfortable, and he pulled out a few blades of grass as he spoke.

"Anyway, what happened to her … it was awful. She went crazy, you know. Completely *insane.*"

He emphasized this last word, clearly anxious to get his point across. Alice, however, was entirely nonplussed: she already knew this.

"And?" she asked, hoping he had something more to add—something that would help her.

"And now you're wearing her dress. When you were upset before, I thought I saw it—saw her … "

"Yes?"

"And I can't help but think that you … what if you're kind of … becoming her?"

Alice stared at him in shock for a moment. Then, an instant later, the tension in the air broke and she actually smiled. Tony smiled back—a hesitant, shaky kind of smile, but a smile all the same.

"Hey, do I look crazy to you?"

He laughed now. Such a nice laugh: deep and rich and comfortable. She, *Alice*, had made him laugh. Alice—the serious girl who never smiled anymore, the girl whom boys avoided—had just made one of them laugh.

"Yes," Tony teased, "absolutely out of your mind. I knew you had crazy eyes from the moment I met you."

They both laughed for a second then, but what little happiness they had squeezed out of the situation faded fast, leaving only ghosts of smiles on their faces. The darkness of the night seemed suddenly impenetrable, as though they had, for a brief moment, been bathed in light, then jerked away from it and tossed back into the black that was the world.

"I don't want to die," Alice heard herself say. The only thing that surprised her more than how calmly she said it was the fact that she had said it at all. "For a minute there, I thought I did. It was the witch—she had me so convinced."

It had been less than an hour since she'd fallen to the ground in tears, but she felt years older—so old now that when she looked back she hardly recognized that girl. Maybe it was Tony. Maybe talking to a real person had brought her back to the self she had lost somewhere in the house. Or was this a new person—someone she hadn't met before? Alice wasn't sure, but everything inside of her was quiet and calm and she wanted to cling to this stillness forever.

"You won't die. Not if I can help it," Tony said. He looked more determined than ever; his jaw was clenched and his lips were pursed. "I think I'm going to have to talk all of this over with my dad. He knows a whole bunch more about stuff like this than I do." He frowned. "He'll be delighted, not that he deserves it."

"I think that—"

But Alice didn't get a chance to finish her sentence. She began to dissolve into the towel that she was lying on.

I think that I'm going to be okay.

And she was—for a moment. Then her head sank into the ground and she appeared once again in the library and remembered immediately what it was to be trapped.

***

She found herself staring at the ceiling and seeing only Tony's face, his eyes. A powerful sense of possibility had come over her and even this dark place couldn't shake it. She had the key and she knew now that she wanted it. She wanted the key and she wanted to live and she wanted Tony to care one way or the other.

Standing up, she found herself staring at the portrait of Elizabeth. "I'm not beaten yet," she whispered. The painted face stared back, deranged.

"Are you ready?"

She turned around and saw the girl approaching—all charm. She held out a hand. "Shall we go?"

Alice shook her head. "Not quite yet. There's one more thing I want to do." There was still a loose end she had to tie up before she could be sure. The attic key was warm in her hand.

The girl looked worried for a moment, but then pasted her smile back on. "Of course, Alice. You do whatever you need to."

"I want you to wait here for me. Can you do that?"

"But I'd like to come with you—"

"Wait here."

Alice watched the girl carefully. She thought she saw her try to take a step forward, but then she pulled back and sat down in a chair. She masked her attempt to move so well that the whole maneuver looked effortless and natural, but Alice was sure now that the witch had been telling the truth about one thing at least:

Alice had power over her. This was why she had had to work through persuasion—get Alice to *let* her into the shadow house. For some reason (and Alice thought she knew why now), the girl had to obey Alice's rules.

"Thanks," Alice said, with an ingratiating smile. She didn't want the witch to know that she knew the truth—not just yet. But there was still suspicion in the girl's face as Alice hurried away.

As she ran out of the library, Alice saw something that stopped her in her tracks: the mist was creeping forward again, faster than ever, as though it knew what she was trying to do and was doing its best to stop her. She sprinted up the stairs all the way to the deer tapestry. The attic room was on an outside corner of the house. If the mist kept advancing at this pace, the attic would be one of the first rooms to be eaten up entirely.

Fingers wrapped tightly around the heavy brass, she rushed down the hall and pushed the tapestry aside. She eased the key into the lock, holding her breath.

It fit.

The door swung open under her hand and she was faced with a small flight of stairs. She hurried to the top and stopped in surprise. Elizabeth had written that she didn't like this room, but whatever Alice had been imagining, it was nowhere near as bad as the truth.

Everything in here was black. The chest of drawers in the corner, the desk, the vanity—even the velvet bed covers. A forbidding iron chandelier hung from the ceiling, holding at least twenty half-melted candles. The triangle bed was pushed against the wall, and the blanket, made for a normal bed, did not fit it well. The corners lay crumpled on the floor, like puddles of tar. The triangle desk faced the bed; it was covered with blank pieces of paper. But the mirror—the mirror was worst of all.

This was the first mirror in the entire house that actually showed her own reflection—probably because the original room no longer existed. And yet this was not her reflection as she remembered it. Each triangle of glass distorted her face in a different way. Once during school, a police officer had come to talk about drunk driving and had made them put on "drunk" glasses to prove how dangerous intoxication was. Staring at the mirror made her feel like she was wearing the glasses again; she couldn't focus on any one part of it—it was all so blurred and strange. There were blank patches of wood between the triangles, as though someone had pried the dividing bars out. There was something somber and dreadful and haunting about the whole thing—something that she couldn't quite explain, even to herself.

She tore her eyes away from the glass and turned to face the other side of the room. Just as she had suspected, the mist already covered two of the walls and, if Alice watched closely enough, she imagined that she could see it inching closer every second.

She had to find the witch's books before everything was swallowed up—gone.

She wished she'd had the foresight to bring Elizabeth's diary with her, but as it was she didn't dare waste time going down to fetch it. She would just have to find the books on her own.

First, Alice dove for the bed and looked under the pillows, but she found only dust. Then she rummaged through the papers on the desk, checking every cupboard and drawer. She found quite a few things there—an old-fashioned fountain pen, a hat, and even a feather boa—but still no spell books. Her luck was no better with the drawers or the vanity. By the time she'd finished looking through the dresses in the closet, the mist was starting to work its way across the bed.

Starting to panic, Alice ran forward and pulled the blankets off the mattress (they fell heavily to the floor). She sent the pillows flying. In desperation, she knelt on the bed only inches from the mist and grabbed ahold of the headboard and pulled so hard that the bed frame shook; the floor whined like a wounded animal. An idea hit her at last. She froze, then leapt off the bed. Elizabeth had first found the books under a floorboard. What if they were still there?

The mist already covered most of the room. What if she had missed her chance? Heart racing, Alice dove for what was left of the floor and started banging on the floorboards, listening for creaks. She found nothing until she was almost under the bed. When she knocked on a board right next to the nightstand, it fell in at least an inch. She pushed on it again, harder this time, and it creaked and slipped down even farther. Alice quickly spotted the crevice that Elizabeth had mentioned in her diary, and she stuck her finger underneath to try to pry the board up. At first it came easily, but then it got stuck and refused to budge. The mist was only a foot away. Alice leapt up and grabbed the only tool available to her—the pen from the desk.

She eased the pen into the crack and used it as a lever. For a second she felt guilty about scratching the floor up like this, but then remembered that this house and everything in it (including her) didn't even exist in the ordinary sense of the word. She gave one final push on the pen and the board came loose. Pulling it free from the floor, she reached into the hole and pulled out two books that looked so fragile she worried they would disintegrate in her hands.

The mist was so close now that she could blow on it and see it bend under her breath. Alice took one final look around the room, trying to cement it into her memory. On a crazy impulse, she pulled the mirror off the vanity and tucked it under her arm with the books. Then she hurried out of the room and locked the door behind her.

CHAPTER SEVENTEEN

Alice sat down at the top of the staircase and thumbed through the book of curses with shaking hands. It was very old, with yellowed pages and that musty smell distinctive to decaying paper. All of it appeared to be handwritten—it had probably been the witch's personal notes. Alice didn't have to read long before she felt shivers crawling up and down her back. There were dreadful things written in this book—spells to cause excruciating pain, spells to kill in the most gruesome ways imaginable. Alice would have stopped if she weren't so desperate to find the binding spell. But she had to admit that, despite the horrible illustrations and instructions, she read the book with a kind of strange fascination. It reminded her of watching horror movies with Jeremy when their parents were out. She would usually cover her eyes during the scary parts ... but she always peeked through her fingers.

Jeremy would have loved this stuff, obsessed with ghosts and hauntings and magic as he was. He'd always been that way—from the very beginning. The first Halloween Jeremy had been old enough to choose his own costume, he had declared he was going to dress up as a witch. Her mother had tried to talk him out of it. *Don't you want to be a firefighter? What about a prince? You could have a sword and a shield and ...* But he had insisted, and between his whining and Alice's arguing, their mother gave up, and Jeremy had left the house on Halloween with a ridiculous wig and a pointed hat and a huge, hairy fake wart right on the tip of his nose.

Now, holding this tattered book, thinking of the portrait over the fireplace—the madness on Elizabeth's face—Alice regretted every creepy movie she'd ever snuck home for him, every magic trick book she'd pointed out to him at the library. Most of all she regretted that her body was lying somewhere just dying. What would he do without her? Who would make sure he didn't do something dangerous when her mom wasn't looking? And her mom was rarely looking.

Alice clasped her arms against her stomach, staring blankly into the distance, thinking of Elizabeth locked in her room going insane—seeing only Jeremy, with his bright red hair, his silly smile. As she watched, he cracked then crumbled, falling slowly to pieces.

She shook her head. *No.* She wouldn't let it happen. Grabbing the book again, she flipped through the pages with new determination, because she could *not* lose this battle.

She found what she was looking for in the very last section of the book. It appeared to be a section for very difficult magic, spells that (judging by all the notes and modifications in the margins) the witch herself had not perfected. The final few pages dealt with cursing objects. Alice slowed down and read very carefully.

***

Laying a curse on an object with no life of its own is very difficult magic indeed, for magic feeds off of souls and off of life. Curses draw their strength from life, and, if there is not a life to use, then they can do nothing. This is why, in order to perform such a curse, the object must be imbued with a life of its own, and that is the difficulty.

A curse on a house is a common request, but one that even the wisest among us hesitates to grant. A house is a very large, lifeless thing and to fill it with a soul requires a human life. But the problem is that simply murdering the person will do very little good, for if the soul is transplanted into the house without knowing and agreeing to behave as it must, then the curse is useless. The soul and the witch must work in complete cooperation. For this reason, it is not uncommon that the witch has no choice but to sacrifice her own soul. Of course, no sensible witch would do such a thing unless forced.

Binding a soul to an object is perhaps the most difficult magic. There are many speculations on the procedure, but I hold with the oldest belief. Life is the most basic magic—the very core of our being. There are many who speak of four elements that make up our existence: earth, water, air, and fire. I believe that there are five. Life is the fifth element and it encompasses all of the others, like a triangle divided into four smaller ones. Melding all of the elements creates a new existence where there was none before.

I am preparing for a great experiment in this area. I believe that, if I am careful, I can split part of my own soul off and use it to fill a small object, a mirror perhaps. I will have to go near to death, and then return before it is too late. Somehow, I must combine all of the elements into one in my death. Hanging, I think, is the best option, for it suspends the victim between the earth and the air. I will have to include water and fire somehow as well.

***

The pieces fell into place—a puzzle, a picture—finished now. The sensation of complete triumph was something Alice had not felt often and, when it hit her now, she was surprised by how it made her heart burn and her lips tingle with a suppressed smile. She stood up and put the book down; she knew that she was ready.

When she returned to the library she saw the girl exactly as she had left her—curled up catlike on the chair, her fingernails digging into the velvet cushions. She jumped to her feet when Alice came through the door.

"How do you feel?" she asked, which struck Alice as a strangely doctor-like thing to be asking given the circumstances.

"You care a lot, don't you?" said Alice, walking past the girl to stand in front of the desk. She looked at the portrait and was calm. Elizabeth's eyes seemed to look just over her shoulder at the witch behind her, and Alice wondered if this then was the solution. The curse needed souls to live, and one soul had been there for longer than all the others. If Alice could get rid of the witch, would the curse crumble? It was plausible, and the thought of being free—it was dizzying.

"Of course I care," said the girl. "We've been over this."

"Then maybe you can explain why you lied to me." Alice still stared at the portrait, but she could hear the girl's soft footsteps behind her. She could not hear breathing. Did the girl even need to breathe?

"I've never lied to you. I wouldn't do that, Alice."

"Maybe. But you didn't tell me everything." She was angry now and grateful for it. Anger and hope made her stronger than she could have been otherwise.

Alice sensed more than heard the girl walk forward; she could see her black dress out of the corner of her eye.

"I showed you as much as you wanted to see," she said, clasping her hands in front of her. Alice turned to face her then.

"But you only showed me what you did because you knew that I wouldn't want to see more. And you changed things—just a little bit. Just enough." The girl's eyes glinted and Alice felt fury tingling in every inch of her skin, because the girl had planned the whole thing so carefully, had known exactly which buttons to push, and Alice, in her desperation, had fallen for it.

"Alice, you're confused." The girl stepped forward, flashed that glittering smile, and tried to take Alice's hand, but Alice had had enough of that. She yanked her arm away and pushed the girl into the desk—hard. The girl did not cry out in pain, as Alice had expected her to. What actually happened was far more alarming.

The girl's brown eyes turned black—so black. The girl blinked furiously, trying and failing to stop the transformation. She placed her hands over her eyes, then grabbed the desk and shook it hard. Bruises appeared—not where she had hit the side of the desk, but everywhere, all over her neck and her face and her arms. Alice, shocked, took a step backwards. The marks suddenly faded away, but the girl's eyes remained black.

"Look what you've done," she cried. "Look!" She held out her arms, which turned purple with bruises as if on cue. She was nervous now, and her performance was far from convincing. Alice looked down her nose at the girl's skinny arms and saw that the bruises were fading in and out, as if the witch couldn't quite keep up the illusion. It made Alice's stomach turn, but not from sympathy. It was pathetic and Alice felt only disgust.

"Enough." All the witch had done from the beginning was play with her—manipulate her. This attempt to make Alice feel sorry for her was nothing more than a desperate miscalculation. "It's too late for that."

The girl screamed, rushed forward, and Alice dodged to the side. Panting, the girl turned back around. "You wanted to know what he thought. I only did what you asked me to do."

"But that's not all you did," said Alice, grabbing the back of a chair for support. Her knees shook but she was not afraid. "You changed what I saw—in the mirrors. You made me see things that weren't there."

The girl was breathing hard and the bruises were gone; she must have gained some control over herself, because she was standing quite still now, clutching her dress in her fists. "I was trying to help you."

"Maybe you thought you were, but I don't think so. Because I think I've finally figured it out—your plan. I know what you're doing and it's not going to work."

The girl widened her eyes. "My plan? I just want to be your friend."

Alice's nostrils flared. Up until now she hadn't been angry, but the fact that the witch would keep up this ridiculous charade infuriated her. Did she think that Alice was so needy that she would fall to her knees at the promise of friendship? Did she think Alice was that weak?

But she had been—this had worked for the witch before. Alice had been needy and entirely pathetic. Her throat tightened as she remembered how she had struggled for air through her tears, sitting on the floor, the witch's hand on her knee. She gulped down some more stale air. The witch stared at her—pleading eyes—and Alice wanted to slap her.

"Wrong," she said. Her voice trembled.

The girl shrugged and looked away, but Alice darted forward and grabbed her face—held it between her palms—forced the girl to look at her. The girl stiffened and pressed her hands to her throat, her mouth hanging open like a gasping fish, and Alice realized that her thumbs were digging hard into the witch's neck. She pressed harder, caught up in her own strength, but then she glimpsed Elizabeth's eyes over the witch's head—they seemed to glitter in approval—and they jarred Alice to her senses. She forced herself to move her hands down to the witch's shoulders, which she held tightly.

"You want me to be stuck here with you," Alice said roughly. "You don't want to help me. You want to have me. Because—do you want to know why?"

The girl tried to pull away now but couldn't break free.

"You want me the same way you wanted all the others. You used them up, didn't you?"

"I don't know what you mean," she said.

"I mean that Elizabeth was wrong."

The girl tried to push Alice away and this time Alice let her. The girl made a mad dash for the library doors and Alice sprinted after her into the foyer, knowing full well that there was nowhere the girl could hide from her. The girl had thrown herself against what was left of the mirror above the couch, her hands pounding against the glass, her head thrown back—a trapped animal.

"If you don't want me here, then send me away," she said, her voice high. Then, seeing the look of disgust on Alice's face, she put her hands down, took a deep breath, and smiled. "I can see that I've made you uncomfortable. Just wish me back to the other side of the mirror—it will be as easy as wishing me in. Remember? I promise if you send me back I won't trouble you anymore."

The girl had a way of speaking that made everything she said sound reasonable and right. She held her head high and threw back her shoulders—the stance of someone who knew she was in charge. But Alice could see past the clever acting now. She saw that the corner of the witch's smooth smile was trembling, and suddenly the pretense seemed desperate instead of brave.

"No," said Alice.

The girl got off the couch and backed away from Alice until she was only a few inches from the edge of the mist. She stopped short, glanced over her shoulder, and took a step forward—away from the puffy white wall.

"Go on," said Alice as the girl's black eyes scanned the room for any escape. "But wait, you won't do that. Because that's exactly what you're afraid of. Moving on. Going forward. I have to say, it's a little funny that you're so willing to encourage me to move on when it's the one thing you fear most.

"I imagine," Alice walked forward, arms crossed over her chest, "that you weren't always this way. I think that once you were powerful—frightening, even. You got greedy. And I don't think you meant to kill yourself—no, that was an accident. You wanted to be better and stronger; you wanted power and it all went wrong."

The girl was not looking at Alice; she had closed her eyes and clasped her hands behind her back. Alice felt a brief flicker of fear, because she had expected the girl to make a run for it again. She wanted to see the witch's eyes—see the fear in them. Now Alice could only see that impeccably composed face and she watched it carefully, like someone waiting for the next trick in a magic show.

"You were right about one thing," said Alice, raising her voice. "You have no power over me. You're so weak now that even I can make you obey. You may have killed your body, but a part of you lived on inside of the mirror. But it started to use you up—not all of you, just most of you—left you a shadow of yourself, just like you knew it would. And you realized that eventually it would consume you entirely, unless it had something else to eat while you looked for a way out. That's where Elizabeth came in. You realized that this was your opportunity and you told her how to bind another soul to this house—you knew it would buy you time. But you didn't tell Elizabeth the whole story. You told her no soul could survive in a curse and she believed you, but she was wrong. It *is* possible. *You* have survived. And when she died, you got what you thought you needed—a little extra energy to sustain the curse while you looked for a way out."

The girl still didn't say a word. Her chest, level with Alice's, went up and down with long, even breaths. This made Alice even angrier. She wanted the witch to tremble—to be afraid. She felt as if she were talking to a statue and it made this whole speech seem pointless, even foolish. But Alice carried on, because now she had to. She had too much momentum to stop.

"And then Elizabeth got used up, too. But now you had more options. Elizabeth did something you couldn't do—she extended the curse. It wasn't just the mirror now. It was the whole house. It fed on victims when it got hungry and as long as it kept on eating away at human lives, you were safe."

Still no reaction. The girl was perfectly still. Alice clasped her hands behind her and squeezed her fingers hard.

"And so whenever the curse claimed a new victim, you were there to greet her. You were there to *help*. How many did you convince to give up? You can be quite persuasive when you want to be. But you've never met me before. And I'm not giving up. I'm done with you."

And then—movement. The witch's eyes opened slowly, like curtains, and her eyes were no longer black. They were brown and warm and large. Alice's heart skipped a beat.

"You're right," said the witch, voice thick as honey. "You win."

"I … what?" Her fingers hurt, she was gripping them so tightly.

"I mean you've beaten me. You've bested me. You've figured out the riddle—all my secrets."

Alice didn't know what to say. Her brain seemed empty; her mouth hung open. She felt partly let down, partly relieved—as if she'd been preparing to battle with a lion, but had been thrown into a pit with a kitten.

"I used Elizabeth, just like I tried to use you. And now, because you've figured it out, I have to do as you say—think of me as your own personal genie. I can grant you whatever you wish. And I know what you wish. You wish to escape this place. Don't you?"

Alice felt herself nodding.

The witch nodded as well and said solemnly, "Then that's what I'll help you do. But you'll have to trust me, just a little bit."

At the word *trust*, alarms started going off in Alice's brain, but they were muted and slow. She wanted to hear what the witch would say—escape hung before her, gleaming, and she wanted it badly. Jeremy's face flashed before her eyes and she realized that she was hungry to see him, ravenous even.

"I know you don't want to believe anything I say, but think back—not everything I showed you was a lie."

The girl had a point—she had shown Alice a genuine snapshot from her own life. But even as Alice leaned in, waiting eagerly for the girl to reveal the secret of escape to her, a dull but relentless voice at the back of her mind pointed out that something was wrong here. It only served to confuse Alice, because hadn't she won? The witch had said she had nothing to fear from her.

"Get to the point," Alice demanded, trying not to let her voice show how much she wanted to hear.

"Of course. I'm sorry. What I mean is that what I told you before about the mist is still true. It's the way out. It really is."

She's still trying to kill me.

The realization hit Alice like a punch to the gut. The girl didn't seem to notice that Alice had stiffened; her gaze was level and calm and ... *conniving, lying* ... Alice could think of so many words. After everything she had been through, that she could still eat up the girl's lies ...

"Will you come with me?" Alice asked. She heard her voice, was relieved that it was steady. "Into the mist, I mean."

The girl smiled, surprised at her luck. "Of course. You go through first—I'll be right behind you."

"No." Alice held out a hand. "Together."

Her smile wavered, but held. "Oh … yes, if that's what you want." Her fingers wrapped delicately around Alice's, and Alice, blood pounding drumlike in her ears, stepped toward the mist. She stood face-to-face with it, nose only inches from it, and thought it looked pillowy but not soft—just suffocating.

Alice, fingers against the girl's wrist, could feel her pulse racing. Taking a deep breath, she forced herself to do what she knew she had to: she lifted her foot and began the long step forward into the mist.

The minute she did, the witch jerked her hand away. It happened in a split second, just as Alice had known it would. And Alice herself whipped around—her toes just grazing the mist—and grabbed the girl by the shoulders. Saw the shock in her eyes.

The girl did not even have time to open her mouth. She had no time to react. Without a word, with one push, Alice sent her careening silently into the mist. It parted to absorb the witch and (Alice couldn't decide if she imagined it or not) she thought she saw white hands reach out to envelop her. The witch, realizing finally what had just happened, tried to pull away. She struggled, flailed, screamed. But, in an instant, the hands were drawn back into the mist and the witch was gone without a trace.

CHAPTER EIGHTEEN

Not without a trace.

Alice sat at the top of the stairs, staring at the triangle mirror. It lay facedown on the carpeting, the wooden back scratched in places, burned in others. Gingerly, Alice reached down and flipped it over with the very tips of her fingers, barely touching it. She dropped it gently onto the carpet, then stepped back, wiping her hand in Elizabeth's dress.

The witch's scream was still ringing in her head as she leaned forward ever so slowly and stared down into the mirror. She saw a self she barely recognized blinking up at her. And, leaning down, she saw around her neck the faintest shadow, like a string ... like a rope ...

Alice jumped forward and grabbed the mirror and the books and ran with them down to the library. Throwing the books onto the couch, she pulled a blanket from a nearby chair, wrapped it around the mirror, and shoved the entire bundle in the closet. Then she closed the door and stood panting for a moment, her spine still tingling. She looked at the diary and considered throwing that into the closet as well, just to get away from it. But she needed it, whether she liked it or not, and so she grabbed the thing and hurried out into the lobby, where she curled up on the padded bench by the mirror.

She sat, waiting. Her breath was rhythmic and she listened to the familiar sound of it, eyes darting around the room, ready to notice the slightest change.

It all felt so wrong. She held the book open in her hands, not even pretending to read. Alice hadn't ever been sure that defeating the witch would free her. But she had expected ... well, she had expected *something*.

What? Expected what?

Not this, she answered herself. A change, some sign of progress. Not more of the same in this lonely, silent place. So much lonelier now. She hadn't expected that—that she would almost find herself missing the girl's company. It had been easier to forget that she had no idea what she was doing here when she'd had the girl to fight against. Now the lack of a visible opponent left her directionless.

Nor were her doubts any less persistent. The girl had given them a voice, said them aloud, hit Alice over the head with them. But even without her they pounded at Alice from the inside, fists against her skull. Her head ached. The longer she sat, the louder they became, shouting at her in the girl's voice.

We are you. I am you. I will always be you.

She closed her eyes.

For seven hours, Alice sat in the lobby. She knew she should be doing something—reading the diary, maybe. But as much as she tried, she couldn't get herself to focus; her thoughts darted from thing to thing. Her heart pounded and would not slow. So she sat there, alternately closing her eyes and staring blankly at the ceiling, waiting for Tony and his dad to come in. The mist covered half of the room now, and it was still creeping across the only remaining mirror. If they didn't come soon, Alice was worried that she wouldn't be able to see or hear them at all, and she needed to know if Tony had told his dad the truth. She needed to be prepared for what would greet her the next and final time that she came alive.

George came down by himself at eight thirty a.m.; he was carrying a book titled *Raising Teenage Boys: How to Be a Father to Your Son*, and he sat down in the sitting room off the lobby with a cup of coffee. Alice wondered at first why he had bothered to come down if he was only planning to do some reading, but she soon noticed that he kept glancing at what appeared to be an incredibly old pager on his belt. It had some strange wiring and what looked like a cell phone screen hanging oddly from the side. Even now, he was taking readings—the picture of persistence. Her dad was the same way—not with ghosts, of course, but with business deals, with work. He fought until the very end. He never gave up on anything.

But he gave up on me, she thought bitterly.

Alice's version of the sitting room was mostly covered by mist, but she set up camp near an antique desk and mirror. The mirror itself was very old and surrounded by laughing bronze cupids, brandishing their arrows and kicking their baby feet. The mist obscured part of the frame, but Alice had a fairly good view anyway. Setting the witch's books and the diary on the desk, she tried to read—opening then closing the covers, flipping through the pages. But mostly she watched George, waited for Tony to show up. The back of her neck tingled and she kept whipping around, half expecting to see the girl laughing at her from some dark corner of the room. When she didn't appear, Alice was unprepared for the pang of regret that came over her.

When Tony came into the room at ten thirty, he looked exhausted. Alice got to her feet, leaning over the desk to get a better view of him as he stumbled across the room and collapsed in a chair across from his dad's. His hair was untidy and there were dark shadows under his eyes.

George eyed his son. "Did you sleep at all last night?"

Tony yawned in response.

"You weren't on the Internet until four in the morning?"

Tony looked up, surprised.

His father shrugged. "I'm a light sleeper."

Shaking his head, Tony said, "Fine, you're right. I was up late—doing research."

"Tony, school hasn't even started yet. Take some time off, for goodness' sake."

"It's not"—another yawn—"for school. I've been researching … curses."

"Really." George frowned.

"I'm not lying. Why do you always think I'm lying to you?"

"When have I ever said I thought—" George began, but then stopped, hand tightening around the parenting book. He took a deep breath. He opened his mouth to say something, but then shut it just as quickly. Tony glowered.

"Dad, if you have something to say, just say it."

George hesitated, then blurted out, "Does this have anything to do with a girl? I don't care if you were up late chatting online— you're on vacation. It's okay."

"I don't believe this." Tony's scowl deepened. "You've been *spying* on me?"

"Spying on you? I'm allowed to talk to your mother sometimes, you know. And if she mentions that you have friends you like to keep up with on those websites and a few of them are girls … I'm allowed to know that. What makes you think I'm spy—" He cut off, mouth in a silent O, then leaned in and said confidentially, "Oh. I see. A girl *here*. You've met a girl at the hotel, haven't you? Well. She cute?"

Tony's expression grew stonier the longer his dad spoke, but Alice thought she saw the tiniest hint of a blush crawling up his neck—pale as an unripe peach.

"It's nothing," he said quickly.

George stroked his parenting book absentmindedly. "You

know, if we want to develop a genuine, trusting relationship, we have to start being honest with each other. You would tell your mother about something like this, wouldn't you?"

"No."

"Well," George seemed pleased with this news despite himself. "Well, um … yes, you should tell her things. But you should definitely tell me. And now's as good a time as any to start forming a lasting bond."

Tony's forehead furrowed and his gaze dropped to the book on George's lap. "Oh no," he groaned. "You've been reading parenting books again."

Too late, George slid his hand to cover the title. Tony shook his head while George, seeing that the damage was done, confessed. "Yes, and I think I've learned some really useful things—things that can help us build our *relationship*." He emphasized this last word, as though introducing an entirely foreign concept.

"Well it certainly worked like a charm last time, didn't it?"

"We can't dwell on the past, Tony."

"Why not? Last summer you were on that whole 'meaningful conversation starters' run. Remember how that went?"

"I really don't see why we have to—"

"'What was a moment when you felt truly loved?'" Tony interrupted. "'When was the last time you had a serious conversation with a family member?' Dad, this stuff doesn't work!"

"Maybe if you'd just give it a chance … "

"Maybe you should stop trying to be my best friend."

George drew back, hurt. Alice, watching, felt her heart sink a little in sympathy—then sink farther when she realized she had done the same thing to her mom before, told her off for trying to get close to her. She didn't understand why she had done it—not really—except that she had felt smothered with expectations, as though her mother was trying to fix her. And though she could understand what Tony meant, she also felt for George, was surprised at how sharp the pain in his face was.

"Well … " said George, calmly, heavily. "Okay. Maybe you could explain what you mean by that, Tony."

Tony, who seemed to realize that he had crossed the line, said in a much softer voice, "I have friends, you know. And they're nice. And I like them. But sometimes I just want … " He paused, then continued. "I want a dad. And if you're never there, if I only see you for a week during the summer, then I just don't see how this is going to work."

George looked away for a moment, then asked, "Then what can I do?"

Tony turned to the mirror. It was strange, making eye contact with someone who couldn't see her. She thought she felt a real connection for a moment, as though a thread stretched through the glass from his heart to hers, transmitting his feelings like a tin-can telephone.

Not that he deserves it. Tony had said that right before she disappeared and she hadn't thought anything of it. But now, staring at his face, she understood why he hadn't told George about her yet. He hadn't been afraid of his dad's reaction; he had been punishing him by holding back. But in the last ten minutes, George had proved himself somehow, and Tony's resolve was broken. He was going to give his dad the only gift he had ever wanted.

"You can help me," said Tony at last.

"With what?"

"With a ghost."

George's was one of those chubby, innocent faces that made adults look like overgrown children, and when he heard this his round eyes widened.

At least I've made someone happy. It was strange that all the pain she'd been through could bring a smile to some stranger's face.

"That's me—a real Samaritan," she sighed.

***

It wasn't until an hour later that George and Tony stood up to leave the sitting room. The mist had crept forward while they talked, and Alice had developed a crick in her neck from standing with her head to one side for so long.

"I still don't know why you didn't tell me earlier. For goodness' sake, Tony! A real ghost—conversational and everything. Do you know what this means? If I document this correctly, my next book could very well change the way the world looks at death!"

Tony looked a whole lot less thrilled about all this than his father did. "Dad, you're forgetting why I told you this in the first place. She needs our help, remember? You can't do tests on her. She doesn't have time for stuff like that."

"Of course, of course," said George, waving his son's worries away. "We'll do our very best to help her out … but while we're chatting with it—"

"*It?*"

"I mean *her*. Sorry."

They walked out and into the lobby, and Alice followed them on her side of the mirrors. She had just reached one by the staircase when the hotel manager looked up from his desk. Just from the way his teeth clenched and his eyes narrowed, Alice could tell that he was in an irritable mood this morning. "Well, well, well," he drawled, "do the ghost hunters return triumphant?"

George was apparently too happy to pick up on the prickly undertones in the manager's voice. "Just got a great tip," he said. "Tony here has seen the same ghost twice now."

"Really," said the manager, eyeing both of them with obvious mistrust.

"It's the girl who got in the pool accident," George said, before Tony could answer for himself. "He's talked to her and everything."

At the mention of Alice, the manager's face tightened even more. "The girl isn't dead yet," he said tersely, "though she will be soon."

Tony's jaw dropped.

"What?"

"She's been declared brain-dead. They're pulling the plug day after tomorrow."

"They—they're going to let her die?" Tony said. He had turned very white. "They can't!"

The hotel manager shrugged. "Well, what do you expect them to do? There's no point in keeping her alive as a vegetable for sixty years. You've got to draw the line somewhere. Hospital bills are expensive. Especially when you're pouring money into a lawsuit against an innocent hotel … "

Tony had already run into the library.

"Tony?" George took off after him, leaving the hotel manager by himself at the desk. When he saw that no one else was around, the manager sighed and rested his head in his hands.

The mist edged forward another inch, swallowing up all that was left of the mirror.

They were going to kill her.

Her own parents … how could they … *why* would they …

She stood. Her entire body clenched—she shut her eyes, pursed her lips, balled her hands into fists. These were her blast doors, shutting one by one, trying to keep the explosion from bursting out.

But why? Why should she keep it inside? There was nothing here to hurt, no one to see, no one to hear.

She let out a scream and it wasn't enough. Throwing the diary aside, she dashed forward and picked up the small wooden table next to the mist-covered sofa.

CRASH.

The table hit the opposite wall so hard that the framed paintings shuddered. A single leg split off and went flying into the mist. Alice bent over her knees, trying to catch her breath, but it seemed to have escaped her completely—flown from her lips—and she panted like a dog, a dying dog on its last leg ...

The leg.

She straightened. Out of the corner of her eye, she had seen the table reappear next to the couch, as she had known it would. But unlike the other things she had destroyed, this one had not escaped completely unharmed. It wobbled on its three remaining legs, falling against the side of the couch.

Alice's breath rattled. She whipped around. The wall of mist not five feet away was still as winter. She turned back and grabbed the table again, pulled it up off the ground, threw it as hard as she could. It went flying into the mist and the white rippled like the surface of a pond. Alice did not breathe, stared at the space beside the couch, waiting.

Thirty seconds later, the need for air became overpowering: She gasped it in.

The table did not reappear.

What went into the mist did not return. It was a one-way road and here was the gate and she could, too ... if she could do it, if she could just push herself through ... there would be an end ...

She sank to her knees—closed her eyes and tried to think, but her brain was awash in a wild mix of fear and excitement. She crawled to the side of the mist. The tip of her nose was only a few inches from it. Her mind spun; her hands pressed into the floor, sweaty against the smooth wood. A dull ringing sounded in her ears. She leaned forward, forcing herself to keep her eyes open wide. Her nose disappeared into the mist and she breathed in, ears ringing louder now, hands slipping across the floor. The mist had no smell—neither the fresh, clean smell of the mountains nor the heavy, asphalt taste of the city—the mist was without flavor. It simply was.

Alice leaned back, then edged closer. The tops of her knees disappeared into the white. She stared at the whiteness the way a diver would stare at the water far beneath and then, taking a deep breath, she almost ...

But she didn't.

She threw herself away, shocked, almost ashamed. Was she really willing to give up that easily?

The diary. She needed a distraction; she needed to get away from the mist. Alice jumped to her feet and her knees shook. *A fit—a storm—that's all it was.* It had passed now, or so she told herself. But the mist was strangely insistent in its silence and she could hardly take her eyes off of it even now. *Stay focused.* She didn't see the diary anywhere on the floor, and she knelt down to look under the couch. There was nothing, not even dust.

She stood up, then knelt back down, then stood up, and the nervous fluttering in her stomach became more of a hurricane—bats instead of butterflies—and she turned once again to stare at that snow-white wall.

"No ... "

Falling to her knees in front of it, she stuck her arm into the nothingness and felt around for the familiar binding, but there was no floor on the other side of the mist, and there certainly wasn't any book lying there.

"*No!*" she said again, pulling her empty hand out and staring at it in despair. That book was not something she could afford to lose. *Read me.* The rules were clear: if she wanted to get out of here, she had to read the diary. And she was only halfway through.

She breathed in, then out. The mist bent forward under her breath like an opening gate. And then—she couldn't be sure whether she was imagining it—a tendril of white unfurled from the solid wall and brushed against her cheek and suddenly ... she could smell it. Nowhere on earth was there a smell like this; it was inviting as fire and calm as glass and light as down ... she leaned into it ...

Her head and shoulders were in the mist now; everything around her was all fog. But her fingers still clung to the floor.

Perhaps she shouldn't ...

Another whiff of peace washed over her and she closed her eyes. If this was death, it wasn't bad. And without the diary, she was as good as dead anyway.

She took one final, deep breath and pressed herself forward into the mist. Her knees were on solid ground for one more second. Then all that was solid simply slipped away.

CHAPTER NINETEEN

Alice could never fully explain what happened next. The only thing that she could compare it to was hanging in a zero-gravity room filled with floating mirrors. Everything glowed white, just like the mist itself. It was light as a summer day—maybe even lighter—and it hurt her eyes. There were no shadows, no darkness to relieve the inescapable brightness. The air wasn't warm and it wasn't cool. It was just there, no temperature at all, that indescribable smell rippling through it like ocean currents. And everywhere were the mirrors, so perfectly smooth, so flawless that she could not tell where one ended and another began. The same girl peeked at her from ten different places. It took her a moment to realize that this thin, tired face was her own—reflected again and again and again.

Perhaps this was what forever felt like.

Alice tried to walk, but there was no way to tell if she was moving forward at all. Swimming worked better, because she could feel her arms pushing the thick air behind her. She hurried up and forward, then dove down as best she could. Could the diary have fallen? How far down did the mist go?

A desk floated serenely by.

"No," whispered a chorus of voices that cut through the brightness like a sharp, cold wind. They echoed through the emptiness, filling everything, rushing across her. Though they sounded neither threatening nor angry, Alice felt a chill run down her back.

She stopped moving.

"Who are you?" she called, as the air grew dense with whispers—or was it wind? No, it was definitely whispers—many voices hissing back and forth, too indistinct to understand. Frightened, Alice hurried to find the diary before she got so lost in the mist that she would not be able to find her way out. Already she wasn't sure she knew which way back was. The whispers grew louder until Alice could hardly bear the sound of them pounding on her ears, bearing down on her as if she were surrounded by invisible loudspeakers. Still she could not understand what the voices were saying; it was as though they spoke a language known only to themselves. She covered one ear and continued making swimming motions with her other arm, gritting her teeth against the noise.

"I've lost something," Alice said, hoping an explanation would somehow appease the invisible whisperers. Out of the corner of her eye, she saw something beige and small and rectangular reflected in one of the mirrors—something that was definitely not her.

She uncovered her ear and pumped both her arms, faster now; she tried kicking her legs. But there was no way to tell exactly where the diary was with the mirrors reflecting both distant and close things. Distance—space—folded in on itself like origami. When she reached the spot where she had seen the diary, the mirror was gone and the book itself was nowhere to be found. She looked around in a panic and caught another flash of it in a mirror close by.

The hisses rose and fell in waves—sometimes unbearably loud, other times softer than Alice's own breath. It was like drifting in the ocean, being carried closer to the land of the voices, then tossed farther away.

It wasn't until Alice had been swimming for what felt like at least ten minutes that she realized that, though she had been paddling furiously, she didn't feel in the least bit tired. She wasn't aching—wasn't even out of breath.

The whispers became suddenly loud, and for a second she thought she understood what they were saying.

"Not yet."

Alice did not bother to answer this time; she dove downward and swam and swam and swam, following even the tiniest reflections of the diary. And then, at long last, she saw it, spiraling downward. She hurried after it and her fingers closed around the binding. *She had found it.* But this didn't excite her at all. *That's odd,* she noted, wondering if she should be alarmed.

Turning around, she began to go in the direction that she could only assume was up, if there was an up here. Faster and faster her arms went; she used the book as a paddle and felt herself go even faster. It was almost enjoyable, feeling the air rush past her, feeling her body move just as she wanted it to, without fatigue. Even her eyes were becoming accustomed to the brightness and, as she swam, she began to forget.

Why must I hurry? she thought, and let herself slow down. It felt so peaceful here. She was tempted to lie back and let herself be carried farther in by the soft, fragrant air. But there was this nagging in the back of her mind that refused to let her stop, that urged her to return to where she had come from.

She looked around her. Mirrors, mirrors. A woman in black, rope around her neck, thrashing wildly, trying to get somewhere. Her distress concerned Alice, who was cocooned in peace. It was wrapped around her like the lightest down blanket. She closed her eyes and, when she opened them again, the woman was gone.

And then the whispers spoke loudly again, startling her. She had grown accustomed to the quiet murmur; she had almost forgotten they were there. She had almost forgotten everything now.

"Leave," they whispered, and the coldness that shot through Alice's body jarred her out of complacency. A burst of icy air by her ear made her whip around, expecting to see someone standing there, breathing down her neck. But she saw nothing more than a tuft of white mist blowing by. She began to hurry again.

"Go back," said the voices, even louder than before. Frustrated by the endless searching, confused by the mirrors and the reflections, Alice began to grow angry. She was not physically tired, not out of breath, but there was a deep exhaustion inside of her, a weight so familiar and steady that she wondered how long she had been carrying it. She wanted to rest, wanted to forget. And what right did this voice have to dictate her fate? What right did it have to force her to return?

"I don't care!" Alice yelled at the voices. "I don't care anymore!"

The voices went silent for a moment, then returned in a chorus, "But you must."

It wasn't that the voices had sounded unkind before, but Alice heard something new in them, something quiet and understanding. She had the distinct impression that somehow the voices *knew*, that they understood her situation better than she did.

"Why?" she shouted anyway, pushing the feeling aside. The mist began to grow thin around her and darkness crept into the white. She almost thought that she could see a wall in the distance.

"The curse will continue, unless you can break it."

"Who are you?" Alice yelled back.

"It is your duty," the voices said.

The reflections were dimming, the mirrors growing smaller.

"*Who are you?*"

Now Alice could almost feel the floor beneath her feet. Her body began to take on weight again; she started to fall.

Just when she was sure that she was free of the mist, Alice sensed a sudden change in the whiteness around her. It convulsed, contracted, and then out of it—out of the heart of it—she saw hands emerge, so many of them, ten, maybe more. They reached toward her and she could not have pulled away even if she had wanted to, and before she could react they had grabbed hold of her—her arms and her legs and her hair. As they did, she felt a startling warmth flood her and suddenly the voices were no longer coming from the mist, but rather from her own head, and she could hear the whispers (only they weren't whispers now, but thoughts) as they came and went, like the sound of singing birds perched in a tree. Her heart pounded fast, trying to absorb it all, trying to understand.

And then the mirrors in the mist shifted and she saw herself reflected ten times over. Only it wasn't her. In each mirror there was a different face, a different woman, and she saw them and she knew them because they were in her head and she was them—all of them. All of the women who the curse had killed, inside of her, counting on her, relying upon her. And now, helping her.

In a grand, synchronized motion, the hands pulled back and pushed forward, pressing against her, pushing her out of the mist and into the safety of the house. As they pulled away, she felt the warmth recede and, at the very last moment, before it disappeared entirely, she heard the voices—the thoughts—the women—chant in unison their final good-bye.

"For all of us," they said.

Her knees hit the solid floor hard and Alice quickly relearned the sharp taste of pain.

***

For many minutes Alice lay on the floor, gasping for air. It seemed that all the bodily fatigue she had not felt while caught in the mist was coming back to haunt her. The diary she kept grasped firmly in her hands, as if it were life itself to which she clung. What had happened in the mist began to fade to simply a confusing blur, as if she had just woken up from a dream and now it was slipping away from her. All she could remember were the mirrors and the white and voices from the distance and the strangest warmth pounding inside of her, fading. A lump in her throat.

After a while, she pulled herself to her feet and left the lobby, which was now almost completely swallowed up by the mist. The library was still untouched and that was where Alice sat down with the diary. Behind her, the clock was chiming the time. Eight o'clock. Had she really been caught in the mist for an hour? She went over to the clock, just to make sure she wasn't imagining things.

She wasn't. With growing uneasiness, Alice returned to the couch, unnerved that time could so easily slip away from her. She needed every second of it. Alice bent down and picked up the diary, but just as she was about to open it, she had a horrifying thought. Clutching the book, she ran back out to the lobby and looked into the mirror. Her heart seemed to have gotten lodged in her throat and she thought it might strangle her. When she saw the dark windows, the drawn curtains of the real hotel, her heart sank stone-like back into her chest. Eight in the *evening*—she had been gone for half the day.

Alice shook her head in disbelief, but the evidence was undeniable.

She had lost thirteen hours. In a little over twenty-four more, she would be sent back to the real world for the last time. And soon after that her parents would let her die.

Determined to lose no more time, Alice returned to the library, opened the diary that had cost her so dearly, and began to untangle the final pages of writing.

***

May 17, 1883

I have decided. The way to break the curse will be through hate—my hate. Only then can the punishment be complete; only then will my hatred be appeased. I have painted a clue into my last portrait. It is so simple, so perfect.

It is still light outside and I am preparing. Tonight is the night. Tonight the curse will be cast. It is a new moon and the darkness is powerful.

Before I cast the curse, there is something I must do. I have been working on it all day, for I must be very careful. I am afraid to scratch the glass. What if I should hurt the witch? But I must get these bars off if I am going to free her. The knife helps, but it is still slow work. I have managed to pry most of the wood off. The witch has been throwing herself at the glass; she is anxious to escape this mirror at last.

I do not think she understands. She believes that I release her to ask her guidance. In fact, I free her to demand her assistance. She will serve me. I used to believe that the witch was powerful, that she was strong and wise. Now I know differently.

The witch was weak and now she is weaker still. The mirror has used her soul to sustain its existence and now she is merely a shadow of herself. She is feeble, and I am strong. But she will still serve her purpose.

Very carefully, I remove the wood—if only you could see how very careful I am. I only use the knife to slice through the very edge of the glue. From there, I use my nails and scrape, scrape, scrape the rest off. Heavens, how my hands are bleeding! The cover of this diary is already quite stained and still they drip.

I have left a trail of blood on the desk. There is but one piece of wood left.

***

She is free! The witch is free. The minute I pulled the last bar away, she rushed out of the mirror and right out of the room. She is running around on the grounds now. From my window, I can see her popping out from behind bushes and trees, reacquainting herself with her old home. She looks dreadful, I must admit. Her hair is all tangled, her eyes wild. Her hands are bleeding from clawing at the glass.

I called her back. I whistled out the window and she came zooming back into the room, fast as lightning. I have never seen a living creature move so quickly. But then again, I am not sure if she is really alive. Would you believe? I can see straight through her.

The witch helps me to prepare. The rope is already strung from the chandelier. The matches are ready for the fire. I sent the witch to fetch earth from the garden and now she has sprinkled it all over the room. We are ready.

Oh! I hear footsteps in the hallway. Someone is knocking on the door. Perhaps it is Lillian. What perfect timing! I shall welcome her inside.

***

It was not Lillian at the door. It was Father.

What terrible luck. Father was not supposed to have anything to do with this. He should be asleep at this hour, but it seems that he saw the witch peeping into his window. How careless of her! I told her to stay hidden.

When he saw what I had done to the room, my father tried to run. Between the witch and me, we managed to tie him to the bedpost with some of the leftover rope. It is a miracle that we were able to restrain him at all. My father is a very strong man, but the witch is wild and that gives her strength to rival his. I wish that it did not have to be this way, but I cannot allow him to go free. What if he alerted Lillian? My plan would be ruined!

Now we all wait together: the witch, my father, and I. We wait very quietly. The witch put a piece of her dress in Father's mouth so that he would stop yelling. It is a shame that he had to get caught up in this. But there is nothing that either of us can do about it now. Not even the witch knows how to erase a memory.

Lillian should be here by now. I told her very specifically to come to my room at midnight tonight. I told her that I wanted to tell her a secret. I even hinted that I might show her the witch's things.

The witch is getting restless. She paces the room, chewing on her bleeding hands. She seems quite distraught.

Back and forth she goes. Back and forth.

Father looks terribly frightened, poor man. He stares at the witch with horror in his eyes. I don't blame him really; she is a frightening sight. Sometimes he mumbles things, but he can't make much of a sound through the fabric in his mouth. He fights frantically against the rope tied around his body, but he cannot break it.

The witch has begun to dance now. She is dancing around the room, waving her bloody arms around in the air. She is chanting something in an old and evil language. The words make my skin crawl in the most delightful way. Father doesn't seem to be enjoying it. He closes his eyes now. I don't think he can even bear to look at her.

Wait! I hear a footstep in the hall.

Stop dancing, little witch. Stop dancing or she will hear.

And we will fail.

It is the witching hour now.

Come in, Lillian!

Good night, ladies!

***

And then, in small, more careful letters, written at the very bottom of the page:

***

The curse is in motion.
But hope is hard to fell.
If you would escape my fate,
You must understand my hate—
Or you will die as well.

CHAPTER TWENTY

Alice ran her finger under the words as she reread them three times in quick succession. *If you would escape my fate, you must understand my hate.* Elizabeth had promised a way to break the curse and here it was. Alice felt sweeping triumph, then a quick rush of disappointment.

This was it!

This was *it*?

But this was only a riddle. Alice tried to dissect the lines but the poem's meaning was both too obvious and too obscure. The words slipped between her fingers. Hate was the only thing that she could grasp onto. She had to understand hate.

There were several pages left in the diary, and Alice flipped to the next one, hoping against hope that there would be some kind of explanation. But on the page after the riddle, the handwriting changed abruptly. The letters here were slanted and small, with little curlicues on the ends. It was the writing of a lady: elegant and careful. Alice could read these pages easily.

***

I have read through my sister's journal and I feel obliged to finish it. I suppose it is odd that I should take the time to do this when I fully intend to destroy this diary, but I feel that I must. After today, I will try to forget that I ever had a sister. Elizabeth and the truth of her madness must fade into memory. But before I resolve never to speak of this again, I plan to purge it from my mind.

I will bury the diary, hide the other books. I can no longer bear the sight of fire.

My sister went mad. I do not know if it was the fact that her lover abandoned her, or simply the strain of her last role that finally unhinged her. Either way, it was not entirely a surprise. Madness runs in my family; I will be lucky to escape the scourge myself.

When I saw the signs, I told Father at once and we decided that rest would be the best thing for her. We left her in her room (alone, most of the time), and that may have been a mistake. Elizabeth grew obsessed with the witch who once lived in that attic. I often saw her reading what appeared to be old spell books. Every time, she would attempt to hide them from me, but she wasn't fast enough. Sometimes when I came into the room, I would hear her talking to herself. On these occasions, I would peep into the room and watch as she carried on entire conversations with the mirror by her bedside. She seemed to believe that the witch lived inside of it. She talked of terrible things—curses and death and murder. Father called the doctor, but the doctor could not be enticed to stay after he saw the state she was in.

As Elizabeth grew worse, I suggested to Father that we commit her to an asylum, but Father would not hear of it. Father, for all of his prickliness, is a soft man at heart, and he always was overly indulgent where Elizabeth was concerned. She was his only comfort when Mother died—she reminded him of Mother so much. Elizabeth always got exactly what she wanted. When she announced that she wanted to be an actress, he scrimped and saved to pay for acting instruction. She was his pet and he doted on her. He even had portraits painted of her in every role that she took on.

That love was the end of him.

When I saw that Father would not listen to reason, I took matters into my own hands and called the asylum myself. Elizabeth, however, was stronger than I expected. She somehow managed to escape from the men who came to collect her. She made such a fuss that Father realized what was going on and called it all to a stop immediately. It was a foolish decision—one that probably cost him his life—but Elizabeth was to stay in the house and he would hear no more on the subject.

After that, I did something rather foolish, I admit. In one of the newspapers, I saw something that made me suspect Elizabeth's lover, William, had not been a lover at all. According to the press, a man of similar description had swindled a girl in New Hampshire just the week before. I gave the paper to Elizabeth to see her reaction and, when she became upset, I goaded her. I did not expect her to attack me; I did not believe she was that far gone. But no sooner had I turned to leave than she wrapped her fingers around my throat and tried to strangle me. She would have succeeded had Father not intervened just in time. In my anger, I am afraid that I threw a vase at her and rendered her completely unconscious.

That, of course, ruined any chance I had of winning Father over to my side. After that incident, he became even more intractable than he had been before.

Things came to a head last night. Elizabeth had spoken with me earlier in the day, when I went to bring her lunch. She requested that I come to her room at midnight. She said that she had some great secret to tell me. I was suspicious, but I was also anxious to get back into Father's good favor, and since the only way to do that was through Elizabeth, I reluctantly agreed. She was very quiet for the rest of the day. I listened at her door every so often, but all I could make out were the oddest scraping sounds, as if she was carving wood.

But when darkness fell, I started hearing strange sounds. They were coming not from inside, but rather from the grounds. I was worried that there might be a thief about and I went to warn Father, but he was not in his room. Thinking that he had heard the sound as well, I went outside to look for him. I had no luck there either, but I imagined I saw a flash of clothes as a person ran from tree to tree. Frightened, I hurried back inside and called the police. Soon I began to hear heavy footsteps upstairs, as though someone was dancing—or leaping. I went to check on Elizabeth.

It was precisely midnight when I walked into the room. There was little light, and at first I could not see much of anything. But when, after a moment, my eyes adjusted, I nearly fainted.

The first thing I noticed was Father. He was tied to the bedpost and gagged. He shook his head at me wildly. Frightened to see him like that, I tried to turn around, but Elizabeth threw me to the side with strength that was frankly inhuman. Before I could recover myself, she had the door closed and locked behind me. Crumpled on the bedroom floor, I had the oddest sensation of sitting on dirt, and upon looking more closely, I realized the floor, the bed, the entire room was covered in soil. It looked as though someone had pulled buckets of dirt from outside and dumped them everywhere.

On top of the bed there was a pile of wood—enough to build a bonfire. And, worst of all, a noose hanging from the ceiling.

I screamed, but it was too late to call for help, and we had so few boarders that likely no one would have heard. Elizabeth was dancing around the room, chanting something that I could not understand. She looked quite wild—her face was white and haggard and her hair tangled. Her clothes were ripped and dirty. I backed into the corner and almost dared to hope that she had forgotten about me, for she seemed to take no notice of me as she leapt back and forth over the edge of the bed. She took out some kind of salve and rubbed it all over her face. I could hardly see her skin under it. It looked very much like mud.

When she brought out the matchbox, however, I knew that we truly were in trouble. I tried to stop her, but she threw me to the floor again with apparent ease. By the time I crawled back to my feet, she had lit a fire in her bedsheets and it was working its way up the wood. I tried to free Father from his ropes, for if the bed burned, so would he. Elizabeth was too fast for me. She soon forced me onto a stool underneath the noose and had my head inside the loop.

I will not try to explain how terrified I was, trapped in an attic about to be consumed by flame with a madwoman dancing at my feet and a noose around my neck. Death, I was sure, was imminent.

I could not move. Elizabeth danced a wild waltz around the room, and I stood, noose around my neck, frozen with fear. I looked frantically around the room and then I saw it. On top of the chest of drawers next to me lay the mirror (covered with what looked like dried blood) and a knife.

It was hope that freed me from my paralysis. The knife was just barely out of reach. I stretched to reach it, but the noose on my neck tightened and, choking, I had to pull away. I was afraid of what would happen if I lost my balance. I was tempted to lift it off my neck, but I knew that Elizabeth would see and would reach me before I reached the knife. All I could do was hold my breath and reach as far as I dared. The tips of my fingers brushed the handle at last; I could feel the rope digging into my skin.

Elizabeth was still dancing around the fire, which had now grown to quite a height. She pulled a jar of oil from her desk and poured its contents over the entire bed. The flames blossomed and my father began to scream, as much as he could through the fabric in his mouth. Elizabeth was completely unaffected. She screamed strange words into the fire. Father's voice rang in my ears, stronger than the pain of the rope on my skin. I reached forward, eyes burning from pain, from smoke, from tears. My hand closed around the knife.

Father screamed louder than ever and Elizabeth leapt onto the windowsill. I did not think too hard about what I did next, for I had no choice. Gripping the knife, I took aim and threw with what little strength I had left.

The knife struck Elizabeth right in the chest and her scream blended into Father's. She fell backward through the open window and I heard the splash of her body hitting the water of the pond. My hands were shaking so terribly that I could barely lift the noose from my neck. I was so shocked at what I had just done that I didn't notice Father's screams fading. When I limped off the stool and attempted to free him, he was already lost in the fire.

I fled from the room and out of the house. That is where I found the police officers. They put out the fire and explained the deaths as well as they could without knowing what had happened. I would not tell them the truth. I will not further besmirch our family name. After the fire was out, I hurried to the attic and found that this diary and the witch's books had survived. I will not allow them to find their way into a curious reporter's hands.

Tomorrow I meet with a man who wishes to buy the hotel. He is offering a pittance, but I will sell it to him anyway. I cannot bear to stay here any longer. I will go as far away as I can—to California, if possible. Tonight I will bury this diary in the garden. No one will ever know what happened. The secret will die with me.

***

Alice stared at the last page of the diary as if it were lying to her. Her fingertips seemed large and clumsy as she fumbled with the page, flipping it over, then back again, staring at the last words Lillian had written as though they were a code that she could crack.

The secret will die.

Will die.

Die. She couldn't get past that word. It clung to her, clawed at her. She bit her tongue, trying to stay calm.

Slamming the little diary closed, she walked back over to the desk. There she threw down the book exactly where she had found it in the first place. It hit the desk with dull finality. Immediately, Alice had the urge to pick it back up—it had been her companion for what seemed like ages. Her hands stretched out toward it and she pulled them back, clasping them in front of her. She turned on her heel, but had only gotten one step away when she whipped back around. In one fluid motion, she grabbed the diary and threw it across the room. It hit the side of the fireplace and fell to the floor, cover bent awkwardly backwards like a broken limb.

Alice breathed hard through gritted teeth. Why should the diary get to rest quietly—peacefully—on the desk when she could not rest at all?

She paced the room, arms crossed over her chest, hugging herself as she used to do when she was a child and afraid.

So the way to break the curse was hate. But what had Elizabeth hated? Lillian, William, even the witch … Alice could think of several things and she thought she understood. William had, after all, abandoned Elizabeth. Every ounce of attention Lillian received had irked her. The witch had been a threat, holding power she craved. But, even though Alice had read the whole diary, read through page after page full of hate, the curse was not broken and she was still here. Would she know when she had understood enough? How? Did she need to do something, say something?

She had read the diary hoping for answers and now all she was left with were more questions.

Closing her eyes, she tried to find something in herself—a deeper understanding, more feeling. She searched for a memory of powerful hate, but the only emotions that surfaced were anger and frustration. Maybe this was the problem: she had never hated something strongly enough to understand. Surely she could hate more. It ought to be easy. She would find what Elizabeth had hated and she would hate it, too.

She was already so angry, it couldn't be too hard.

Lillian, William, the witch. Alice opened her eyes.

She looked around the library and her gaze came to rest on the portrait of Elizabeth. She tried not to think about what had happened to her. And yet she could imagine all too clearly that woman with the madness in her eyes, dancing around the dark attic room, face painted black, lighting a fire that would burn her own father to death.

Hate. I hate her. The more she thought about it, the angrier she became, and she let it boil up inside of her. It was all-consuming and she did not fight it. She let it burn.

She marched over to the closet and opened the door; reaching inside, she pulled out the cloth-wrapped mirror and carried it over to the couch. She unwrapped it; she could see no blood on the glass. Perhaps Lillian had cleaned it up so that the police wouldn't become suspicious. Now that Alice looked closely, though, she could see scratches that looked quite a lot like claw marks. She reached out to brush the surface with her hand and, to her shock, realized that it was warm. Not cool like glass should be—warm like human skin. She pulled her hand away.

Alice looked at her distorted reflection in the glass and was surprised to see the anger there, magnified somehow by the imperfections in the glass. Her eyes were overlarge—her mouth small and lopsided. Deep shadowed hollows made her cheeks look skeletal. In the mirror, the ceiling caved, rippling down so that it seemed about to crush her beneath it.

She moved and the reflection changed. Her eyes shrank to mere pimples of brown. Her face was piggish and pink. She saw nothing worthwhile, nothing worth fighting for—only helplessness, emptiness. Her heart sank and some of the anger fizzled into despair. She couldn't blame her parents for giving up on this girl. Moving again, she became a witch—right there. There were her long nose and her pointed chin—perhaps even a wart or two dotting her face. Her eyes were brilliant and a little bloodshot and they looked positively evil the way the glass reflected them back.

Jumping to her feet, she fled the glass. She didn't make it to the armchair, but simply fell to the rug and curled up, pulling her knees to her chest, burying her head. It made her feel small. Alice wished she could cry. The despair was too heavy and though she could feel the weight of it against her chest, she was too tired, too empty. The tears would not come.

She ached to talk it over with Tony, with anybody, really. She just needed another voice besides her own to tear her out of her head—new eyes to help her see clearly. "I don't know," she said, thinking that perhaps just hearing a voice (even her own) would help. It didn't. She thought she could hear her voice echoing in her chest and it made her feel hollow.

Tony's voice was strong—warm. Her own seemed thin and pale in comparison, like a pastel swatch in a room of bright colors.

She imagined what he would say to her if he were here now. (*Don't worry, Alice. It'll be okay. We'll be okay without you.* No. No, he wouldn't say that.) She could recreate his voice so clearly in her mind—every nuance. *I was worried about you, Alice—so worried, I—*

Gong. The clock was sounding. She jumped; she had completely lost track of time in her rush to finish reading the diary. Had it really taken her that long? Then, just as she was sitting back, just as her heart was starting to slow, she realized that the ceiling was getting higher—she was sinking into the rug.

Panicking, Alice tried to grab hold of the couch, but her arms went right through the cushions. This wasn't—couldn't be right. There was another full day before she would come alive again. She had more time than this! Unless …

The mist. Her breath stopped short. It hadn't been thirteen hours. It had been a day plus … twenty-four plus thirteen.

No.

Lost. Was she lost?

And though she was worried that she was, her last thought as she sank through the floor was not of herself, but of Tony. He would be able to help her, to see something that she had missed. Buried in her fear, she found a stubborn, throbbing hope, so sweet that she could taste it—smell it—rich and scented and strong.

She was in to her neck now, and then she was submerged in water.

CHAPTER TWENTY-ONE

Again, Tony was ready for her. No sooner had she fully materialized on the bottom of the pool than she felt his arms loop around her and rush her to the surface. He was so fast that she didn't even have a chance to swallow any water before she reached the air.

"Thanks," she said to him. He didn't answer; he actually looked a bit nervous.

"Tony," Alice said, "is something wrong?"

"The witch?" he asked instead of answering her question. He helped her out of the pool, then pulled himself out.

"Gone."

"Bring her over here, Tony," shouted a voice from the side of the pool. George. He sounded excited beyond all reason.

"Oh." Alice had forgotten that she and Tony would not be alone tonight. She quickly realized, though, that what she needed most was advice and the more people who could help her, the better off she would be. George—who studied hauntings, who probably knew all about curses—might be just the person she needed.

But still she had a vision of just her and Tony, whispering urgently, his hand on her back. She couldn't shake it—it was like a movie she had seen ages ago but couldn't quite forget.

"I thought he'd be able to help you," said Tony, who sounded as though he regretted it.

Alice looked up at George. She was about to launch into her story and tell them both everything she had learned, when she realized that George's eyes were wet. His mouth was ajar and his face was aglow with something Alice had rarely seen on adults— awe. George gulped and took a half step forward. He reached out a finger and touched her hair, then jerked his hand away.

Alice was silent, because it hit her that this was the moment he had been waiting for all his life. It was strange to be at the center of it—to have someone look at her like that.

Tony went to grab a towel from the pool deck. George came closer and Alice couldn't stop herself from leaning away. Shivering from the cold water dripping down her back, she hesitantly allowed George to kneel down next to her and grab her arms, examining them in the light of his flashlight.

"Look at this," he said in an excited, high-pitched voice. "They seem so real! It's unbelievable. Look at the transparency of the skin. I could almost see straight through this hand!"

Uncomfortable, Alice got to her feet, hoping to put some distance between them. But George stood up as well and continued to stare at her, hands clasped together in front of him.

"Dad!"

Tony handed Alice a towel and George asked, "Are my video cameras on? You checked the batteries, right? I need to make absolutely sure this is documented."

"I checked them three times, Dad."

"Excellent, excellent." He looked at Alice again—a shiver ran through him. Clearing his throat, he turned to face a nearby tripod. "As you can see," he said, his voice a little hoarse, "we have here a living, partially corporeal ghost." He sounded unable to believe it himself. Stopping, he glanced back at her, rubbed his hands together. Then he turned back to the camera. "I will now begin to question the spirit."

"Dad! This is to help *Alice*, remember?"

"Yes, yes, Tony. I know. So, what is your name?"

"I told you her name!" said Tony, indignant.

"My name is Alice."

George, glowing, hissed at Tony, "Did you see that? It talked! It talked! I don't believe this is happening."

"*IT?*"

"Sorry, sorry—so sorry."

"How long is this going to take, Dad?"

George shrugged the question away, gesturing to Tony to get out of the camera's range. Tony gave his dad a grudging look but went to stand behind the camera as well.

"So, Alice," said George, now in the casual, conversational tone of a journalist doing an interview, "tell us a little bit about how you came to be in your ... um ... current state."

Alice frowned and looked at Tony for support. Tony dug his hands farther into his pockets and shrugged, as if to tell her that it couldn't hurt to indulge his dad for a little while.

"Well, I'm not dead," she said.

"No—of course not. But you aren't quite alive, either?"

"Please," she blurted out—partly to him, mostly to Tony. "I don't have much time and—"

"Don't have much time?" George asked eagerly. "What exactly is it that is keeping you from staying here for long? What does it feel like?" He turned to Tony and whispered, "*Feeling*—that's the key. People are dying to know what death feels like. No pun intended." He laughed at his own joke; Alice saw that his hands were shaking.

"It's the curse. There's a curse," she looked directly at Tony now, "and a riddle to solve."

Tony's eyebrows went up and she nodded.

"'If you would escape my fate, you must understand my hate.' Elizabeth wrote that in her diary."

"Elizabeth Blackwell had a *diary*?" George cried, nearly hyperventilating now. "What ... how ... Where can I read it? What did it say?"

"But what did she hate? Did she mention that?" Tony asked.

Alice pulled the towel more tightly around her. It was hard to tell if the pressure against her fingers was the towel stretching or the sensation of her hands going through the fabric. Either way, it seemed to help with her nearly uncontrollable nerves. "It's not that simple. She hated lots of people."

"But someone in particular. She must have mentioned ... she must have left more clues."

"She didn't—"

The camera beeped and Alice jumped, startled. A bird cried in response to the noise and the sound set her teeth on edge.

George nearly leapt to the camera's side. He squinted at the screen.

"*Tony!* The battery's low. *I thought you said you checked.*"

Tony shrugged, but he didn't look sorry. He caught Alice's eye.

"Better finish the interview off soon."

"*Tony, I don't believe—*" The camera beeped again and George cut off. He looked at the screen, then at Alice. Taking a deep breath, he collected himself. "We'll have to circle back to the curse if we have time. For now, let's get to the important stuff. Tell me, would you call yourself a ghost? And please remember to be honest—many people are anxious to hear what you have to say."

To the side of the camera, Tony pressed his palm into his forehead and whispered to his dad, "How many times do I have to tell you? Alice is not dead. Ghosts have to be *dead.*"

George shushed him, pointing to the camera screen.

Alice was temporarily stunned by the question—all thoughts of the curse fled her mind. She wasn't a ghost. She wasn't dead. She wasn't *going* to die. And yet there were some moments when she felt that she understood what it was to be unseen and uncared for.

"I feel like a ghost," she said at last, heart pounding as the confession slipped unbidden from her lips. "I feel ... torn—broken. When I first realized that I was trapped, I started yelling at the people in the mirrors, trying to get someone to pay attention to me. And no one could hear. I was afraid." There she was, being open again—and not just to Tony. George was almost a complete stranger. And there was a camera, an open window for other, nameless people to watch through. A week before she would have been embarrassed to share so much; now she felt invigorated, alive. "I think I understand ghosts. At least, I would, if I believed in them."

George's mouth dropped open and he stammered, "Surely you believe in ghosts? After all you've been through?"

Tony looked equally confused.

"People who really die don't become ghosts." She didn't know how she knew this, didn't know where this was coming from, but she felt it was important. She remembered from somewhere a world of white mist and mirrors and voices that she didn't recognize. "People who die move on. To be a real ghost, you would have to be trapped somehow."

"Like you—you're trapped. But you said you aren't a ghost."

"I have direction. I just don't know which way I'm headed."

George immediately started trying to steer the conversation out of these dangerous waters. He probably hadn't planned on having his ghost discredit his entire field of research.

"Yes, fascinating. And moving on … can you tell our viewers anything about death?"

"I'm not dead."

"She's *not dead.*"

George brushed them off, looking flustered. "I mean, were you to speculate, based on your experiences as a … not-dead person, is there anything you would care to tell the world?"

And Alice did have something to say. The moment the question began to sink in, the moment she began to think about it, answers started emerging out of nowhere—winking from dark corners, from memories that she could not recall.

"I don't think that you go away … when you die. You just, you know … " But they didn't know; she had to tell them somehow. "It's like waking up, I think. It's like the first day of school. It's like your past and present and future are staring you in the face, mirrors on white walls that disappear when you get too close to them. And when you reach out you can touch any moment because they're all inside of you—all time, in here," she pointed at her heart, "inside."

There was complete silence. Not even a bird. Not even a rustle.

"But I don't know that," she said meekly.

She wondered how she knew that.

The blinking red light flashed quickly three times, then was solid, then turned off. The night was silent.

"I guess that's it," said Tony. He glared at the dead camera, then at his dad.

"But ... but ... " George protested, still staring at Alice as though mesmerized.

"Dad, that should be plenty of footage. Think about it—you've always wanted a spirit on film. Now you have one. Isn't a few minutes better than nothing at all?"

Alice nodded, though no one was looking to her for an opinion. Now that her unexplained moment of understanding had passed, she wondered why she had let George convince her to speak about this in the first place. Death was not something she wanted to even think about, much less lecture on. She could feel it hanging over her like a dark storm cloud, and the only thing she could think to do was stare in the other direction.

"We promised to help her. You promised. Let's help her now."

George stroked his video camera absentmindedly.

"I guess ... it will be enough."

"We can't let her die." Tony gave his father a meaningful look and George looked up in surprise.

"Oh," he said, and it was clear the thought had not occurred to him. "Of course not. Absolutely not."

Warmth—sweet, strong—heated her from ears to fingertips. Though she had never felt any particular love for George, a growing affection for him filled her now. She had help, at least. All she needed now was a little more time.

Would there ever be enough time?

"Tell us everything you learned from the diary," Tony was saying, "and between the three of us we'll figure it out. It'll be fine—you'll see."

So she began to tell them, as quickly as she could, about how Elizabeth had cursed the house, how she had tried to kill her own sister, how she had killed her father, how she had died. And the riddle—the hate. It was so simple and yet so terribly impossible.

"How can I possibly know what Elizabeth hated?" Alice moaned. "I mean, I know she hated—"

"You!"

Alice jumped and Tony hurried to her side; he grabbed her shoulder. Still at his cameras, George froze. The hotel manager marched across the lawn, staring at George. Alice, frozen, couldn't be sure if he had seen her. She wished she were more invisible than she already was.

"You!" he repeated, pointing a finger at George. "I thought I might find you here. Well, you'll have to clear all this stuff away by tomorrow morning. I've hired my own lawyer. He's coming to examine the signs around the pool tomorrow morning and I thought I should check to see if you had left anything out here. Sure enough—"

He saw Alice.

He stopped so suddenly, he nearly fell over his own feet.

"What ... Wha ... y—you ... "

His jaw hung open rather stupidly as half-formed words

tumbled out of his mouth. His small brown eyes bugged out in the oddest way; he looked a lot like a bullfrog, Alice thought. It would have all been very funny had it not been so terrible.

For a moment, the four stood frozen, scattered around the pool like lawn statues. Tony was gripping Alice's shoulder so tightly that she could feel his nails digging into her skin. George had his hand on the video camera. The hotel manager's cheeks were white.

The manager turned and sprinted back toward the hotel.

"No! Stop!" George yelled, hurrying after him. Tony jumped up and ran after his father. Alice dropped the towel and hurried to catch up to Tony.

"I don't know what kind of prank you three are trying to pull," the hotel manager yelled as he ran. "I don't know if you're trying to fake a ghost story or what, but I swear the police are going to find out about it."

"But it's not fake!" George said in a breathless yell. "She really is a ghost!"

The hotel manager had reached the door now and he whipped it open.

"Ghosts don't exist!" he yelled as he dashed inside. "But that girl does and she's trying to ruin my life!"

He slammed the door shut just as Tony was about to barrel inside. Tony screeched to a halt in front of it and yanked on the knob, but the manager had locked it. George stopped at Tony's side, breathless, and Alice darted up right behind him.

"Go," said George, turning on the two of them. "Quickly now, while there's still time."

Tony looked, dumbfounded, at his father. "He's calling the police," he said, as though this were something new.

"He'll be back. Do you really think that he's going to let her out of his sight for one minute? The minute he gets off that phone, he'll come right back out here—he doesn't trust any of us. He'll try to make sure she stays put. He'll threaten us if he has to."

"But I need—" Alice began.

George cut her off. "I know. You need quiet. You need to talk and not be disturbed. You don't have the time for this, so go! I'll keep the manager occupied. I can buy you time."

"But he'll be furious," said Tony. "When he sees Alice is missing—"

"*Go*," George repeated, more insistently this time. He took a quick step forward, brushing his hair off of his sweaty forehead, gesturing toward the trees at the end of the hotel property. It was oddly quiet in the yard now, without the hotel manager's screaming. Alice thought it might have been peaceful if her heart hadn't been pounding, if every nerve in her body hadn't felt suddenly wired.

"Dad," said Tony, and he moved closer to Alice. His hand brushed her back. "What are we going to do? If the police come … if they find her … "

He didn't have to complete the sentence. There would be

confusion—panic, even. And even if she were seen, even if her parents heard that she'd been spotted, would they believe it? Or would they pull the plug even sooner, just to end the torment of having their daughter's life dangled in front of them when they knew there was no hope?

And when she disappeared tonight, as she knew now that she would, what would happen then? It was her last night alive, her last chance. If she went back to the shadow house having learned nothing new, without a single idea, what then? She would die. That's what would happen.

Her breath came in short gasps.

"You want to know what you're going to do?" said George harshly. He grabbed Alice's hand. "You're going to take her and you're going to run. Try to help her while you still can."

Alice looked back and forth between them. George talked about her as though she weren't even there. And for some strange reason, she herself hardly felt that she existed. She couldn't say a word, couldn't force anything out of her lips.

"But what about you?" asked Tony, taking Alice's hand. "You could help—you should come."

"And have the manager hunt us all down like dogs? Someone needs to hold him off. I'm staying, Tony. And you need to go."

Alice thought she heard the sound of running feet inside the hotel. Her hand tightened around Tony's and he looked over his shoulder at the closed door.

The footsteps came nearer—quick—a sharp patter.

Tony went then, dragging Alice along with him, but he kept looking back at his dad as he ran. Alice hurried to keep up with him; the pull of his arm on hers was the only thing that kept her moving forward. She was exhausted, winded, and the farther she went from the hotel, the worse the sensation became. It was strange that she should be so tired when every part of her was burning with adrenaline and all she wanted was to get away from this place. Now that she was actually doing it, she couldn't find the energy to move forward.

It was when they reached the trees at the edge of the yard that she noticed it—the burning sensation in her fingertips. It spread quickly, with every tree she passed, every step she took, running up her hands and her arms, coursing through her like a ton of glass shards, cutting her, hurting her. By the time they reached the fence, the pain was almost unbearable, and the moment Tony let go of her hand to jump over the low brick wall, she collapsed on the grass, hugging her knees to her chest, gasping for air, willing it to stop, wanting anything that would end the pain.

"Alice! We have to run!" Tony reached a hand over the wall, his voice an urgent whisper. And Alice willed her hand to reach up and grab his, but nothing happened. A moan escaped her lips. She couldn't move. She couldn't breathe. She was panicking now and the only thought in her mind was to get back to the hotel. The idea took hold of her with surprising force—back to the hotel. Once she was back at the hotel, the pain would go away. She knew it. She just had to get back. Alice began to crawl toward the hotel, almost without her own consent. It was as though her body had taken over.

But Tony didn't understand. He leapt back over the fence.

"Alice, we have to go *now*. We need to get just a little farther away," he said, eyeing her with a worried frown. And she couldn't explain to him what was wrong because she had to get back there, back to the place where the pain would end.

Then there was an arm under her, around her, lifting her. Carrying her to the fence. She couldn't stop him and every inch he moved the pain spun to an even higher pitch, and she couldn't believe that she could hurt so much, that inside her there was the ability to feel so much pain.

"*No!*" she heard herself scream. "Please, no!"

She was struggling, fighting him, and he couldn't hold her now. She fell out of his arms, landing with a dull thump, sinking into the dirt, the grass. She felt him lean over her and then there was a kind of fuzziness all around her—her vision was blurry, and his voice came to her as if through a long, dark tunnel.

Alice?

Alice.

When she woke again, the pain was gone.

CHAPTER TWENTY-TWO

"Shh." Tony's hand pressed against her lips as she stirred feebly. Her vision gradually came into focus. Tony's face looked down at her, framed by trees. She pushed herself up and saw that she was sitting in the darkness behind a bush. Through the leaves she could see the pool dimly, where the hotel manager was screaming at George, waving his arms in the air as if he were hailing an airplane. His voice was distant.

"You've only been out for a few minutes," whispered Tony. "I think it had something to do with the hotel—you couldn't cross over the fence. I carried you back here."

"But we have to get away. I ... I have to get away ... "

"Right now we have to stay quiet."

Her arm was pressed against his; she leaned on him heavily. Although the pain was gone, the exhaustion remained, and she hardly felt strong enough to hold herself upright. She glanced over her shoulder at the low brick wall in the distance and wondered for a brief moment whether she ought to try jumping it again. Now that the pain wasn't so absorbing, she even thought she could make it. Maybe. She could push through it.

But as she moved to stand, the weakness in her arms was so overwhelming that she gave up the idea at once. She was as good as trapped here on the grass.

"You were videotaping something," the manager was yelling. Alice could just see the back of his dark red shirt. George was standing next to the tripod, his hand on the camera. "It was her, wasn't it? You got her on film."

"These are *infrared* cameras," George said, with just enough irritation in his voice to make it sound nearly believable. "They don't pick up anything but heat signatures."

"Do you think I'm an *idiot*? That's the same video camera I got my wife for Christmas years ago."

"Your wife wanted an infrared camera?" asked George, clinging gallantly to his lie.

The hotel manager made a sound like an angry horse and reached for the video recorder. Instead of trying to stop him, George stood back and let him grab the thing.

"'Infrared camera,'" the hotel manager scoffed. "This is a video camera—an ancient one too. Worthless piece of crap. Still uses tape. Couldn't afford to spring for digital, huh? Ghost business really must not be going well. Is that why you decided to invent a haunting? To get in the headlines at last? Well, the game's up now.

When the police get here and I show them the tape, then they'll see that the girl's alive, that this is all some kind of hoax, that—"

He stopped. He was looking down at the camera in his hands. His shoulders were nearly to his ears, and his whole back seemed to arch, like an elongated letter c with a little hunch at the top.

"Where is it?" he said, the rumble of barely suppressed rage making his voice sound gravelly.

George stood with his hands behind his back. "I like tape. It's more reliable. You can touch a tape, feel it with your fingers. Digital recording is a mystery—just numbers stored in a case so tiny you have to *believe* it's there. But tape ... tape is solid. I like things that are solid."

The manager threw the video camera to the ground. It hit with a crash, then bounced several feet. The view screen flew off and landed in the grass a few feet away.

"What did you do with it?" he demanded, marching forward.

George backed away toward the pool. "You would think a ghost chaser wouldn't care much for solid things." He spoke casually, and if Alice hadn't been watching him for days now she wouldn't have caught the hint of anxiety that told her he was far more nervous than he was letting on. "But that's what ghost chasing is all about. People want to see ghosts because they're looking for proof that when they die the world won't melt away completely. They need to believe that there's something solid there—something to hope for."

"You give it to me. *Give me the tape!*"

George was on the very edge of the pool deck now, his heels hanging over the water. The hotel manager stopped a few feet in front of him and Alice could see his beet-red ears. George's chest moved up and down in hurried little leaps; his tongue ran across his upper lip.

He was holding something behind his back—something square. He leaned back over the pool (Tony inhaled sharply) and Alice had just begun to realize what he was going to do when his fingers loosened and the tape fell like a small dark bird into the water.

It landed with a surprisingly loud splash. It sank down a few inches, then came to rest on the surface, bobbing up and down as ripples pushed it toward the center of the pool.

"*No!*" screamed the manager, running forward, shoving George to the side. He leapt into the pool (the splash was tremendous) and pulled the dripping tape out of the water.

"No!" he said again, more quietly.

He ran a finger across the edge of the tape, then, with a cry, he threw the tape as hard as he could.

It fell onto the lawn, where it lay like a dead thing.

Tony's hand tightened around Alice's and she looked up and saw the shock on his face. She was sure her own expression was similar.

"Here," said George, leaning down and offering the manager a hand. His eyes kept wandering to the ruined tape on the ground.

The hotel manager just turned his back.

"The police are coming. You'll pay. You'll pay."

George stood back up. "I already have," he said.

The manager slogged through the water toward the step, his wet shirt hanging heavily around his torso.

Alice whispered; her voice was hoarse.

"Why did he do it?"

She wasn't sure if George had acted for better or for worse. Wasn't showing the world that ghosts were real what he had always wanted? Would it have been such a bad thing for the manager to show the tape to the police? Maybe it would have convinced her parents that she wasn't dead … to wait for her … but—she realized almost at once—her parents would not believe even a video. They would call it a forgery. They would be angry, probably, that someone had gone to such lengths to torture them further.

But George … the tape was his evidence. Surely it would have only helped his cause if the tape had been seen.

"My dad used to tell me that when someone doesn't want to believe something, you can't make them. You can offer them as much evidence as you want, but if they shut their eyes and cover their ears, there's nothing you can do about it." Tony was very tense; Alice could feel the tightness in his arm as he put his hand to her back, supporting her.

"But the videotape. I thought … I thought it would prove … "

"What would it prove? Life after death? You're not dead."

"But at least it would show … something … "

"It depends." He shrugged. His voice was tight. "To some people it would just prove that some lunatics would do anything—

even fake a death—to prove a point. There would be lots of people who would believe it, sure, but they'd be the ones who always thought there was something more to death than just disappearing—the ones already looking for proof. And then, when you wake up—"

She noticed he said *when*, not *if*.

"—it won't mean anything. People will say my dad filmed it after you came out of the coma and no one will believe it at all."

"But I still don't understand why he destroyed it."

Tony frowned. "I guess he just didn't want his best evidence taken by the police. Maybe he'd never get it back."

The manager was wringing out his shirt. He eyed George closely, as though worried he was going to make a run for it.

"Do you believe?" Alice asked. She knew that she should be talking with Tony about the witch—using her time to figure out how she was going to save herself—but her mind was tired of puzzling over the witch's cryptic note. Her body ached for rest and she wished she could sit there forever, leaning on Tony's arm. She envied statues, how they rested for ages, frozen in time.

Time. Time was flying by, and even though there were things she needed to figure out, there were other things she needed, too— things that she wanted to take with her if she was to die. She craved moments to cling to, moments unsullied by the witch. A mental gag reflex that she could not control strangled the questions she knew she should be asking. The minute she even thought of the curse, something inside of her clenched up and pushed back.

"Do I believe what?"

"That there's something else. You know … after."

His frown deepened. He readjusted his legs. "It doesn't matter." He wouldn't meet her eyes. "Who cares what I think? We need to talk about you and the curse. This thing about hate—could you tell me again?"

"Not now," she sighed. Thinking about the curse made her stomach spin like a hamster wheel. And she was just sick … so sick … "Can't I have *one* moment?"

"I can tell you how many moments you have. Sixty. And thirty of them are already gone." Tony's voice sounded unnecessarily harsh to her. Her hands went cold the way they did when her dad yelled at her, even though Tony was barely whispering.

She pulled away from him and hunched over her legs, steadying herself. Her head spun the moment she moved—from anger or from weakness, she wasn't sure.

"Is it possible in order to understand her hate, you have to feel it?" asked Tony. "Maybe if you could just try to hate all the things that she didn't like, that would do it."

"I've been trapped for six days with nothing to do but think about this. Tell me something I *haven't* thought of," she snarled.

He reached out and put his hand on her shoulder. "I'm sorry," he said, and she felt a gut wrench of shame that passed in an instant, "I'm sorry to push you. I just … I really want to help you. I need to know that you'll be okay."

"Why?" she said dully.

He pulled his hand away.

"You really don't know what other people see in you, do you?" asked Tony.

She refused to meet his eyes. Her own were burning. There was too much inside of her and some of it had to come out and it was coming out as water.

"Do you know what you need?" continued Tony, when Alice said nothing. "You need someone to tell you all the good things about yourself every day, every hour—on the hour. You need someone telling you that you're wonderful until you finally believe it." His voice faltered, but he pushed on regardless. "You need someone telling you that they love you."

There was something about the certainty in his voice that made her feel warm—heat in her chest that unfurled up and down her body. It made her want to burst out in tears. It welled up inside of her and she tried to stop it from gushing out, but she couldn't.

A loud, piercing sob escaped her lips.

She froze. Tony stiffened.

A few tears rolled down her cheeks.

"What was that?" asked the hotel manager.

George looked a little paler than usual, but said calmly, "A bird, most likely. Lots of birds around here. That's why you put them on the room keys, right? Very clever of you. Really charming—"

But the manager was not listening. He was marching toward the copse of trees. Alice clung to Tony's arm.

"Are you hiding there, girl?" asked the manager. He was coming straight toward them. He was close enough that she could see his rounded belly jiggling under his soaked shirt. She leaned forward, hand pressed against the grass, fingers wide—like a runner crouched at the starting block.

"Check it out if you want," said George coolly, hurrying to catch up to him. "But I think I know a bird when I hear one."

The manager acted as if he had not heard.

He was coming close. She could hear his feet when they hit the ground ... bare feet, he'd taken his wet shoes off ... he was smiling. Why was he smiling? Smiling like a man who had just won. Could he see them? Oh God, he could see them.

Her muscles tightened. Panic was raging like a wildfire in her mind and she didn't think about what she was doing—all she knew was that she screamed and leapt to her feet and that she, who had only a moment ago been barely able to hold herself upright, somehow managed to drag Tony up with her. She ran and he began to run with her, his hand in hers.

Only this time it was not Tony pulling her, but rather her leading Tony toward the only place she could think to go. The hotel loomed forbiddingly before her, but it was familiar, and Alice, in her alarm, sought only familiarity.

The hotel manager was close behind them, and though Alice did not dare to turn around, she could hear his footsteps as he pounded the lawn, hot on their trail. He let out a shout so gleeful that it sent Alice's nerves spinning to entirely new levels of terror. George shouted something indistinct in the distance.

"The back," Tony panted, pulling her to the right. "We left it unlocked."

They dashed to the door. Tony pushed Alice inside first, then hurried through and locked it behind him. Fists pounded the wood.

"My key—where is it?" the manager was screaming. "It was in my pocket—"

"I haven't touched—"

"The pool ... it must be—"

Alice glanced back out the window and saw the manager sprinting away. He would find the key soon; she was sure of it. She needed a better hiding place. She needed to run. Alice grabbed Tony's hand and pulled him through the hotel. The library. She would go to the library. Exactly why the idea appealed to her so strongly, she could not explain; perhaps it was because, somehow, the library was the center of all of this. That was where she had found the diary. That was where the mist had walled her in.

She dragged Tony inside, closing the door behind them. Then she hurried over to the couch, tried to lift it, but found that it was heavier than she expected.

Tony hurried over and picked up the other end.

"The door," Alice said.

"I know."

Alice struggled under her end of the couch; Tony did most of the heavy lifting. Between her stumbling and his, they managed to get it pushed against the door—a makeshift blockade. Alice bent over, hands on her knees, trying to catch her breath.

The hotel was silent. At least for now.

She walked numbly to a wall and sank to the floor, her brain just beginning to process what she had done. She wrung her hands, then slammed a fist into the rug. She had tried to run away from the manager and there she was—hiding right smack in the middle of his hotel. A locked door would not keep him out for long. He would find the key in the pool. Or he would break down the door.

"It's over, isn't it?" she said. "It's too late. My time's almost up and here we are. Stuck. And I don't know anything new about the curse. And I just don't see how … " She was sitting with her back crushed against the library wall. Huddled up in that dark, musty room, Alice didn't think she had ever felt quite so helpless, quite so alone. Tony came and sat down next to her and she still couldn't shake the feeling that she had nothing and no one; she put her hand on Tony's knee and felt the comforting heat of his skin under hers, and the warmth inside of her burned even more furiously and she felt tears making little paths down her cheeks because she was so afraid to lose him and be alone again.

Tony reached out and brushed them away; he left his hand on her cheek for a second too long.

And Alice cried harder, because somehow this made everything worse.

"I told you my parents are divorced, didn't I?" Tony finally said.

"Yeah."

"Well, some relationships just fall apart, you know? But my

parents ... well, they sort of ... exploded. They don't just not love each other any more—they *hate* each other. My mom said once that the only reason she hates my dad so much is because she used to love him. She says that's what happens when you completely love someone and then they disappoint you—hurt you so deeply that you can't forgive them. When you don't care about someone, it just sort of stings. It's love that makes hate possible. Maybe you shouldn't be asking what Elizabeth hated. Maybe you should be asking what she loved. She loved William, didn't she? Maybe you need to hate William, too."

Alice didn't say anything. Hate William? Even if Tony was right and Elizabeth had hated him most, then it wouldn't do Alice any good. She hadn't ever loved William. He was a lying, cheating scoundrel.

"It won't work," Alice said in a half whisper. "I'm never going to get out of this. I'm going to die tonight. I'm going to die."

"No." Tony surprised her by taking her shoulders and staring her straight in the eye. "No, Alice. You can't talk like that."

She actually laughed—threw her head back and laughed.

"How? Tell me how! Give me the answer! Now would be a good time."

But Tony only tightened his grip on her shoulders, as though if he held on tight enough he could keep her there—single-handedly drag her away from the inevitable.

"It matters, Alice. You don't even know how much it matters." His voice was quiet, strong and smooth as steel. Alice looked at his eyes and felt her heart give the strangest leap. A tingling sensation rushed through her, starting in her chest and sweeping all the way to her fingers and toes. She shivered.

"Does it matter?" she asked. She was digging for an answer and she didn't care. She had to know, once and for all. "Who does it matter to?"

"To your family, your friends, everyone you know," Tony said. But Alice shook her head and repeated, a little desperately, "Tony. Who does it matter to?" He gulped and looked away for a second. Alice sat there silently. Her mouth was hanging open and she was breathless; the tingling rushed through her again.

At last, Tony spoke.

"It matters to me."

There were footsteps in the hallway—loud, pounding footsteps. They'd gotten inside even faster than she had expected.

Maybe it didn't even matter because they were here either way. She glanced up at the grandfather clock—identical to the one in her own version of the library. Only a few minutes left until one. Only a few minutes left to be truly alive.

"Where did they go?" she heard the hotel manager demand.

"Please!" said George. "Please, will you just listen to me?"

But the manager wasn't listening anymore. Alice clutched Tony's hand as one pair of footsteps came closer, then stopped outside the library doors.

"They're in here," yelled the manager. "I know they are! I never close these."

The doorknob jangled as he tried to open it.

"No matter—I have a master key!"

He hurried off. Alice looked halfheartedly for a window—an escape—but she already knew it was useless. The library was the heart of the hotel. There was nowhere to run. Nowhere to hide. Alice felt the world spin around her—a confusing blur of sound and time. Senseless.

"Alice." Tony grabbed her shoulders. "I don't care what you have to do—what you have to believe—just tell yourself that you're going to make it. Don't give up on me, Alice. Don't give up on yourself."

"You really do care," she said, and this was the very first time she had truly understood that. The revelation was a beam of sunlight in the dark room. She felt it warm her bloodless face, lighten the darkest corners of her mind. She was dizzy.

"Of course I care. And that's why I need you"—he was having trouble speaking—"I need you to promise me that you won't give up. That you'll keep trying."

"I never thought that anyone could care," she said dumbly.

"Then that's your mistake."

A key jangled in the lock.

Tony turned to look at the door, but Alice grabbed his arm and he swung back to look at her. The dizziness had now become so bad that Alice could have sworn the room was spinning around her, that she was at the center of everything, perhaps of the entire world.

The lock turned.

Alice knew it was her last chance; she had death in front of her and everything behind her and none of it mattered except for the fact that Tony liked her. Loved her, even! It was marvelous. The whole world was twisting round and round and Alice couldn't tell up from down or left from right.

"I've never been kissed," she whispered.

He almost laughed, but his eyes were red and when he spoke he sounded more sad than amused.

"Well, why didn't you tell me that earlier?"

He leaned toward her; the door began to swing open and Alice leaned in, could feel the warmth of his breath on her lips. There were people running toward her and shouting and flashing lights and Alice didn't care about any of it. She closed her eyes.

The clock struck.

"Tony!" she cried, but it was too late. Just as their lips were about to meet, she began to slip into the floor. Tony reached out for her desperately and grabbed hold of her hand, but Alice's arm slid out of his grasp like water. In fact, Alice was all water. She slid through the real floor and dripped into the prison hotel, dripped back into that awful place.

She landed on the floor and Tony was gone. Alice was entirely alone.

CHAPTER TWENTY-THREE

Alice crumpled onto the floor, her hands making nonexistent handprints in the nonexistent carpet. In her mind, she could see Tony, still standing where she had left him with his arms stretched out and that terrible, helpless look on his face. And now he truly was helpless. No matter what he would have liked to do, there was no way Tony would be able to help her now. There wasn't even a way for her to help herself anymore.

The mist on the wall opposite her glowed faintly, like moonlight. She curled up into a tiny ball on the floor; her heart ached and hopelessness filled her—water into an empty glass. As much as she tried not to think about him, Tony's face ... his eyes, his smile ... haunted her. Her family smiled at her from far away and she could barely see them through the fog. She wanted to escape the images, but somehow she couldn't.

Wasn't that funny? She, the ghost, the shadow, was being haunted by reality. But, the more she thought about it, the more sense it made. If you were alive, you could still make things right. But, once you stopped living, you were stuck with yourself—stuck just the way you were when you left. Living people had no need to be haunted by anything; it was the dead (or not-quite dead) that lived in memories—always remembering what they once were.

"And what am I?" Alice whispered to the heartless room. "What am I?"

It was a good question, but Alice didn't have any answers. The only thing she was sure of was that she had always had this angry voice in her head, shouting that, whatever she was, it wasn't enough. She wasn't good enough. Somehow, despite her best efforts, she was doomed to be forever inadequate.

"I can't do this," she said to herself. The riddle was too vague and she was too confused to come up with any good answer. Maybe there wasn't one. Maybe this nebulous promise of escape was just another way for this place to eat her up—destroy her completely. Another cog in a killing machine. She thought of her own body in the hospital, kept alive by a machine that had taken the place of her heart. Was she too only a machine? And when they pulled the plug, would that be the end of it?

"Just let me go, will you?" she shouted, breaking the dead silence around her. "It's over, Elizabeth—you win. I can't solve your riddle, so just let me die." Tony wouldn't mind. Her family didn't need her. It wouldn't matter.

I am you. Maybe the witch had been right about everything after all.

The sound of her voice died away into the stale air that seemed too frail to support much of anything. She closed her eyes and waited for something—she was not sure exactly what. Curled up on the carpet, she waited for what seemed like a very long time. But she felt nothing. There was no slow breeze against her skin, dissolving her body into nothing but dust in the air. Nor was there a ripping pain to tear her away from the world. She opened her eyes and saw the room around her, calm and quiet as ever.

So this was it? She was supposed to sit and wait until the fatal moment when she really did die? Was she expected to simply contemplate the hopelessness of her situation while, miles away, her heart thudded out the rest of its numbered beats? No. She would not stand for it.

She thought of the mist. She only had vague memories of it now, but she thought she remembered peace and white and softness. Maybe if she just walked in, she could forget all this. Though last time it had left her right back where she started. No, the mist was no escape. It was the house that she needed to fight.

She shook her fist at the ceiling. "Do you hear me?"

There was no answer, so, pulled to her feet by a quiet, last surge of energy, Alice rushed over to the fireplace, reached up, and ripped the painting from the wall. She threw it to the ground at her feet, where it lay silent as Elizabeth's wild eyes stared into hers.

"You've failed!" Alice said. "So much for your revenge. Because you know what? It's better if I die. He doesn't deserve to have to put up with me! He deserves someone better. I don't care! Didn't know that would happen, did you?"

The woman in the painting stared and smiled a twisted smile, just as she always did. Furious, Alice took a fountain pen from the desk and, even though she knew it would do no harm, stabbed the beautiful painted face.

"I hate you!" she shouted, stabbing it again. Before she could say anything else, the canvas mended itself and the madwoman was standing by the river again. Staring at that woman, those black curls and wide eyes, something inside of her snapped.

"Damn it! Damn you! Damn everything!" she screamed, almost incoherent. She stabbed again and again and again, then sank down onto the ground, hitting her head against the edge of the couch. She just wanted it to end. She wanted the whole torturous ordeal to be over.

"I'm not going to get better," she whispered to herself.

She thought of Tony and his blue eyes, the color of deep water. He would find some other girl—a girl who could give him everything he deserved. Not a phantom, hovering somewhere between life and death, heaven and hell.

"You can kill me just like you killed the rest," Alice whispered to the walls. "Just do it. Do it now."

Of course, there was no answer.

Alice fell backward onto the floor and felt a tear slip down her cheek. It felt so real, so warm, that for a minute she could have sworn that she was really, truly alive. She felt whole. It was strange that, now that she was about to die, she felt alive in a way that she had never felt before. She couldn't explain it, but everything around her seemed so much more vibrant. Maybe she simply hadn't noticed it before.

"I lose," she said to the empty room. She had lost the game. She had lost her family. She had lost him. She couldn't believe this was how the story ended; it felt all wrong—as if someone had dropped the pages of her life and picked them up at random and everything was shuffled together and none of it fit.

Or maybe this was the way it was supposed to be: her lips forever frozen an inch from his. Maybe this was the universe's way of telling her that this wasn't meant to be, and part of her agreed. The two of them were puzzle pieces that might never fit. It wasn't him that she had a problem with. It was her—with all her imperfections—that she wasn't sure about.

Could she actually deal with death? Being just herself forever? Would dying be as lonely as this past week had been?

"Oh God," she whispered, and her eyes popped open in horror. She pulled herself to her knees and felt more tears drip down her cheeks and off of her chin. "I can't do this."

She looked up and was startled to see her own reflection staring back at her with wet cheeks and wild hair. For a second, she wondered if she really was starting to lose her mind, but she quickly realized with a jolt of relief that it was just the mirror that she had left propped up by one of the couches.

"This is your fault," she said to it, and her reflection said the same to her. "You caused all of this! You drove her mad!"

The reflected face in the mirror was so distorted that she felt as though she was confronting all the evil inside of her—everything disturbing, everything that she had ever questioned. It made her squeamish; she didn't want to look—she didn't want to know—and yet she felt that she had no choice. Seeing that reflected in a mirror would be enough to drive anyone mad.

And maybe it had.

And then, with a suddenness that took her breath away, the thought came. It rushed through her—rushed through her veins and her bones and her very heart. It flooded her mind. It burned without a flame and without mercy.

It's love that makes hate possible, that's what Tony had said. But maybe she had been thinking of the wrong kind of love. For there was another person Elizabeth cared for, probably even more than she had loved William.

I am you, the witch had said. The witch was her. And if the witch had been her …

The witch had been Elizabeth—and the witch had shown her the worst side of herself. What if Elizabeth hated the witch—hated what she saw in the mirror? What if that was the answer?

The witch was Elizabeth. Elizabeth hated the witch.

And—oh! The fire burned her! It was so easy to be the witch. It was frighteningly simple. So terrifying. So many terrible things that

Elizabeth didn't even realize, that she feared were there, that she tried to hide inside herself ...

But they had escaped.

At first it was a dull, dim kind of comprehension, but it throbbed and grew and grew and soon it was shooting through her like physical pain. It possessed her—ran through her in perfect, flawless, golden flames. It ate her up.

She knew.

The energy she had found before now left her in throbbing waves. It slid out of her body and floated away. Alice lay on the floor, exhausted, but she knew that there was no time to waste. With a strength that she didn't know she had, Alice forced herself to roll onto her stomach and crawl toward the mirror. Dizzy with weakness, Alice held it in her hand and looked at herself. She saw the witch glare back at her, with barely open eyes and a huge, laughing mouth.

I am beautiful—Elizabeth had written that so many times. She had written about her talent, her brilliance. She had written about the reviews of her performances. And above all, over and over and over again, the constant refrain of beauty—repeated so emphatically that Elizabeth herself could not have believed it entirely.

The lady doth protest too much ... Alice thought weakly of the lines from *Hamlet*.

Elizabeth's greatest fear must have been that William had left her because she wasn't beautiful enough, wasn't good enough somehow. And then she had looked in the mirror and seen the terrible reflection of her face—the ugliness of distortion. The hideous witch that she feared to become.

Elizabeth hated the witch—the witch who was both the girl Alice had known and Elizabeth herself.

She hated her ugliness. She hated her powerlessness, trapped as she was on the other side of the mirror. Helpless to help herself. That was what Elizabeth hated.

She didn't hate William, she hated herself.

If you would escape my fate,

You must understand my hate.

And Alice understood. She understood at last what she had to do. She had to hate herself, or at least the parts of her that she secretly knew about, but was afraid to reveal. She had to hate her inadequacy, her imperfections. She had to hate the parts of her that made her feel that she could never, ever earn the love of someone like Tony—or anyone else.

And yet there was something else, too—something that came with the understanding, something that she now saw so clearly— how had she missed it before? Hate, simple self-hate, would never free her from this curse. Hating who she was would leave her no better than Elizabeth. She would live a hollow life, going through the motions, never secure, never able to truly feel—to truly love.

You really don't know what other people see in you, do you?

He had asked her that and she had been ashamed then, because she didn't. She looked in the mirror now and couldn't see anything worthwhile—only the ugliness, the faults, the broken parts of herself that she had so often swept under the rug but had never truly confronted.

You need someone telling you that you're wonderful until you finally believe it.

He thought that she was wonderful. But other people had thought that Elizabeth was wonderful, too. She had had pages upon pages of praise to hold close to her heart, to try to feed off of until she could finally believe it herself. And despite all of it, she never had.

And then Alice realized that Tony could tell her she was wonderful all day long—he could tell her every minute, every second—and none of it would make a difference. He couldn't make her believe that she was better than what she thought she saw in the mirror.

"It's a lie!" she shouted at the mirror. "That's not who I am."

A lie, a lie.

She thought she could hear a woman laughing—laughing wildly in the distance—and she whipped around. There was no one there but Elizabeth, staring at her from the painting, smiling her crooked, cruel smile. Hating her. Elizabeth hated her.

Alice looked back at the mirror and saw that nothing had changed. Because it wasn't a lie—not entirely. There were things that she genuinely did not like about herself, and she knew that they would always be there, lurking. Every moment of her life they would be there, some things that she could change, some things that she could not.

Her face changed and there was the girl staring at her, her face young and bright again. "You see," she said, "you can't escape me. I'm inside of you."

"No," Alice whispered.

She turned the mirror over and threw it down; it landed dully, crushing the carpet underneath it. Her legs shook and she let herself fall to the floor, pulled her knees in against her chest, hugged them to her. She rocked back and forth, stinging tears pricked her eyes, tumbled down her cheeks, the cheeks that the mirror had so disfigured. So empty—she was so empty, and yet she was overflowing. Everything that she had locked away, every hidden thought, came streaming out, and she could not stop them.

She sat that way for many minutes—how many she did not know—and when the last tear fell from her chin onto her knees, she felt quieter. She opened her eyes and saw that everything around her was obscured by mist—the whole room was soupy white, as if a cloud were sitting inside of it. The realization hit her with surprising force: it was too late. The mist had come, just as she had imagined it. It was closing in on her. Soon there would be nothing but whiteness; she knew this because even now, with every passing second, the mist grew thicker and the furniture began to disappear. For no apparent reason, Alice grabbed the mirror from the floor and held it close to her.

Then came the other mirrors. They hovered around her and she turned away, looking steadfastly at the mist-covered carpet underneath her. She didn't want to see her own reflection—didn't want to be reminded. The witch's mirror was cold against her body. But then, even as the chill of the mirror pressed against her, she felt a surprising warmth sweep over her. A pure white hand stretched out of the mist to touch her own. The sight of it clutching her fingers did not frighten her; it was almost comforting. Then, inside her own head, the voices spoke.

"Watch," they said.

She looked up, hesitantly at first, darting frightened glances at the surrounding mirrors. But what she saw was not her own reflection. Many different women, all beautiful, stared down at her. A mirror swept down in front of her, taking her by surprise, and before she could look away she saw herself in it, reflected as she truly was. Strong and powerful and wonderful. Perhaps there were faults there, hidden in that shining person, but they were absorbed into the whole. They made the girl deep and meaningful and alive. And the other women in the other mirrors smiled at her and she saw them now too—didn't just see, but also comprehended—how they were all different but all so very breathtaking.

She felt a twinge of fear, but also purpose now. She grabbed the mirror and turned it over. There she was again, staring back at herself, ugly, awful. She didn't look away this time. She knew that she had to move now—had to act now. Because this was her last chance. The house was trying to stop her, trying to get to her before she got to it.

But she wouldn't let it. Because now she understood.

Heart pounding, Alice raised the mirror in the air. It was so heavy—her arms were like lead and she could barely hold onto the thing. The higher she lifted it, the heavier it seemed to become, but she refused to let go. She looked up at it and there she was, staring back at herself—deformed and frightful. And as she looked, she felt the hatred flood her heart. All of her lies, her pettiness, her weaknesses … they all came rushing through her in a great wave. She saw them, she acknowledged them, but she knew also that she was more, that they were a part of her but that they did not define her. She closed her eyes and saw herself as she truly was—held onto that knowledge in that white room inside of her. That was the truth.

The waves surged; she tightened her grip on the glass. And, with a cry that tore through even the thickness of the mist, she threw it down at the mist-covered floor.

CHAPTER TWENTY-FOUR

The mirror shattered, and as it did the whole house seemed to heave a great sigh of relief. The bits of glass hung frozen in the air, glittering like diamonds. Beams of light were tearing great gashes through the walls of the library; Alice shielded her eyes from the brightness. Then came the rushing wind that tore the room apart— it lifted the walls and tossed them, tumbling, into the distance. The floor was ripped from under Alice's feet and she hung there next to the suspended fragments of the mirror. Then the glittering glass dissolved into the light and Alice began to fall.

She was spinning, spinning down an endless tunnel of blackness and tiny pricks of light. Voices echoed in her head, cracking her skull, and she couldn't move to plug her ears. She tried to look down to find her body, but it was gone. She gasped, or thought she did, but she felt no air in her throat.

Was she ... dead?

She felt horror, but had no body to react to the emotion. She had no stomach to lurch, no eyes to widen, no teeth to clench. What she felt was purely mental and stronger somehow—waves and waves of raw emotion with nowhere to go, ripping through this cloud, this nothingness.

"Good night, ladies, good night, sweet ladies, good night, good night!"

Another voice, female this time, shot through her mind. Alice felt as though she had heard it before, but she couldn't remember where. The lines she remembered. They were Ophelia's, the last she ever spoke.

"Good night!"

Alice continued to fall. Was there an end to it? Or was this an eternal rabbit hole? She tried to call for help, but she had no voice. She knew she was telling her body to move, but nothing was happening. If she could have screamed, she would have, but her cries never left this formless mass of thoughts.

"Good night!"

The voice rang in the darkness once more, and then, quite suddenly, it all stopped. The lights, the sounds, the voices. And Alice slept.

***

The first thing that Alice noticed was the pounding in her head. It overpowered everything else and she moaned. Her head was full of beeps and rustlings and whispers. She couldn't sort them out and, for one panicked moment, she thought she was back in the darkness of the rabbit hole. But then her eyes popped open and what she saw was so wonderful and shocking and unexpected that she almost started to cry.

"Tony," she tried to say, but her voice came out as a mangled gurgle from deep in her throat.

He smiled a smile so large that it seemed to split his face in half. "Hello, Alice," he said. He reached out and stroked her hair. Alice closed her eyes again as his hand ran from her forehead all the way down to her ear. The warmth of his touch shot through her entire body and, for a moment, she felt completely happy. But, slowly, thoughts began to form in her muddled mind and uncertainty banished the warmth.

How was this possible? Was this another one of Elizabeth's tricks? She *had* died, hadn't she? Maybe this was some sort of heaven—an imaginary world where everything turned out just the way she wished it would.

"You aren't real," she gasped out. She wanted to reach out and grab this fake Tony's hand; she wanted to make him stop stroking her hair like that. Having him touch her as if she were really and truly alive was more than she could stand. She had given up on him once; she wasn't sure that she would be able to do it again.

Tony laughed.

"Of course I'm real."

Alice shook her head as best she could; her body wasn't

cooperating as it should have. "I've died."

He laughed again. "I think the doctors would disagree."

At that very moment, a nurse came rushing into the room.

"Did you call?" she started to ask Tony, but then she saw Alice and she stopped dead in her tracks. "I don't—I don't believe ... Mrs. Montgomery! Mr. Montgomery!" Her voice echoed down the hallway, frantic. A second later, Alice heard the sound of running feet and her mom's face appeared in the doorway, closely followed by her dad's, and then Jeremy's, with his tangled mop of bright red curls.

"Alice?" Her mom clutched at her heart. "Alice!"

And then Alice lost track completely of whose hand it was on her head or her arm and who was hugging her. She couldn't understand a thing anyone was saying because her entire family was trying to talk, and laugh, and cry, and hug her at the same time. Tony watched from the side of the room with the nurse, who was wiping tears from her eyes.

"I don't understand," Alice said as best she could. Her voice still sounded strangled and tired. "How did I get here?"

"You hit your head in the pool," her mom said, though she was crying so hard that it was a miracle she could talk at all.

"You've been in a coma!" Jeremy piped up, as if this were certain to impress her.

"But that's not what I meant," said Alice. "How did I get out of the hotel? What happened?"

Everyone except Tony smiled; they all seemed to think that this was an extraordinarily silly question. All the same, her dad sat down on the side of the bed and explained very patiently how someone had called the paramedics after the accident and they had put her on a stretcher, carried her out of the hotel, and then driven her to the hospital, where she had been ever since. Alice realized that her parents were not going to understand the question that she was really trying to ask, so she decided to give up on it and talk to Tony later. He, at least, would know what she meant.

"I'm really alive," she said, more to herself than to anyone else.

Her mom took her hand. "Yes, you're alive, thank God."

She had really escaped. She had really broken the curse. Alice twisted around to look at the window behind her. It was see-through. She sighed in relief.

"I need a mirror," she blurted out. "Does anyone have a mirror?"

"Honey, you look fine," said her mom, smoothing her hair. But the nurse pulled a handheld mirror out of her pocket anyway and handed it over to Alice. She flipped it open; she had to know, she had to make sure.

"Normal," she sighed, when she saw her tired-looking but real, undistorted reflection staring back at her. "All normal."

"Of course. Everything's going to be fine," said her dad.

"You don't have to sue the hotel, then?" Alice said, feeling that she owed it to the poor manager. The last time she had made a trip back to reality, she'd left him close to a nervous breakdown.

Her parents looked at each other, shock evident in their eyes.

"How did you know about that?" asked her mom.

"Tony ... Tony told me," said Alice, looking to him for backup.

"Um ... yeah," he quickly filled in. "I told her all about it."

"Well," said her dad, eyeing him suspiciously. "I'm sure we can call it off, if that's what you want, of course."

"Yes. I think that's exactly what I want."

Her mom leaned in and whispered confidentially in her ear, "Alice, how do you know that young man? He came in here just last night, demanding to see you. Says he met you somewhere."

Alice smiled. "Oh yes. We're friends. We're very good friends."

***

It was a long time before Alice managed to get some time alone with Tony. When her parents weren't talking to her, it was Jeremy, jabbering about how he'd been so bored all week and no one had done anything with him and he was so glad she had woken up because everyone had been so *boring*. Alice wasn't fooled by any of this. She knew Jeremy well enough to see that in his face there was genuine relief.

But late on Monday night, when her mom had gone to take a shower and her dad and brother were back at the hotel, Alice heard a knock on her door and Tony's familiar voice coming from the hallway.

"Can I come in?"

"Tony!" Alice cried, and he took that as a yes. He came inside and closed the door behind him, then sat down in the chair by her bed.

"No one else is here," he said, nodding at the empty room.

"Thank goodness! I've been getting so tired of company."

"Well, I can leave if you—"

"No," Alice interrupted. "No, I want you to stay."

"That's good, because I've been wanting to ask you what happened when you got back into the hotel."

Alice told him the whole story in great detail, relieved she could at last tell someone the complete and entire truth. It felt good to get the experience out of her mind, to cleanse herself of it. When she finished, Tony sat back in his chair.

"So it wasn't William that she hated after all."

"No," said Alice. "Funny, isn't it?" she asked, though she wasn't sure that it was.

Tony appeared to be lost in thought about this; Alice waited, then asked a question that she had been wanting to ask.

"What happened to you—after I left? The police didn't do anything to you and your dad, right?"

"Oh no," said Tony, waving off her concerns. "Let's just say they got the impression that the manager wasn't a completely reliable source. They scolded him for calling them and told him to see a doctor."

"I guess it's good he didn't get the videotape after all." It was easy to say that now, when all she wanted was as few complications as possible. The tape would have been just one more thing to explain.

Tony grinned. "Well, about that … Turns out my dad still has it."

Alice gaped. "But he threw it in the pool! It was destroyed."

"He threw *a* tape in the pool. He switched the real one with a blank—kept the actual tape in his pocket the whole time. He was pretty shocked that I thought he actually damaged the real one, said he thought I knew he was smarter than that."

"What will he do with it?" she asked, alarmed. The questions she would get if anyone saw that tape …

"Well, now that everyone knows you're alive, it's not going to have much weight, is it? If he tries to use it, people will just say that he made the film after you recovered from the coma. But he says he's hanging onto it anyway—he's just going to show it to a few close friends, ones he knows will believe it."

The idea that random people might see what she had said, know what she had gone through, left her feeling exposed. But Alice knew she owed George for what he had done to help her, and so she swallowed hard and bit her tongue, hoping fervently she would never run into any of George's "close friends."

"Where is he now?" she asked.

"Oh, he's locked himself up in the hotel room—a *different* hotel. I think the manager might have killed us in our sleep if we'd stayed there after the ghost fiasco. He says hi but he's on one of his writing kicks. He says he wants to record everything that happened before his memory degrades." Tony pointed to his forehead and said in a mock older voice, "'Don't have a hard drive in here, son. Gotta write it before it turns to mush.'"

"And what are you still doing here? Don't you have to go home sometime?" Alice asked, although she was fairly certain that she already knew the answer.

"I'm here for you. Once you get out of the hospital, I'll fly back to my mom's place."

Suddenly Alice had no desire at all to recover. "Oh."

"You live in California, don't you?"

She sighed. It hardly mattered where she lived if it wasn't next door to him. "Yeah. How did you know?"

"Your mom told me."

"I see."

He smiled, like a little boy with a great secret to reveal. "Did I ever mention where I live?"

"No," Alice said. She almost didn't want to know.

"California," he said, and Alice took in a sudden gulp of air. Did she dare to hope?

"And I figured out," Tony continued, "I only live about forty minutes away from you."

Alice would have hugged him if she had the strength. She would have jumped out of the bed and clapped her hands like a little kid.

"That's wonderful!" she said.

The sides of Tony's mouth twitched, as though he was having a very hard time keeping his nonchalant grin from exploding into a gigantic smile.

"Alice," he said very seriously, "there's something else we need to talk about."

She felt a few butterflies pop into her stomach.

"What?"

"Well, you should know that you can't just demand that a guy kiss you and then disappear before he has the chance."

The butterflies tripled in size.

"Would you like me to make it up to you?" she asked.

Tony pretended to consider this very carefully. He ran his finger over his chin and looked thoughtfully at Alice for a very long minute before answering.

"I guess so," he said at last.

Alice gulped and closed her eyes. Her heart was pounding and, for perhaps the first time in her life, she couldn't seem to think at all. She was only aware of how loud her heartbeat was and how her ears were ringing so that she couldn't hear anything. She felt Tony's lips meet hers and everything—every sensation—ripped through her like electricity. Tony's hand was around the back of her head and she could almost feel each and every one of her hairs bending under his touch. So much awareness at once—it overwhelmed her and she could hardly stand it.

She had no idea how much more time went by before Tony pulled away. She fell back against her pillow.

"Are you okay?" Tony asked her. She must have looked pretty bad for him to sound so concerned.

"I—I'm … " But what was she? Every single bit of her was tingling. Everything around her, every light, every color, every texture seemed so much more real than ever before. Alice took a deep, exhausted breath and let it all sink into her. She felt the reality of everything around her and she was a part of it. At last she was a part of it.

Opening her eyes, she looked at Tony, still bent over her with that concerned look on his face. She smiled at him, seeing him now as she had never seen him before—every twinkle in his eye, every curve of his face.

Alive, she thought. *Finally alive.*

***

When Tony finally left, Alice lay back on the hospital bed; the butterflies in her stomach were gone, but she was still full of tingling, fluttering happiness—its intensity surprised her. She stretched, her arms pulling backward, upward, fingertips brushing the glass of the window and the wood of the ledge underneath. They ran up against the pocket mirror the nurse had left and Alice picked it up. She opened it hesitantly and looked at the image inside. For the first time in many years she looked at her reflection and didn't feel anything other than the simple joy of being alive. She felt no hate; it was as though the curse had ripped it out of her.

You are wonderful.

And she believed it.

ACKNOWLEDGEMENTS

Thanks go first to my agent, Carrie Pestritto of the Prospect Agency, who has believed in this story for a very long time and worked inexhaustibly to get it to this point. This finished book would not exist without her support and great advice.

A huge thanks also to Mandy Schoen, whose spot-on editing was invaluable in shaping this story. And thanks to all the great team at Month9Books for their hard work.

Thank you to my family for putting up with my editing grouchiness and for supporting my crazy writing dreams. My love to all of you.

JESSICA ARNOLD

Jessica Arnold lives (in an apartment) and works (in a cubicle) in Boston, Massachusetts. She has a master's degree in publishing and writing from Emerson College.